"Mr. C[...]
sibly w[...]
ously [...]
puzzle[...]

New Statesman

JOHN DICKSON CARR
Available in Library of Crime Classics® editions.

Gideon Fell Novels:
BELOW SUSPICION
HAG'S NOOK
HE WHO WHISPERS
THE HOUSE AT SATAN'S ELBOW
THE PROBLEM OF THE GREEN CAPSULE
THE SLEEPING SPHINX
THE THREE COFFINS
TIL DEATH DO US PART

Non-series:
THE BURNING COURT

Writing as Carter Dickson
Sir Henry Merrivale Novels:
THE JUDAS WINDOW
NINE—AND DEATH MAKES TEN*
THE PEACOCK FEATHER MURDERS*

forthcoming

JOHN DICKSON CARR

THE HOUSE AT
SATAN'S ELBOW

INTERNATIONAL POLYGONICS, LTD.
NEW YORK CITY

THE HOUSE AT SATAN'S ELBOW

Copyright ©1965 by John Dickson Carr.
Reprinted with the permission of the author's estate.
Cover: Copyright ©1987 by International Polygonics, Ltd.

Library of Congress Card Catalog No. 87-80304
ISBN 0-930330-61-7

Printed and manufactured in the United States of America
by Guinn Printing.
First IPL printing June 1987.
10 9 8 7 6 5 4 3 2 1

For
CLAYTON RAWSON

Dear Clayt:

I offer you this little story because of our mutual interest in tricks and impossibilities. For the sake of verisimilitude much of the action has been made to occur in real places. It is hardly necessary to add, however, that there is no William Rufus College at Southampton University, no hospital at Blackfield; and that, though Lepe Beach does very much exist—it may be reached by bus from Southampton—both Satan's Elbow and Greengrove, like the characters of the story itself, have no existence in Hampshire and could not exist anywhere outside my own distorted fancy.

Yours as ever,

John Dickson Carr

Lymington, Hants, September 1964

1

AND SO, early on that Friday evening in June, Garret Anderson packed a bag in his flat at Hampstead and rang for a taxi to take him to Waterloo.

It would not be true to say that he had *no* knowledge of the Barclay family or of the house at Satan's Elbow and, therefore, that he could have had no premonition of coming events.

Besides, considering the inexplicable business of Fay Wardour . . .

Fay, Fay, Fay! He must forget Fay and put her out of his mind for good.

Still! . . .

It had been two days ago, on the Wednesday afternoon, that the 'phone rang in that same flat. Garret, rattling away at his typewriter, cursed the telephone as he always did when its clamor punctured his thoughts during a difficult paragraph. But his expression changed as he answered.

"Look, Garret," began a hearty voice, vaguely familiar without being at once identifiable. "I won't ask you to play guessing games. This is Nick Barclay."

"Nick! How are you?"

"Never better. And how are *you,* you old horse-thief?"

"I mean, where are you?"

"I'm in London, of course," answered Nick. "I don't casually telephone across the Atlantic, as others in my job have been known to do. To be exact, I'm at Claridge's."

"Is this another flying visit to your former homeland?"

"Well . . ."

Garret Anderson stared at the telephone.

"Up to four years ago, about this time in the summer of sixty," he said, "I hadn't heard your voice or set eyes on you for just under twenty-one years, when both of us were boys of not quite sixteen. You 'phoned out of the blue, as you're doing now. Even then I didn't see you for more than twenty minutes or half an hour. You were at London Airport; you took time to drive into town for a drink. Immediately, all in a bustle and with a photographer in tow, you were off to Morocco to see how the Moors were making out as a new country after they gained their independence in fifty-six, and to write a spread for that glossy rag you've since inherited: *Flash,* isn't it called?"

"It's a pretty damn good magazine, Garret."

"Well! Is this the same sort of flying visit?"

Again Nick Barclay hesitated.

"No," he said. "I can't stay long, it's true; not more than a week or two, anyway. But this is family business; it's dead serious; there are things I don't like. Look, you old mossback. Are you so wrapped up in musty historical records that you don't even see the newspapers?"

"I see the newspapers, thanks. Even if I didn't, the news on TV . . ."

"Yes; there's always television, isn't there?" Nick spoke with full-blown bitterness. "Anyway! As you do seem to have heard, I inherited my father's and Bill Willis's so-called 'magazine empire'—which doesn't seem to be any more popular, nowadays, than most empires—when the old man dropped dead of a heart-attack last March."

"Sorry to learn of your father's death, Nick."

"Yes; thanks for the letter of condolence; I'm afraid I was too tied up to answer it."

Then a new note of urgency crept into Nick's voice.

"But I wasn't talking about that," he added. "It concerns old Clovis—my grandfather, if you remember, who died at the ripe old age of eighty-five in the very same month as my old man. Now it seems I've been saddled with something I don't want and won't have. And very ugly events are under way. But I don't want the whole situation to blow up in my face; I don't want Uncle Pen committing suicide, or any bloody foolishness like that."

"What?"

"Look," Nick said abruptly. "Can't we get together and talk?"

"Yes, by all means. Why not have dinner with me tonight?"

"It'll be a pleasure, Garret. When and where?"

"Suppose you meet me at the Thespis Club about seven-thirty."

"Thespis Club?"

"In Covent Garden; it's the oldest theatrical club in London. Listen, Nick! You've been away in America for a quarter of a century, ever since Nick the elder hoicked you out of school and emigrated at the outbreak of the war, after he had that blazing row with your grandfather. But don't tell me a leading newsman can't find the Thespis Club in Covent Garden."

"O.K., old horse. Many thanks. See you."

It greatly amused Garret Anderson that he himself should be a member of the Thespis Club, and fitted into the ironic comedy his life had become. Garret, that learned historian, wrote the popular biographies of Victorian worthies in politics and literature which—though excellent books, not without wit or insight—had earned him much reputation but only a modest measure of financial success until his American agent conceived the notion of turning one of them, *Macaulay,* into a Broadway musical.

The famous team of Halpin & Peters, commissioned to do the show, had their own sweet will. Thomas Babington Macaulay, Sydney Smith's "book in breeches," became a romantic hero whose passionate affair with a (fictitious) earl's daughter inspired him to write both his *History of England* and, in particular, *Lays of Ancient Rome.* Lady Holland, the formidable hostess of early Victorian days, capered as a figure of broad farce; one of her songs, "Read Any Good Books Lately?" almost every night afterwards would stop the show. Macaulay's own lyric, "Little Bird from a Bough," sung to his lady-love on the terrace at the House of Commons, made sentimental hearts palpitate. And so, against an alleged background of literary and political London in the eighteen-thirties and -forties, was born *Uncle Tom's Mansion.*

Garret, invited to New York by the backers, saw how matters were going but had signed a contract and was powerless to stop them. Despite some protests, the critics were conquered, *Uncle Tom's Mansion* became a smash hit.

"But didn't it annoy you," more than one friend afterwards asked Garret, "when they butchered the facts right and left?"

"It did at first, yes, until the ridiculous side grew more entertaining than embarrassing. If you can't change things, laugh at 'em. Besides—"

Besides, as he might have added but didn't, the fantastic success of *Uncle Tom's Mansion* had removed all money pressures forever. Not only did it send rocketing the sales of his earlier books, but he could now, without protest from anyone, write biography as accurately as he liked.

Thus Garret Anderson, at just past forty—sometimes telling himself, without strict truth, that he was beginning to feel his age—might be accounted a fortunate man. Not altogether a happy man, but assuredly a fortunate one. Lean, vigorous, and not ill-looking, perhaps a little too easy-going and over-imaginative, he had nevertheless a balance in his sardonic sense of humour. He was a solid citizen, reasonably sober and with a sense of responsibility. Some, in fact, were inclined to regard him as a little stuffy.

"And yet," those same friends had said to him, "I'll bet *Uncle Tom* embarrassed you more than you've ever admitted. In many ways, Garret, you're a blasted old Victorian yourself."

Victorian, eh? If they had known about Fay . . .

But they didn't know, nor was he likely to tell them. The situation with *Uncle Tom's Mansion* could be dismissed as merely funny.

Not so funny might be the situation of Nick Barclay and the Barclay family, Garret decided when he received that telephone-call on Wednesday, June 10, and invited Nick to dinner at the Thespis Club.

In south-eastern England, where the waters of the Solent stretch in deeply between the Hampshire coastline and the Isle of Wight, at one point the coast juts out into a flat spur of land called, for reasons lost in the mist of centuries, Satan's Elbow. If no sinister meaning was ever attached to the name of Satan's Elbow, a more dubious reputation—Why? Garret Anderson had never been told—came to surround the country-house, Greengrove, which an eminent though disreputable high-court judge, Mr. Justice Wildfare, built there shortly past the middle of the eighteenth century. Presently the judge died, perhaps by violence; the Barclays bought it from his heirs and had been masters of Satan's Elbow ever since.

They were not really an old family, as families go. The first Barclays of whom there is definite record—brisk, no-nonsense men of business—came down from the north about 1795. They made a fortune selling shoes to the French Army during the Napoleonic Wars, and by judicious investment throughout the nineteenth century so increased their holdings that, even with taxes and the cracking of all ordered props after World War Two, old Clovis Barclay, last of the patriarchs, remained a wealthy man.

Old Clovis, when still very young Clovis, had shown the family acumen by marrying a well-to-do girl. Of this marriage there were three children, two sons and a daughter: Nicholas, born in 1900; Pennington, born in 1904; and Estelle, born in 1909. Mrs. Clovis, a gentle and ineffectual soul, departed this life during the early nineteen-twenties. She left her own money entirely to Pennington, the younger son, who would be provided for whatever happened.

And there, to all intents and purposes, began the modern story.

For old Clovis, latterly a bearded tyrant, very much the head of the family, was a tough proposition. Though never quite sure what he wanted, he was always sure—and stated loudly—what he didn't want. His favourite among the children was the robust, energetic Nicholas, who became the father of Garret Anderson's friend young Nick. Despite this favouritism, or perhaps because of it, old Clovis and his elder son quarrelled incessantly. Nicholas wanted to go into business for himself, and that was wrong. Nicholas made an early marriage to a dowerless bride, and *that* was wrong. True, Nicholas might drive racing-cars for which the old man paid; Nicholas smashed up his left leg so badly that he never afterwards regained its full use, and no word was said. But independence? Striking out for himself, with a family of his own to support? Never!

On the other hand, old Clovis could barely tolerate Pennington, the "artistic" one, who had been Mrs. Clovis's favourite. He called Pennington feeble and ineffectual, which was untrue; but there matters stood. About Estelle, a born spinster of the kittenish variety, who idolized her father and always supported him, he seldom seemed to think much one way or the other.

"Essie? Oh, she's a girl; the others will take care of her; she'll be all right," Clovis said. Then a still younger generation entered in.

Young Garret Anderson and young Nick, who at that time longed to be a newspaper reporter, became close friends when they were at Harrow during the later nineteen-thirties. Between old Clovis and Nicholas the elder friction sparked into open trouble as the world swung towards hostilities of a deadlier sort. Billy Willis, an American acquaintance who recognized Nicholas's immense business capacity, was in New York preparing to launch a modest pair of magazines which in time, with some luck, might become many magazines; and he wrote constantly urging Nicholas to join him. His last letter arrived shortly before the Nazis stormed into Poland; war was declared; the air-raid sirens moaned on a sunny Sunday morning in September, thirty-nine; and one day later Nick the elder tackled old Clovis.

"I'm out of it, you know," he declared, leaning on his cane in the long, dusky library at Greengrove. "This damned game leg will keep me from active service, which is the only possible kind of service here. If I'm ever to do any good at all, I must go and join Bill. Let me have a thousand pounds as a stake;

you shall have it back in six months, and then we'll see. Well, what do you say?"

Old Clovis complied, after his own fashion. He did not reply immediately or write a cheque. For a full week he brooded. Drawing from the bank at Brockenhurst a thousand pounds in fivers, he made the notes into a thick bundle held together by rubber bands. Again he confronted Nicholas in the library. Even then he did not contemptuously push the money across the table or fling it on the floor at Nicholas's feet. He flung that wad of notes, in fact, straight and hard into his elder son's face.

"There's your money," roared Clovis. "Now get out. What do *you* say?"

Nicholas did not hesitate either. What he flung into his esteemed parent's face was the full content of an inkwell on the library table. What *he* roared was, "Go to hell and stay there."

And he stalked out, slamming the door. Within twenty-four hours Nicholas, his wife, and his son were aboard the *Illyria*, bound from Southampton to New York.

Most people knew the sequel. War or no war, the affairs of Willis and Barclay prospered almost at once. Nicholas, immediately useful, soon grew indispensable. By the end of hostilities he was a partner; their modest two magazines had become four. In the early nineteen-fifties, when he bought out a partner who wanted to retire, Nicholas controlled half a dozen important periodicals with one-word titles, led by *Flash*, the heavily illustrated news-slick, and *People*, whose intimate glimpses into the lives of eminent men and women were never so intimate as to be distasteful.

"I knew he'd do it," said Nick junior.

It was young Nick's prosperity too. They had sent Nick to another school—the American Harrow, at Gottsburg, in Pennsylvania—and then to Princeton. Afterwards, since he still cherished his passion for reporting, his father saw to it that he had several years' knockabout experience in various cityrooms and then took him on the staff of *Flash*.

Nick made something of a name for himself as a special correspondent. He was sent everywhere to see everything. Good-natured, quick of sympathy, pretending to a cynicism which was far from his actual nature, Nick really had found his niche as a newsman.

Meanwhile, in England, and in the house at Satan's Elbow . . .

An embittered old Clovis, after Nicholas's departure, behaved much as might have been expected. He was no more bitter than Nicholas, who afterwards held no communication whatever with the patriarch except to return his thousand pounds and add interest at the current bank-rate. But Clovis, apparently, remained more than adamant. The name of his elder son, he said, must never be mentioned again; he had no elder son. Much as he might dislike the suave, bookish, highly civilized Pennington, yet Barclay possessions must remain in Barclay hands. To Greengrove he summoned Andrew Dawlish, that hard-headed if impressionable solicitor who served the Barclays as faithfully as his father and grandfather had served them for nearly a century. Mr. Dawlish, though the same age as Pennington, had a gravity which matched the patriarch's own. Old Clovis's will, full of comments which the solicitor tried in vain to suppress, left everything unreservedly to Pennington. Faithful Estelle was not even mentioned.

The years rolled on; Clovis, bedevilled by growing intimations of mortality, grew at once more secretive and more cantankerous. And then ...

In New York, during the early spring of 1964, Nicholas Barclay, who had never ceased to boast of his health and strength, was climbing hand over hand up a rope in the gymnasium of the Apex Club when he suffered the heart-attack that killed him a few months short of his sixty-fourth birthday. Old Clovis, pottering through the garden at Greengrove under buffeting March winds, contracted bronchial pneumonia and was gathered to his ancestors in Beaulieu Churchyard. That was not an end; it was merely a beginning.

Garret Anderson in London heard of both deaths. Nicholas's passing made something of a splash in the British press; that of old Clovis occasioned only a modest obituary in the *Times*. Bits of gossip informed Garret that Nick's Uncle Pen had inherited not only Clovis's money, which he didn't need, but also Greengrove, which Uncle Pen loved and cherished, just as Nick himself had inherited his father's enterprises and become rather a tycoon at forty.

Garret could never understand Pennington Barclay's devotion to the house at Satan's Elbow. During the one visit he had paid there, as Nick's guest many years ago, the place depressed and disquieted him. Despite modern improvements, despite the beauty of the surrounding countryside, Greengrove was too shadowed and cheerless. You always wanted to glance round over your shoulder after dark. Rooms and passages, bleakly luxurious, were awash with disturbing currents which seemed not altogether of modern origin.

It was none of his business, Garret told himself; he had

been only a boy at the time, probably mistaken; and, anyway, who was he to make such confident pronouncements?

All the same, when Nick unexpectedly telephoned on that Wednesday, June 10, Garret felt a twinge of disquiet from more tangible causes. He had little knowledge of what had been happening at Greengrove during the intervening years. But Nick, the alleged cynic, clearly had something on his mind, and to judge by his words, it could be nothing good. Garret, resolved not to be late for their dinner-appointment, got out his car in plenty of time to rearch Covent Garden, drove round interminably—as you always do in London nowadays—before finding a place to park, and entered the Thespis Club a few minutes past seven-thirty.

His guest had not yet arrived. It was a quarter to eight when Nick Barclay strode into the little ground-floor bar, where eighteenth-century theatrical protraits (an omen?) crowd their great gilt frames round the walls.

Except for themselves and the barman, the room was deserted. Though Garret had met his old friend only once before in just under twenty-five years, he again felt he would have known the newcomer anywhere. Nick still ordered his clothes from London. Dark-haired, square-jawed, alert of eye, he was well above middle height, like all the male Barclays; but as he neared middle age, unlike his grandfather or his father or even his uncle, he had begun to put on a little weight.

"Ho!" said Nick.

They shook hands heartily and cursed each other with real liking. Garret ordered Martinis, carrying the drinks to a table, where they sat down facing each other. Nick, after clinking glasses for a toast, swallowed the Martini almost at a gulp. Then he sat up straight, with lines of worry drawn slantwise under his eyes, and looked hard at his companion.

"Well?" he said.

2

"Well, what?" Garret demanded.

"How are things going, you lucky so-and-so? Since I saw you last, it seems, you've become quite a famous man."

"For all the wrong reasons."

"Well, who cares? Why fight it? *Uncle Tom's Mansion,* whether you're responsible or whether you're not, is quite a show. I've seen it twice; congratulations. When are they bringing the show to London?"

"Not yet, if ever. The Lord Chamberlain won't license it."

Garret called for a refill of the Martinis, and they both lighted cigarettes. Nick chortled across the table.

"Who'd have though old Macaulay was such a rip-roaring film-hero, though? Remember what Lytton Strachey wrote? 'There he is—squat, square, and perpetually talking—on Parnassus.' What's the Lord Chamberlain got against him, anyway?"

"In the second act, if you recall, Macaulay defies the Viceroy of India: first with a long speech about democracy and then with a rousing song whose title escapes me."

" 'Don't Tread on 'Em, Viceroy; They'll Kill You.' Shall I whistle the tune?"

"No, thanks."

"But I'm still not with it, Garret. What's bugging the Lord Chamberlain?"

"The Viceroy in *Uncle Tom,* presented as the heaviest of heavy villains flogging and torturing Hindus for the glory of the Raj, was a real-life official whose descendants are still alive. Unless they rewrite him into an obviously fictitious character, the Lord Chamberlain won't play."

"Tough luck. But that's not what I really wanted to ask you. How's your private life, old horse? Married yet?"

"No, not yet. You're married, or so I heard?"

"I *was* married," answered Nick, blowing out smoke with a philosophic air. "I *was* married, yes, but it didn't take. Irma and I split up long ago, and since then I've been playing the field. Love 'em and leave 'em: that's my motto, if not a very original one.

"I'm getting on in years, Garret," he added rather portentously. "If I'm not very careful I'll develop a corporation. And the hair's going a bit thin on top, as you can see. But *you,* old mossback! You look fighting-fit; you're as thin as a rake; you've got hair as thick as you ever had, you thrice-fortunate son-of-a-bitch."

Again they clinked glasses.

"You're a fine one, aren't you," Garret retorted, "to call anybody a thrice-fortunate son-of-a-bitch? 'Tycoon Barclay, Monarch of All He Purveys.' 'I may own the joint,' says Barclay, 'but I still cover any news-stories that interest me.' "

"That sounds like *Time.*"

"It is *Time,* cover-picture and all."

"Well, well! It must have hurt 'em like hell to boost a competitor, but they played up like gentlemen. I still think you're a heel, though. You were in New York for the opening of *Uncle Tom,* weren't you? Why didn't you look me up?"

"I tried to. They said you were out of town."

"Yes, I guess I was. That was the fall of sixty-two, wasn't it: the Cuban crisis? Still, as far as being a heel is concerned . . ."

"Look here, this has gone far enough. Come off it, Nick; drop the act. If something is troubling you badly, as what you said on the 'phone more than indicated, why don't you tell me about it?"

"You really mean that, don't you? You'd rally around just as you used to?"

"Yes, of course I mean it."

An abrupt seriousness had struck the grin from Nick's face. It was very warm in the bar, and, as usual, heavily stuffy. A shaft of late sunlight, penetrating past the edge of a window-blind, touched the corner of Nick's left eye. Strained, jumpy, he finished the drink and crushed out his cigarette.

"I can talk to you," he said. "Most people are total strangers after twenty-five years; but I don't feel you're a stranger. I can trust you; I can trust Andrew Dawlish. . . ."

"That's the family solicitor, isn't it?"

"Yes. Still, since I'm a suspicious kind of guy, you're just about the only people I can trust. Anyway, it's true. There is trouble. It's what's been happening at Greengrove and elsewhere; it's Uncle Pen, it's Aunt Essie, it's everything all at once; and I only hope I can handle it."

"Well? What *has* been happening at Greengrove?"

"Ghosts," said Nick, abruptly rising to his feet.

"Ghosts?"

"An alleged ghost, at least. But that's not all. A new will. Mysterious women, flesh-and-blood women, appearing for a time and then vanishing as though they'd never existed."

"What the hell do you mean," demanded Garret with equal abruptness, "by flesh-and-blood women appearing and then vanishing as though they'd never existed?"

"Whu-o!" Something of Nick's chortle briefly returned. "Did I touch you?"

"Meaning what, I asked?"

"The fact is, Sobersides, I *thought* you looked a bit peculiar when I asked if you were married. Is it possible, as your friends in show business might put it, that you've met a dame?"

"Well . . ."

"Is she a blonde, Garret? Remember little Milly Stevens,

who used to live near you at Watford? You were as gone on her as anybody can be at the age of fifteen. Milly was a blonde, and you swore . . ."

"Whomever I've met or whomever I haven't met," Garret said grimly, "bears no relation to the present problem. What is it, Nick? What's bothering you so much? Have another drink?"

"No, thanks. I'm not quite myself; I haven't eaten much all day, and I don't want to get stoned before dinner."

"All right: whatever you say. Sit down and tell me about it."

"I wrote you once, I think," continued Nick, relapsing into the chair and reaching for his cigarettes, "that there had been no communication between my family and my esteemed grandpa's after my father cut the painter and lit out? I told you that, didn't I?"

"Yes."

"It wasn't quite accurate. My father never wrote to Clovis, except to fire back his thousand quid with full interest, and God knows *I* never did. But sometimes Aunt Essie would drop a line to my mother, who always conscientiously answered. It wasn't often—once a year, perhaps, or maybe every other year—but it did give an occasional glimpse of affairs in the dear, happy, tight-clenched ancestral home. Old Clovis—of whom, probably, the less said the better . . ."

"On the one occasion I met him, many years ago, he didn't seem as bad as all that."

"He wasn't half bad, of course, provided you never crossed or annoyed him in any way. Is there anybody on earth of whom the same thing can't be said?"

Lighting a cigarette, Nick stared across the table with extraordinary intensity.

"He was a terror, I'm telling you. We're a peculiar lot, Garret, unstable and possibly not quite sane, but my grandpop was the outstanding oddball. Aside from one sentimental little custom when somebody had a birthday (never mind what the custom was; for all I know, it's still being kept up), Clovis kept the place in an uproar with alternate sulks and rages. It seemed bad enough when my father and mother and I lived at Greengrove. Afterwards—holy cow! You had to read between the lines of Essie's letters; she thought the old boy was God Almighty; and yet you couldn't miss it. He played merry hell with everybody, but in particular, always and incessantly, with Uncle Pen."

"Although," interposed Garret, "although, as I understand it, he still left everything to your Uncle Pen."

"Yes, by a will drawn in forty-eight and deposited with Andrew Dawlish for safe-keeping. Clovis made no secret of that. 'You don't deserve it, Pennington, but you're my son.' Even Essie knew about the will and commented that Pen didn't deserve it."

Nick paused, amid tobacco-smoke and floating dust-motes.

"I *liked* Uncle Pen," he added with sudden defensiveness. "I liked him then; I like him now. He's a damned good sort, and always was; I won't see him bypassed or swindled."

"In what way is he being bypassed or swindled?"

"Wait, can't you?"

"All right: go ahead."

"I *liked* Uncle Pen," Nick repeated. "He had something of a stagy manner, it may be. With his passion for the theatre, in all probability, he'd still give his ears to be a member of this club. But in the old days he treated me as though I were fully grown up, which is the way to win any kid. He always had time to talk; and God, how Uncle Pen could talk! He told me stories: ghost stories, most of 'em, and rather frightening. He had no belief in the supernatural; he scoffed at any notion that the dead return; and yet, like so many other people of the same sort, he was always fascinated by the cauld grue.

"I can still see him as he looked then: thinner than you—but frail, which you aren't—and never in the best of health. I can still see him pacing the garden and reciting poetry, though my idea of poetry at that time, I'm afraid, was something out of Kipling or else *Horatius at the Bridge* by your friend Macaulay. And this was real poetry: Keats, Donne, Shakespeare. But Clovis hated the poetry, just as Clovis hated the theatre. Secretly, we now know, the old devil admired my father for standing up to him."

"Did your Uncle Pen ever stand up to him?"

"That's a hard question to answer. Adolescents hear a lot from the sidelines, of course, but they don't understand the adults of their own families, who seem merely unpredictable and hardly human. It was a long time before I devoted thought to it or could pry any information out of my father and mother.

"Years before, it seems, Pen *had* kicked over the traces just once. It was in the spring of nineteen-twenty-six, when I was still a child in rompers and Uncle Pen himself couldn't have been older than his early twenties. My grandmother had died in twenty-three, leaving him a sizeable wad if he cared to spend it. One day, after a notable fit of temperament on Grandpa's part and even a row with Essie, he quietly packed his bag and left home. The next thing they heard, he had rented a villa at Brighton and was living there with a little actress whose name I forget or never learned.

"Jesus H. Christ!" exclaimed Nick, spreading out his hands. "Can you picture Clovis's pious horror and the twitterings of poor Essie? But it didn't last. The pull of Pen's ancestral home—or something—proved too much. By September of the same year he was back at Greengrove, with his waywardness and his little actress temporarily forgotten."

"Temporarily?"

"If I can put it that way. We must now jump over a great number of years—thirty-odd, in exactness—to the summer of nineteen-fifty-eight. Clovis had long ago made his will. If the situation at Greengrove was no better, at least it seemed permanent. And then, at the mature age of fifty-four, Uncle Pen unexpectedly and secretly got married."

"Married?"

"That's what I said. To a bride more than twenty years younger than himself."

The words, though commonplace enough, stabbed through to the secret mind and heart of Garret Anderson. It was as though the walls of the stuffy little bar had begun to close in on him.

"Twenty years younger?" he repeated. And then: "Who's the girl, Nick? What's she like?"

"How the hell should I know? Have *I* talked or written to anybody in the family?"

"Easy, Nick!"

"Her name is Deidre." Nick crushed out his cigarette. "All I can tell you is that she comes of a very good family. No money, but quite acceptable in every other way; even old Dawlish admits that. 'A charming young lady,' Dawlish says, 'and most tractable. She has been good for Pennington, if one may venture so much, and had a good effect on your grandfather too.' As far as I can gather, Uncle Pen met her at a concert or something; they made a runaway marriage at a registry office, just as my father did with my mother in twenty-two, after which Pen brought her home to live."

"What did old Clovis say?"

"What *could* he say, with the girl so obviously what **she** ought to be and Pen himself not exactly a young rooster in any case? If you think all things became sweetness and light, you don't know Clovis. But he even seems to have liked her and to have been a little less impossible towards the end. Anyway, he could afford to wait. For now we come to the last act and the explosion.

"I don't have to tell you that on March twentieth, present

year, my father had a seizure in the gym of his club and died at the Presbyterian Hospital an hour later. In the following week, when we were still occupied with the funeral and with straightening things out, a last letter for my mother arrived from Aunt Essie.

"*'I grieve to report,'* something like this, *'that poor Father passed away on Tuesday evening. But mourn not; he is at peace.'* (At peace; what do you want to bet?) Clovis had been prowling through the grounds in an east wind, enraged and screaming his head off at some gardeners; and with all our wonder drugs nowadays, bronchial pneumonia is no joke even when you're not eighty-five. Anyway . . ."

"Well?"

"Clovis ceased from troubling, or at least so we thought. Then came the explosion. It was the middle of April when another letter arrived from England. Not for my mother, but for me. Not gushingly from Aunt Essie, but a formal screed from Dawlish and Dawlish of Lymington. It took several airmail exchanges to get the business clear, but we finally did. Things were *not* all right at Greengrove. They'd discovered a new will."

"A new will?"

"A holograph will, drawn up by Clovis without witnesses, but in his handwriting and incontestably legal. Clovis had never ceased to brood, you see; he'd been biding his time. He wrote the will; he hid it in the house in a place where sooner or later it would be discovered. The finding of the will, it seems, makes quite a dramatic story, of which I haven't yet had the full details.

"Anyway! Dated nineteen-fifty-two or thereabouts, this new document revoked the previous will. Uncle Pen was out in the cold, and again Aunt Essie wasn't even mentioned. Everything of which Clovis died possessed, cash, securities, property —including, of course, Greengrove—was left unconditionally to his 'elder son, Nicholas Arden Barclay,' or if the said Nicholas Barclay should not then be alive, it was still left unconditionally to . . . to . . ."

"Yes?" prompted Garret. "Yes? To whom?"

"To *me*," roared Nick. " 'To my beloved grandson, Nicholas Arden Barclay the younger, in the hope he will prove a worthier man than his father and the certainty he must prove a worthier one than his uncle.' Can you beat that, for God's sake? Did you ever hear anything like it?"

The dusty old room with the gilt-framed portraits, the dusty old premises on the south side of Covent Garden, trembled slightly to the roar of a jet plane high in the sky. Nick Barclay had jumped to his feet. Conquering a shaky throat, he pointed to the two empty glasses.

"Look, Garret! I can't pay for drinks at somebody else's club; I can't even order 'em. Still, considering your offer awhile ago . . ."

"Yes, sorry. Fred, two more of the same!"

The barman mixed Martinis, poured them, and discreetly vanished. Nick, a swaggering, good-natured figure of earnestness, leaned one hand on the bar-counter and lifted his glass with the other.

"Well, down the hatch."

"Good luck."

"Do you see, Garret? He left it to *me*, the old coot, when I don't need it and don't want it and won't have it. It won't do. And that's why I'm here: to put things right."

"I see. But how will you put them right?"

"Hell's bells, what kind of greedy bastard do they think I am? Uncle Pen will get his inheritance, once Aunt Essie is well provided for. And Pen, whatever else they say of him, is no tightwad or skinflint. When he still thought he was the heir, during nearly all of a calendar month, he was arranging to have three thousand a year settled on Essie for life. That must stand, if it's enough. Otherwise Pen will get the bulk of the estate, and above all things he'll get Greengrove. He lives in the past; that's why he loves the place so much. All this will entail some legal hocus-pocus, Dawlish says. But it can be done."

"You've talked to Mr. Dawlish, then?"

"I phoned him long-distance when I got in this morning. We've been exchanging air-mail letters at a great rate. He's coming up to town tomorrow to tell me the whole story. And that reminds me. Look, Garret! Can you come down with me to Greengrove for the week-end, train leaving Waterloo Friday evening, and lend a little moral support?"

"Yes; glad to. Any special reason why you need moral support?"

"I'm afraid so. There's been all hell to pay since they discovered that will in the tobacco-jar. It was Essie who found it, by the way. Uncle Pen's not been well. He goes round the house in one of those old-fashioned smoking-jackets people wore sixty years ago; he's even got a tame doctor in attendance. And when he learned that apparently he wasn't lord of the manor after all, it just about knocked him for a loop.

"Mind!" added Nick, as though carefully defining his terms. "Uncle Pen *may* be a little neurotic; these nervous temperaments usually are. In my opinion, he's more intense than anybody's ever suspected. He *might* have gone haywire and done something foolish, like putting a bullet through his head, if he'd thought he was going to be kicked out bag and baggage. But the first thing I wrote the solicitors, weeks and weeks ago, was to tell Uncle Pen he must keep Greengrove as he deserved to keep it. So that's settled, or I hope it is. All the same! If Mrs. Pen has been worried about him, can you blame her?"

"No."

"And that's not all that's been happening, either."

"Oh? What else has happened?"

"Haven't I indicated it? The so-called ghost! Something has been on the prowl, playing all kinds of ugly and inexplicable tricks, ever since they found Clovis's second will."

"Just a minute, Nick! You're not suggesting old Clovis himself has crawled out of his grave and is walking?"

"Lord, no!"

"Well, then?"

Nick pointed his glass at a half-length portrait of David Garrick playing Macbeth.

"The eighteenth century!" he said. "Sir Horace Wildfare, Mr. Justice Wildfare, the wicked old judge who built the house two hundred years ago. Although as to why *he* should be on the prowl, and at this particular time too, your guess is as good as mine."

"You don't believe in this ghost, I take it?"

"No, of course not! Any more than Uncle Pen believes it or Andy Dawlish believes it. Somebody's been masquerading, that's all. But who? And why? And how is it done? Melting into solid walls! Walking through locked doors! I hope this doesn't turn into a case for your old pal Dr. Gideon Fell, about whom you used to write letters. How is Dr. Fell, by the way?"

"Older, like the rest of us, but not much subdued. He and his friend Elliot, who's now Deputy Commander of the C.I.D., sometimes honour me by dropping in for a chat."

"Anyway, there you are. The cook and the maids are threatening to leave; Deidre is badly rattled; Aunt Essie's got the pip. In short, what with one thing or another . . ."

"Yes, I understand. One last drink before dinner?"

"Why not? I might as well get cockeyed as feel the way I do now. *Fred!*"

The discreet barman bustled in, mixed, poured, and discreetly scuttled out. More cigarette-smoke drifted up under the bar-hatch.

"And you ask me," pursued Nick, sipping rapidly, "why I want moral support? It's not ghosts, mind. There's something about this whole business that turns my stomach. I'm going down to that house, which after all is somebody else's house, being so all-fired lordly and priggishly magnanimous . . ."

"It's a very decent thing to do, Nick."

"The hell it is. It's plain justice, as you know very well. Jesus, Garret, what else *can* I do? The money means nothing to Uncle Pen; he's loaded anyway. But I can't take his beloved Greengrove away from him, even though—" Nick stopped abruptly.

"Even though . . . what?"

"Nothing; forget it; it's the drinks talking."

"I don't think it's the drinks talking, Nick. What's wrong?"

"Wrong?"

"There's something else on your mind, bothering you worse than all the rest put together, and for some reason you won't even mention it. What's wrong?"

"No, Garret, I can't have that."

"You can't have? . . ."

"No, I can't. *You're* the one with something on his mind. I knew it when you flared out about mysterious women, and again for certain when I spoke of Pen's wife being so much younger than he is. Something's eating your insides out; it'll do you good to talk. Come, old muse of history and biography! Come, my Victorian mossback with the potentialities of a hellion! Haven't you got anything to tell *me?*"

Garret stared at the past.

"Yes, possibly I have. You'll treat it in confidence, I hope?"

"You know I will, Garret. What's the beef?"

"It's not what you might call a beef, exactly. . . ."

"All right! What is it?"

Invisible blue-devils gathered and beat their drums. David Garrick, Mrs. Siddons, a whole host of theatrical celebrities from the eighteenth century to the end of the Victorian era looked on in frozen posturing. The spurt of a match, as Garret struck it, made a small core of light in the darkening bar.

"It's not much, I suppose, but at the time it meant a good deal. Last May a year ago, being at something of a loose end after finishing *Disraeli,* I went over for a brief holiday in Paris."

"Fair enough. Well?"

Again Garret stared at the past.

"Well, as you suggested, I met a dame."

3

AND SO, early on that Friday evening in June, Garret Anderson packed a bag in his flat at Hampstead and rang for a taxi to take him to Waterloo.

Friday, June 12.

Warmth and sunset held the town. Garret's cab rolled down Rosslyn Hill and Haverstock Hill; at Camden Town it cut to the left through Bloomsbury, past the new Euston, across Russell Square, round Aldwych into the Strand for Waterloo Bridge and the station beyond. The streets, always traffic-tangled at any hour following those latest regulations which forbid you to make left or right turns at any reasonable and sensible place, occasioned frequent halts at red lights.

Garret noticed none of this. He was preoccupied with thinking of what he had told Nick Barclay on Wednesday night, or, to be exact, with what he had not said on Wednesday night. Faced with the decision to tell his old friend about Fay, he had found himself so tongue-tied, what Nick would have called inhibited, that his account was as discreet and edited as that of any family lawyer.

Still, even if he had been willing to explain everything, how could he? He simply didn't know.

In the taxi he remembered reality.

It had been in the glowing month of May, a little over a year ago, when he found himself on an early-afternoon flight to Paris. Beside him next the window sat a half-dreaming girl, absurdly young and innocent-seeming—could she have been more than twenty-one at most?—who asked him some question about the flight.

He looked round into her eyes: dark-blue eyes, shy, sidelong of glance, yet with a certain intensity behind their naïveté; at the clear colours of health in her fair complexion; at heavy, glossy fair hair worn shoulder-length; at a figure slender but sturdy and beautifully shaped in the light tweed travelling-suit. Before the plane touched down at Orly they were talking twenty to the dozen.

Her name, she said, was Fay Wardour. She had left an (unspecified) job, she told him, partly because a small legacy from a deceased aunt enabled her to do so; she was spending the whole legacy for this adventure abroad—ten days in Paris, a week in Rome—before returning to another job in June. Then they discovered that they would be staying at hotels close to each other: he at the Meurice, a favourite of his, and she at a larger if less flamboyant hive not far away in the rue de Rivoli.

"Hotels St. James et d'Albany. *Sic!*" said Fay with her little laugh. "It sounds terribly incongruous, somehow."

"Like 'the Grand Hotel of Little-Marmalade and of the Universe'?"

"Yes! They're always using names like that, aren't they? Not that *I* would know. I'm a very ignorant and untravelled person; when I speak French, it's of the most dreadfully primitive schoolgirl kind."

"Would you care to exercise your French by going to the theatre tonight?"

"I'd love to!" breathed Fay.

So they had dinner at Fouquet's and went on to the Théâtre Sarah Bernhardt, where both were held enthralled by a spectacular Sardou melodrama done with that convincing *panache* which only Gallic actors know how to manage.

Thus began an enchanted ten days before Fay must go on to Rome. They prowled the quais. They inspected the waxworks at the Grévin and the Punch-and-Judy off the Champs-Elysées. They visited the opera as well as several striptease nightclubs. They dined in the open air, with a high pallor of streetlamps sifting down through chestnut-trees; Garret, usually abstemious, drank rather more wine than was good for him, and Fay too needed little urging in this respect.

Above all things he was enchanted by Fay herself: her good humour, her eagerness, her intelligence and sense of fun, no less than a power of sympathy which seemed to hang on every word he spoke. She would walk for miles at his side, uncomplaining. But she would never permit him to assume avuncular airs. This became manifest when he took her on a walking-tour through Old Paris, that maze of grey streets from the Middle Ages and the Renaissance lying at a very long stone's throw round the Musée Carnavalet in the rue de Sevigné.

"The next turning, Fay . . . getting tired?"

"Good heavens, no! How could I be, when you go on telling me these things? That last place, where Henri Quatre kept What's-her-name in the house across the way: it's absolutely fascinating! What were you saying?"

"The next turning, Fay, will be the rue Simon Le Franc, Simple Simon Street."

"What are we going to find in Simple Simon Street?"

"That will appear in a minute. You see, young lady . . ."

"Oh, don't! Please don't!"

"Don't what?"

"Don't talk like that! As though—as though I weren't quite grown up!"

"You're not quite grown up, are you?"

"But I am! Oh, I am! *You* know that, don't you?"

And in most respects, he had to admit, she was right. The most important feature of that ten days' delirium he could not tell Nick Barclay; he could not tell anybody. In the dining-room at the Thespis Club, with more theatrical portraits, he could only indicate Fay's more obvious perfections, and Nick, assuming an air of profound age and wisdom, tried hard to translate.

"Look," Nick said. "Apart from the qualities you just *liked* about her, this Miss X of yours, I gather, was uncommonly attractive? Damned attractive? Physically attractive?"

"Yes, all of that."

"In short, quite a dish. And you're plainly a man of experience, though you look like such an inhibited stuffed-shirt. I hope you improved your opportunities, old horse. Did you . . . er? . . ."

"Damn it, Nick, do you expect me to answer a question like that?"

"So you won't talk, eh?" inquired Nick. "You're a perfect gentleman, and you won't talk. But I'm no gentleman; I never was. *I'd* talk my head off, believe you me, if a dish like that threw herself into *my* arms without saying boo. O.K.; keep your secrets. But I'll draw my own conclusions, you rat. With Paris making its medicine as it always does, I still wonder if she didn't slip off her clothes and get down to it."

As a matter of fact, Fay had. Their affair began on the very first night, when Garret escorted her back to her hotel. He had no intention of seducing her, or so he believed until it happened; there seemed too great a difference between their ages. But he could not help himself. Whether inspired by night or wine or Paris making its medicine or some deeper cause, no sooner had he touched her than Fay's shyness and diffidence were submerged in an utter abandon which startled him as much as it delighted him and turned his brain. If some inner voice of caution warned him to be careful, he stifled the voice. He had lost his head; he didn't care. Nor, it appeared, did Fay. It was not so much what she said or did; such things can be counterfeited; in the delirium of intimacy there were unmistakable physical signs that she shared his own emotions to the full. And so commenced a delirium which gave no sign of abating. Despite casual affairs in the past, it was as though another voice whispered to him, 'This is it.'

But was it? Not quite grown up, had he suggested? At the act of love, anyway, Fay was skilled, rapt, and so experienced that he felt more than a stab of jealousy towards others she had known. During the ensuing days she displayed different, less comprehensible moods. Fay would never allow herself to be photographed, even against one of those comic contrivances where you put your head above a cardboard motor-car and look foolish. The mere mention of marriage, anybody's marriage, provoked in her a bitterness, a kind of acid gibe, as puzzling as it seemed foreign to her gentle nature. Occasionally, too, would occur black night-time humours from no apparent cause. There would be alarms, depressions, sometimes even a fury of tears.

"Darling," she once whispered, "suppose I weren't really what I pretend to be?"

"What you pretend to be?"

"What if I had no right to the name I'm using? What if I'd already got myself involved in a frightfully sordid business—innocently, it's true, but a really ghastly mess that would only make you hate me?"

"Have I asked any questions? Do you imagine any of those things could make the least difference, even if they happened to be true?"

"They would, darling. You think they wouldn't, maybe, but I *know* they would."

"They wouldn't, I tell you!"

"Oh, Garret!" And then, presently, "Well! We're ending on a high note, at least."

"Ending? What do you mean, ending?"

"Darling! Have you forgotten I'm flying to Rome on Monday?"

"Well, what if you are? I'll go with you."

"You can't! You mustn't! I'd give anything on earth if you could, but you mustn't. I'm—I'm visiting an old friend from school, and somebody else from the same year is flying out to join us. You know what would happen if you were there. It mustn't happen, Garret; they'd be shocked. They're wonderful people, but they'd be terribly shocked. I must preserve *some* outward show of decency, though I'd like to spend the rest of my life just as I am now. And it's not really ending; please say it isn't! We'll meet in London, won't we, just as soon as I get back? Let's make a date now."

Such were the details he did not divulge to Nick Barclay, though he could tell the sequel. In the dining-room at the Thespis Club, hurrying over indifferent food but making deep inroads on a bottle of claret, Nick had assumed an even more portentous air.

"Do you realize," he struck in, "you've not even told me her surname? This 'Miss X' business, first name Fay, has gone far enough. Since you're still so romantically interested in a disappearing charmer, would it do any great harm if you told me her name?"

"None at all. But I'm not even sure I know what her name is."

"A fake name? You think she was giving you the run-around?"

"I don't know what to think. It was hard to believe at first, human vanity being what it is. But—"

"But you never saw her again after she left for Rome?"

"Never again. She was supposed to join me for dinner at the Ivy on June twenty-fourth—in another fortnight that will be just a year. After I had waited there for two hours beyond the time any companion could be expected to turn up, it was plain I'd well and truly had it. End of comedy."

"Comedy, eh? Did you try to find her?"

"Her name's not in the telephone-book, though I've got no reason to be sure she lives in London. What else could I do?"

"You're acquainted with the Deputy Commander of the C.I.D. You could have gone to the police."

"With what information? They'd only have said it was no business of theirs, and they'd have been right. Or, even if they had helped me and had found her, what might have been the result? For Fay, possibly only embarrassment—or worse."

"In case she's married already, you mean?"

"That's one possibility. I don't know."

"There are private detectives."

"There are. But the result might be just the same. For Fay . . ."

"And you won't have the lady upset in any way. Is that it?"

"That's it."

"I'll bet *I* could find her for you if I put the boys properly to work. But you won't have that either, or will you?"

"No, I will not. I tell you, Nick, I've tried to think of every possible explanation. I've tried to think she wanted to turn up but that there was some simple reason why she couldn't. I've even tortured myself thinking of accidents that might have happened to her! . . ."

"Have you, now, poor devil?" Nick said earnestly. "Look,

Garret. You're in a bad way, and you've got to snap out of this. Take advice; consult the oracle."

"That's what I'm doing."

"Then the great man will speak. After careful consideration of this recital, judgment is hereby given that what sent you overboard was nothing more or less than plain, simple, old-fashioned sex."

"All right, all right, supposing it were so. What's wrong with that?"

"Look, my lad! This is your Uncle Nick speaking! There's *nothing* wrong with it, for God's sake, nothing in the world. Encounters like yours with Fay are happening all the time. That's the whole point. Relish it; enjoy it in retrospect. But don't take it too seriously, as it's plain she didn't. Don't confuse the issue. Don't magnify a sound, healthy biological urge into a romantic grand passion out of a Victorian novel. Provided you can see your idyll in proper perspective, it's the best thing that could have happened."

"Common sense suggests you're right. Common sense also agrees it was probably for the best, considering the difference between Fay's age and mine. All the same . . ."

"Grow up, Garret. You'll live to thank me for this. And bear in mind, old son," pontificated Nick, gulping down more claret, "that you're now committed to an encounter of a very different kind. On Friday evening, unless you renege on your promise, you're going down to Hampshire to help solve several problems—concerning a suicidally minded Uncle Pen and his frightened wife, concerning Aunt Essie and her vapours, concerning an alleged ghost that can walk through locked doors without leaving a trace."

The train, Nick had said on Wednesday, confirming it after talking to Andrew Dawlish on the following day, would be at seven-fifteen. Many towns and villages lie close together in or round the fringes of the New Forest, Brockenhurst and Lymington among them. Their station would be Brockenhurst, the next stop after Southampton Central. They would arrive about nine-thirty-five; they could get something to eat in the train, which should not be crowded because by Friday evening any rush of holiday-makers would already have gone. At Brockenhurst, Mr. Dawlish was quoted as saying, a car would be waiting to take them the seven or eight miles across country to Lepe Beach and Satan's Elbow.

And so? . . .

Waterloo, shuffling with echoes under its glass roof, held only a sparse crowd. Garret bought a first-class return ticket and pushed on through. Two companions, as arranged, were waiting by the bookstall.

"My dear Nicholas—" began a grave, heavy voice.

"Look!" said Nick Barclay.

Nick, hatless, in sports-coat and slacks, carried a heavy suitcase. Facing him, his back to the bookstall, stood a squat, square man—"like Macaulay," Garret could not help thinking —with the *Evening Standard* in one hand and a brief-case in the other.

Mr. Andrew Dawlish, a widower of sixty with a grown son who was the other member of Dawlish & Dawlish, wore the professional uniform of short black coat, striped trousers, and bowler hat. For all his gravity there was a certain lightness about him; his wiry fair hair seemed hardly tinged with grey. If his manner showed more than a trace of complacence and pomposity, you could not treat this too seriously because you sensed immense dependability underneath. Yet he stood and pontificated as Nick had done on Wednesday night.

"I will allow, Nicholas, that I find you not *quite* so Americanized as I had feared. You use these vulgarisms, it is true, as we all tend to do under the influence of television, but you preserve much of the old intonation. As I was saying . . ."

"Whoa, steady!" interrupted Nick, swinging round. "Here's Garret; here's the wandering minstrel at last." Rapidly he performed introductions. "Now the whole Dirty Crew is assembled, and we can get on with it."

"May I suggest, Nicholas, that you lower your voice a little?"

"Didn't you hear what I said? This is Garret Anderson. He's my oldest friend. Anything you tell me you can tell him too."

"But might I further suggest that it is not necessary to tell the whole station? Mr. Anderson," pursued the solicitor, looking exactly like pictures of Macaulay, "it is a great pleasure to make your acquaintance. I have read several of your books and enjoyed them all. Our young friend Nicholas, I greatly fear, considers me too cautious and close-mouthed. But one has certain duties to perform. And I flatter myself he will follow my advice, if I may add *that*."

"Yes, you may add it," said Nick. "I'm all for Duty, Stern Daughter of the Voice of God, and I'll follow your advice when I know what it is. But will you, in one word, answer a straight question without any whereases or as-aforesaid stipulateds?"

"In one word," replied Mr. Dawlish, "yes."

"Uncle Pen . . ."

"Ah, yes, your Uncle Pennington!" Mr. Dawlish spoke to a point between Nick and Garret. "We once expected great things of Pennington, or I confess *I* did. He again talks of writing a play, just as he used to do in the old days, though actually all he seems to do is compose long letters to literary weeklies and dictate them to his secretary. It has been a trying time, you know. His health ... his heart ... the shock of these past weeks ..."

Nick waved a mesmeric hand.

"Now look, Blackstone's Commentaries!" he interposed. "You're cautious, all right. And you may be close-mouthed, though I hadn't particularly observed it. Can the man who's asking the question get a word in edgeways?"

"Yes. I beg your pardon. What is it?"

"Well! We're all right, aren't we?"

"All right?"

"You *did* tell Uncle Pen he's not being thrown out like an old toothpaste-tube? That he can have his beloved Greengrove and keep it to the end of his natural life and beyond?"

"I told him, yes. I told him long ago, as you instructed me. I also took the liberty of informing Miss Deidre at the same time.

"Miss Deidre, I should explain," the solicitor added to Garret, "is actually Mrs. Pennington Barclay. The servants began calling her that at the instigation of Mr. Barclay"—*Mr.* Barclay, evidently, was the late old Clovis—"and some of us, alas, have contracted the habit. She is a charming young lady of whom Pennington *ought* to be proud.

"Yes, Nicholas, I informed him. But this is a wicked world, as so far you would have little cause to learn. Men cling with greedy fingers to the things they inherit by law, and Pennington is not altogether of a trusting nature. I delivered to him the message you sent; yours was a generous gesture. The question is: does he believe you meant it?"

"Look, for God's sake! Of course I meant it!"

"*I* believe that. But does Pennington? He is an unpredictable man, an imaginative man in a corner. What, precisely, is your definition of 'all right'? And what, by loose terminology and still looser thinking, might he himself consider to be the end of his natural life? If by any chance ..."

"Nuts, Counsellor!" roared Nick. "Nuts, balderdash, and in your eye! If you're saying Uncle Pen is crazy enough to knock himself off ..."

"I don't say it. I don't even think it. I say only that my old friend is moody and unpredictable. And I further say," Mr. Dawlish added with some urgency, "we must not dawdle here. We must make haste now if we are to catch that train."

"Nonsense! There's plenty of time!"

"Your pardon, but there is not. Look at the clock. I would

not press you, Nicholas, but we have another reason for not missing the train or distressing the household. Do you know what today is?"

"It's Friday."

"It is June twelfth. And tomorrow?"

"Unless they've been monkeying with the almanac, tomorrow will be June thirteenth."

"As you shrewdly point out, it will be June thirteenth. It will also be your Aunt Estelle's birthday."

"The ceremony, eh? They're still keeping up the ceremony?"

"They are."

"Remember, Garret? When anybody there has a birthday, there's quite a ceremony at the old place. I told you, didn't I?"

"Yes, you told me. What sort of ceremony?"

"On the night *before* the great day, the current cook prepares an elaborate cake. It's carried with state into the dining-room; there's speech-making and present-giving. This is always done at eleven o'clock on the night before. Uncle Pen used to claim it ought to be at midnight, but Aunt Essie said it would be keeping 'the children' up too late. Since I was the only kid ever to haunt the joint, it seemed rather a sweeping statement. . . . Her birthday, eh? I don't imagine Essie will relish being fifty-five, if that's what she is. But you're quite right, Blackstone, we can't disappoint the old girl. Come on!"

Nick beckoned to a hovering porter and swung the heavy suitcase into his hand.

"Here you are, my lad," he continued. "Ours is the seven-fifteen. Which gate?"

"Number eleven, sir. Just over there. Bournemouth, sir?"

"We're not going as far as Bournemouth, but it's the same train. Shove that bag into a first-class smoker, preferably an empty one."

"Got your ticket, sir? Front of the train, sir; that's best. I'll nip on ahead, and you follow. Right?"

"Right. What's the matter with the rest of you? God's teeth, come *on!*"

Nick, once determining on a course, plunged at it. Past the barrier, flourishing his ticket, he hurried off down the platform at a stride that was almost a run. Mr. Dawlish, who despite pomposity could move rapidly when he chose, trotted beside him swinging the brief-case. Garret brought up the rear.

The sun had gone behind a cloud; the platform and the train, on their right—a long one with cream-and-chocolate-coloured carriages of surprising cleanliness—lay shadowed and rather chilly-looking under a begrimed skylight. They strode towards the head of the platform, through little knots of other travellers drifting in. They passed the restaurant-car, where somebody's disconsolate face looked out through a barred pantry-window; they had reached the leading coach and were veering towards it in the wake of the porter when Nick Barclay spoke again.

"It won't be much of a party, things being what they are. I'd clean forgotten the old girl's birthday, if I ever knew what it was, and there's no time now to get her a present."

"On the contrary, Nicholas. You bring her the handsomest and most welcome of birthday gifts. Need I say that I refer to the settlement? Pennington proposed this; you confirm it; and Estelle at least has no cause to doubt your good faith. Things should go pleasantly enough, I think, provided you and Pennington refrain from clever comments. Miss Deidre is most anxious things should go pleasantly. Did you speak, Mr. Anderson?"

"Yes," said Garret, who was about ten paces behind them. "Forgive this intrusion, but—the lady you mention! Mrs. Pennington Barclay! What's she like?"

Unchecked in his stride, Mr. Dawlish answered with head half turned.

"Surely, sir, I have endeavoured to make that clear? Pennington's wife is charming, entirely charming. Despite the disparity in their ages . . ."

"Yes, of course. But that was not quite what I meant. What does she look like? How should you describe her?"

"A difficult question, sir."

"Yes, but—"

"The most captious critic," declared Mr. Dawlish, "would be obliged to concede that she is quite pretty. Miss Deidre looks even younger than she actually is. In person she is of medium height for a woman, light-haired, with a fine graciousness of manner which . . ."

Nick Barclay stopped short.

"A blonde, is she?" Then Nick whirled round. "By all the unholy ironies that couldn't be, *a blonde!* God's teeth, Garret, what's got into your head now?"

"Nothing! Nothing at all!"

It was Garret's turn to stop short. Led by the porter, who had opened a door at the extreme forward end of the coach, the other two climbed up inside. A little stir animated the platform. Garret still stood motionless, with an idea that wouldn't go away, when somebody touched his elbow from behind. It was another porter, massive of face and conspiratorial of manner.

"Beg-pardon, sir. But the lady said—"

"What lady?"

"Last compartment o' this kerridge, sir. It's a kerridge, sir, with the corridor on the far side. If yer wants to go into that compartment, see, yer goes in by the door on the right, 'ere, and straight ahead, and round the corner to the left. 'Fore you join the other gentlemen, the lady says, will yer please stop and see 'er for just a minute?"

"Thanks." Garret gave over the small case he was carrying, together with half a crown to prompt good service. "Take this to the compartment where the others went. Tell them I have no intention of missing the train and I shall be with them as soon as I can."

It wasn't possible, of course, and yet! . . . He glanced round. Then he went racing.

Against the broad window, in shadow like the other train-windows here, showed a triangular red wafer with the white letters *No Smoking*. Somebody inside had glanced back at him. Standing there, one hand on the window but head now half averted as though trying not to look at all, was Fay Wardour.

4

ANTI-CLIMAX? Or worse?

"God's teeth!" Nick might have said.

Nevertheless, as Garret rolled open the door of the compartment and faced Fay, it was certain that his entrance produced an emotional explosion of some kind. He might have laughed. They might both have laughed. But they didn't.

She was alone. In a blue-and-white summer dress, stockingless and with blue shoes, Fay cowered back towards the upholstery of the corner seat by the window. She looked even more alluring and desirable than he remembered, but it was as though she were expecting a physical blow. With trembling fingers she fumbled at the clasps of a white handbag and snapped it open. Though they might be in a non-smoking compartment, from the bag Fay juggled out a tortoise-shell cigarette-case and fumbled to open this like a nervous conjurer trying to palm it. Then incongruous things began happening all at once.

Outside, where a luggage-cart rumbled on concrete, a prosperous-looking business-man suddenly ran past the window, pelting hard towards the front of the train; he stopped, turned, and for some reason frantically dashed back along the platform in the other direction. At the same moment Fay flipped open the tortoise-shell case. From what cause Garret could not tell, a filter-tipped cigarette flew out and up as though propelled. It made an arc in the air and fell on the seat opposite.

"Oh, dear!" blurted Fay. "Oh, d-dear!"

Trembling all over, choking back other words and perhaps poised on the edge of hysterical laughter, she sat down abruptly. In somewhat lofty fashion, with the care and deliberation of his own shaken nerves, Garret picked up the cigarette and handed it towards her.

"Yours, I believe?"

"But *I* don't want it!"

"Well, do you think I want it?"

"Oh, d-dear! This is rather ridiculous, isn't it?"

" 'Ridiculous,' Fay, may not be quite the right word; but let it go. Now, look here, my girl———"

"No, wait! Listen to me; do please listen to me! Will you?"

Dark-blue eyes, dark-lashed against the fair complexion, swam up towards him and unsettled his judgment.

"Well?"

"That elderly man just ahead of you . . . he spoke to you, though I couldn't quite hear what was said. . . ."

"The one who looks like Macaulay?"

"Does he? Anyway! That was Mr. Dawlish, wasn't it? The lawyer? Then the young man with him . . ."

"Young man?"

"Yes! That must have been Mr. Nicholas Barclay. Wasn't it? I thought so! You mentioned him once as being a great friend of yours and said you'd been at school with him. Oh, Garret! You're on your way to Greengrove, aren't you?"

"I am. Whereas you're already *at* Greengrove?"

"Well—yes. Why do you ask?"

"Why do I ask?"

A faint noise of slamming doors ran along the line of carriages. A whistle blew. Smoothly gliding, Diesel-engine-powered, the train rolled out of the station. Fay gestured nervously towards the seat opposite. But Garret did not sit down. He stood in front of her, a little unsteadily as the train swayed under gathering speed, and contemplated her like a schoolmaster.

"Since you have no remotest idea why I ask, I'll try to tell you. But there is just one question, Fay, if that happens to be your real name...."

"Of c-course it's my real name! It always has been! Why ever shouldn't it be?"

"You once said——"

"I was talking about my surname! And I've got a p-perfect *legal* right to that too, whatever you may hear in the future."

"Then your first name's not Deidre? Are you Pennington Barclay's wife?"

"Oh, good heavens! This is *awful*. This is worse than anything I'd dreamed of, and I've dreamed of a lot of things. No, Garret! I'm not Pennington Barclay's wife; I'm not anybody's wife and never have been, thank God. Who ever told you I was Mrs. Barclay?"

"Nobody told me. It was a random lunacy out of nowhere. Then I heard a description of Mrs. Pen, and it seemed to fit. 'Medium height,' Dawlish said, though you're on the small side. And also 'fair-haired.'"

"Please, Garret! I've met Mr. Dawlish; he's nothing if not precise. Did he actually *say* fair-haired?"

"No, he didn't. In the strict detective-story sense, come to think of it, he said 'light-haired.' But it amounts to much the same thing, doesn't it?"

"No, not really! Listen, won't you? Deidre Barclay—she was Deidre Meadows when I first knew her—has *brown* hair, a really pretty and attractive shade of light brown. She's taller than I am; she has better manners; she's of good character and altogether much, *much* more presentable. 'Medium height, light-haired' is a good enough description of Deidre, but it wouldn't fit me nearly as well. If you *will* get these wild ideas . . ."

"If I have had wild ideas, Fay, I submit there has been reason for 'em. Then, in the matter of mistaking you for Mrs. Pen, there was also the disparity in ages. And yet age, apparently means nothing in your young life. Awhile ago you referred to Nick Barclay as 'young,' though he's actually the same age as I am: a dull, flat, unmistakable forty. Whereas you—"

"Darling, darling," Fay burst out, "do you know how old I actually am?"

"Twenty-two at the most, maybe? Since my guess a year ago was twenty-one . . ."

"I am *thirty*-two," cried Fay with a kind of vindictiveness towards herself, "and I shall be thirty-three in September. Any woman could have told you that to look at me. But it's not the same with men. They can't see or they just won't notice. Provided a woman's not actually hideous, and *seems* young, and has all the use of her . . . her . . ."

"Faculties?"

"Well, yes. Allow so much, and they'll convince themselves of anything. Still, there's the truth. I'm a dull, flat, aging thirty-two, and rather an odd hag in soul and spirit. What do you say to that?"

Garret lifted a fist in which he had violently crushed the cigarette picked up from the seat.

"I say, madam, it's the best news I have heard in my own advancing centuries. I also observe that by some curious slip of the tongue you are again addressing me with the intimacy of old days. May I sit down beside you?"

"No, don't! I can't stop you if you insist, but please don't!"

"Why not?"

"Because I don't want you to. No, that's not true; I'm lying again!" Fay's hands flew to hide her face and then dropped. "I do want you to, more than anything, even in the stuffiness of British Railways and with Clapham Junction going past. But it can't be. What I'm thinking about mustn't happen; it mustn't!"

"What are you thinking about?"

"Garret, the same thing you are. But it mustn't happen, I say, because the whole situation is horrible and will only get worse. Shall we—shall we settle a few things between ourselves?"

"By all means, if you feel up to discussing them."

"Well!"

Fay sat back, crossing her knees and smoothing down her skirt. Beside her, in the extreme corner of the seat, had been wedged a parcel whose wrapping-paper bore the label of a famous West End bookshop. For a moment the fingers of her left hand idly tapped this parcel. The colour rose in her face and then receded. Garret sat down opposite, watching her.

"I am Pennington Barclay's secretary," she told him. "I'm not his wife or—or anything like that. I'm his *secretary* and have been for about a year. Didn't I *say* that after my holiday I was going back to another job?"

"Yes, but it's all you did say."

"Well, Garret, if you weren't even interested enough to ask . . ."

"No, woman, this is *not* going to become a logical demonstration of how much I am in the wrong. Every time I approached the subject, or tried to, you veered off into clouds and said it wasn't important."

"I'm sorry! I really am most terribly sorry! But I did tell you, surely, I was going to Italy to visit a girl I had known at school? And that another friend from the same year was flying out to join us?"

"Yes. You got that far."

"The first one was Alice Willesden, who's now married to the Conte da Carpi and lives outside Rome. The other was Deidre Meadows: Deidre Barclay, she's been since nineteen-fifty-eight. It's rather ridiculous, isn't it"—a faint bubble of humour welled up through Fay's nervousness—"that this should be a case of old school friends meeting as they pass? You were at school with Nicholas Barclay. Whereas Deidre and Alice and I . . .

"You see, Garret, it was Deidre who got me this position as her husband's secretary. She'd arranged it before either of us left England last year. Mr. Barclay—Mr. Pennington Barclay—doesn't know who I really am. Deidre does know; she never believed what they said; she was willing to take a chance, and she's absolutely loyal. Mr. Barclay, I repeat, doesn't know a single thing about me."

"Well, neither do I."

"What's that?"

"I said: neither do I. Who are you really, Madam Sphinx-without-reason? What do they say about you that's so terrible, and what's the 'ghastly mess' you hinted you'd walked into? In short, why all the mystery and what are we arguing about?

"Seriously, Fay, isn't it time you dispelled this tempest-in-a-teapot with a little plain speaking? For God's sake, don't behave like the heroine in a story, who for no reason at all won't say a word when two sentences would have cleared up most of the difficulties to begin with. But it's not easy to work out the evidence here. When you wouldn't hear of my accompanying you to Rome, just in case your friends might notice we hadn't been the most casual of acquaintances or dinner-companions in Paris . . ."

"Oh, Garret! If *that* were all! . . ."

"It wasn't?"

"If that were all, or even a tenth part of it," Fay cried in a passion of earnestness, "do you think I should have cared what they thought or anybody thought? I'm no Puritan maid, you know."

"Agreed. Neither the noun nor the adjective."

"Besides! I told Deidre about us; I mean, I told her how I felt about you and—and what we'd been doing."

("Did you, now?")

"Deidre may be a trifle strait-laced, or like people to think she is. But she's human and she's understanding. She understood everything, Garret; *she* won't give us away." Fay broke off. "Why, darling? Wasn't that all right?"

"Yes, of course it was! But—"

"However could I guess I'd meet you here? Do you think I didn't *want* you to go to Rome? Do you think I didn't *want* to meet you at the Ivy as we'd arranged? I did; I did a hundred times over! But I resolved never to see you again (and I'll keep that vow, so help me, as soon as you've left Greengrove), because I won't have *you* involved with *me*. I won't see you hurt, I won't have you suffer because of me, as you're bound to do if the truth ever comes out."

"Fay, stop this damned nonsense!"

"Nonsense, is it? That's all you know! And don't be cross; don't be cruel to me; please don't. For the truth may come out whatever I do. If anything happens at that dreadful house, if Mr. Barclay should kill himself or come to harm in some way . . ."

Again Fay stopped, hand to mouth. Above the drone of wheels, above the creak and lurch of a train speeding through open country, footsteps approached in the corridor. Outside the door's glass panel appeared the grey coat and sleep-walker's face of a restaurant-car attendant, who slid open the door and looked blindly in.

"Dinner now being served," he intoned in a vacant voice; "dinner now being served."

Then, apparently seeing nobody, he rolled shut the door and went sleepwalking on. Late sunlight flooded through from the other side. Garret Anderson got up.

"You hear that, Fay? We can . . ."

"Oh, but we can't! We mustn't!"

"Mustn't have anything to eat?"

"Garret, you don't understand! I had dinner before I left town; I *couldn't* eat anything; it would choke me. But that's not what I meant. Go up ahead and join the others. But don't tell them I'm here; don't say you met me; and, in the future, don't even *hint* we were acquainted before!"

"Hang it, Fay, why make more mysteries? Besides, even if I wanted to pretend you're not here, how could I? We're all bound to meet when we leave the train at Brockenhurst."

"No, we needn't meet at all. I'll get out at Southampton Central, which is twenty minutes before Brockenhurst, and get a bus straight to Lepe Beach. I can say I took another train; I can make some excuse. Anyway, at Greengrove we can be introduced as total strangers."

"But what's the good of the hocus-pocus? Was there any very sinister reason why you were in London today?"

"Oh, for heaven's sake, *no!*" Fay touched the parcel beside her. "Mr. Barclay wanted some books; he asked me to go up this morning and fetch them. He could have got them sent down by post, I suppose; that's what he usually does. But he asked me to go, and so I did."

"Then why conceal it? As for meeting as total strangers, I'm beginning to wonder whether that's possible. Since your friend Deidre already knows . . ."

"Yes. And, now we're on the subject, I should like most awfully to ask a question too. Have *you* told anybody about us?"

This was one in the eye, jarring him a little. "Well, yes. I told Nick Barclay. After all—"

"If I can tell my friend about you, why shouldn't you tell your friend about me? Isn't that what you're thinking?"

"Not in those terms, exactly. Something like that, though."

"Garret! Did you tell him *everything* about us? Did you tell him we . . . we . . ."

"No, I did not. From anything I said or admitted, it might have been a meeting out of Victorian fiction. Women, it seems, have less reticence in these matters."

"What's he like, this Nick Barclay? Is he nice? But I don't really mean that; I mean: is he truly your friend and can you trust him?"

"Yes, I trust him entirely. So can you. Nick has a peculiar sense of humour, that's all. But he's clever; he guessed a good deal. Also, when I had the wild idea that Mrs. Pennington Barclay might turn out to be you, he had the very same idea too."

"Oh? Whatever gave *him* the notion?"

"The same thing that made me wonder: Mr. Dawlish's description of Mrs. Pen as light-haired. Nick burst out with some exclamation about blondes and asked me what had got into my head, with a plain indication of what had got into his."

"He thought Deidre might be a blonde? Oh, that's impossible! He can't have!"

"Well, he was shouting along the platform. If the window had been open you'd have heard him."

"I don't say the words weren't used. I only say . . ."

Fay had sprung up to face Garret. The train lurched at high speed, almost throwing them into each other's arms. Both flinched; both drew back and sat down again.

"He can't have thought that, I tell you!" Fay insisted. "And I'm not making mysteries again, either! Up to March of this year, anyway, Miss Estelle Barclay occasionally corresponded with your friend Nick's mother."

"Yes, so I've heard. Well?"

"When I first went to Greengrove, about this time last summer, old Mr. Barclay was still alive."

"Grandfather Clovis? He was something of a terror, wasn't he?"

"He could be very trying if you didn't know how to handle him. Usually he was as nice as pie both to Deidre and me. He went for everybody else, especially Pennington and Estelle, and he didn't restrain his language in any way. However, that's not the point. Last year it was an unusually fine autumn, after that wretched summer weather. I had my camera, and I took some very good colour snapshots."

"Without allowing your own picture to be taken?"

"Oh, what's that got to do with it?" Fay sat forward intently. "As I say, I took some very good snaps in colour. One was of Deidre and her husband in the garden; another was of Miss Barclay herself. Miss Barclay asked me to have duplicates made of those two, and I did. She sent them to . . . to . ."

"Nick's mother?"

"Yes! A few days later, when I was typing one of Mr. Barclay's usual letters to the *Spectator* or *Time and Tide*, she came to me with the duplicate set and said, 'I think my dear nephew might like to have these. But it's no good writing a note; he won't acknowledge it. Will you type the address I give you, please, and put these into an envelope and send them?'

"Well, that's what I did. On the back of one was written, 'Pen and Deidre, nineteen-sixty-three,' and on the back of the other, 'Essie,' also with date. The picture of Deidre was especially distinct. So your friend Nick *knew* the colour of her hair, didn't he? He couldn't possibly have thought she was a blonde!"

"I don't know, Fay. Nick's a busy man. If those photographs went astray in the post, or you sent them care of Willis-Barclay Publications . . ."

"But I didn't! They were sent to his flat. I even remember how she gave me the name and address American style: 'Mr. Nicholas Barclay, Junior, Fifty-two East Sixty-fourth Street, New York something'—a zone number. And how often do letters really go astray in the post?"

"Even so, there are all sorts of explanations."

"Yes, I dare say. Stop a bit, though! Garret! You don't suppose? . . ."

"Suppose what?"

"What if this man should be an impostor, like the Tichborne Claimant or somebody, and not really Nick Barclay at all?"

"Good God, woman, who's getting the wild ideas *now?* Do you think I don't know the bloke I was at school with?"

"Still! If you haven't seen him in all this time . . ."

"I saw him four years ago, when he stopped in London in his way to Morocco. He's the real Nick Barclay and nobody else; take my word for that."

Fay was covered with a pouring contrition.

"Oh, Garret, do please pay no attention when I begin maundering! Or hit me; wallop me; take me by the shoulders and shake me. All right! He's the real Nick Barclay, and I don't really care what you tell him, provided you tell him privately. He's the real Nick Barclay, returned after a quarter of a century to dispossess his relatives."

"In another minute, Fay, there'll be good excuse for walloping you. Nick has not come back to dispossess anybody. On the contrary, he's here to hand over the whole estate to his Uncle Pen and his Aunt Essie. Hadn't you heard?"

"Yes, I heard. The lawyer told Mr. Barclay. He also told Deidre, and Deidre told me."

"Well, then?"

"I'm still not making myself clear, I'm afraid. It isn't what you really mean in this world; it's what people think you mean. This friend of yours, the real heir, may have the best and kindest of intentions. I don't doubt he has, if you say so. But does his uncle believe one word of that? No, he does not. 'Young Nick, Miss Wardour,'" Fay mimicked stately speech, "'was a very decent lad when I used to know him. What he has since become, among so many go-getting Yankees, will be a different matter. I am in his way; I have always been in the way.' There you are, Garret. And the look on his face!"

"*You* say that too?"

"I say it! Deidre says it! Mr. Barclay says it!"

"It's not only you. Everybody else, almost without exception, has been posturing and dramatizing things into high tragedy."

"You won't call it posturing or dramatizing when you've been there and talked to them. Mr. Barclay's a strange man. When old Mr. Barclay was alive he was never quite as subservient as people seemed to think; he would make sly little digs the old gentleman didn't quite understand. And of course he's never . . . never made advances to *me;* that's utterly absurd and ridiculous! But he *is* a strange man. He believes everybody on earth, especially his own family, is leagued against him and always had been. I think he'd like to get back at them if he could. He has heart-trouble, apparently the same kind that killed his brother, and he keeps Dr. Fortescue

THE HOUSE AT SATAN'S ELBOW

as a permanent guest. He wears an Edwardian smoking-jacket; he talks forever of the play he never gets round to writing. All the same, he seemed contented enough until the afternoon they discovered that second will of old Mr. Barclay. Then every mood exploded at once."

"How did the second will come to be found? Did you hear that too?"

"Hear it? I was there!"

For a moment Fay stared out of the window at flying fields and hedgerows.

"It was one day in April," she went on, "and we were all in the library. I can't remember why we were in the library. Since old Mr. Clovis's death it's been sacred, mostly, to his son's use. Mr. Barclay was there dictating to me: pacing up and down and dictating, as he usually does. Deidre was there looking out at the weather. Old Dr. Fortescue was there; and I don't know why I call him old. He's not really old, but he has a vagueness of manner that makes you think so. And Mr. Dawlish was there too. He doesn't often drop in, in spite of being a friend of the family. Deidre wanted to consult him about something. He's the one person Deidre trusts entirely, including her husband, and I think she's right. Then Miss Barclay put her head in, saying she thought she'd left some knitting there. It was a dark, wet afternoon with a high wind. None of us, I swear, had given a thought to those two jars on the mantelpiece.

"On either side of the mantelpiece, I ought to explain, old Mr. Clovis had kept an elaborate china jar with a lid. The left-hand one contained cigars, the right-hand one pipe-tobacco. The old man didn't often smoke, but he kept them for his guests.

"They weren't much good to any of us. Dr. Fortescue says that's a shocking way to treat tobacco; in a china jar without moisture, he says, it gets so dry as to be unsmokable. *I* can't say; I keep myself supplied with cigarettes because it makes me feel less nervous just to have them. The others, except Dr. Fortescue and Mr. Dawlish, take only cigarettes too. But Dr. Fortescue would positively have sneered at a dry cigar; and Mr. Dawlish, who smokes a pipe, wouldn't have dreamed of helping himself to tobacco in what he called a house of death.

"And it *felt* like a house of death, I can tell you, that day Aunt Essie put her head in to ask about the knitting. Does this make any sense at all," Fay broke off to demand, "or am I only maundering on in my customary way?"

"You make very good sense when you stick to narrative,"

Garret assured her. "Fire away, then! Good old Aunt Essie put her head in with a question. What happened next?"

Fay made a mouth of distaste.

"Mr. Barclay broke off dictation to say, 'There would appear, Estelle, to be some knitting on the mantelpiece; get it, please.' Miss Barclay said, 'Yes, yes,' and fluttered over. There was a crash that made us all jump a foot in the air. In reaching up for the knitting, she had dislodged the right-hand jar.

"It smashed to pieces on the hearthstone. About a pound of tobacco spilled out across the edge of the carpet. Sticking up from the tobacco, where it had been hidden, was a long sealed envelope with a name written on it. I was sitting in a chair near the fireplace with my pencil and notebook; I could see it was addressed 'A. Dawlish, Esq.' Miss Barclay cried out, 'That's Father's handwriting, that's Father's handwriting.' She scrabbled down to get it. But Dr. Fortescue anticipated her, picking up the envelope and reading the name aloud. 'This seems to be for you,' he told Mr. Dawlish. 'If it is for me,' said the one you claim looks like Macaulay, 'I had better take it.' 'And keep temptation out of somebody's way, eh?' asked Dr. Fortescue. 'I had better take it, I say. With your permission, Pennington?' Aunt Essie kept crying, 'What's in that, what's in that?' Mr. Barclay seemed suave and easy, though for a moment he looked as black as thunder. All he commented was, 'With my blessing, Andrew.'

"*She* made a grab at the envelope. Mr. Dawlish said, 'Forgive me'; he put the envelope in his pocket and went out to his car. But he came back that night to disclose the contents of the new will.

"Pennington Barclay only said he wondered if 'the old devil,' meaning his late father, 'had been up to a dodge like that.' But there's where the worst began. The tensions, the depression, the awful suicidal humours you could only half guess at, began in that very minute. Then, when the ghost started walking, and was seen by Mrs. Tiffin and by Miss Barclay too . . ."

The train hurtled round a curve, making them bend to its motion; the shrill cry of its whistle floated back.

"Yes, the famous ghost!" Garret interposed. "Mr. Justice Wildfare out of the eighteenth century! Did you see this too? And who's Mrs. Tiffin?"

"Mrs. Tiffin is the cook. No, I didn't see anything and I don't want to!"

Fay sprang to her feet, turning away as though about to run out of the compartment and steadying herself with one hand on the back of the seat. But she looked round past her shoulder, the blue eyes intent and the pink mouth unsteady.

"Oh, Garret, I *know* it's somebody masquerading. Or at least I think I do. But that's almost as bad, isn't it? The horrible, wicked *malice* of somebody who just wants to scare people. And the effect of this new will on poor Mr. Barclay, who tries to laugh ha-ha but can't quite manage to laugh at anything. And he's bought a revolver, you know."

"Pennington Barclay has?"

"Yes! When he applied for a firearms-licence he had to say he was afraid of burglars. And it's not burglars at all. If the ghost shows itself to him he swears he'll drill holes in a spectral body. It's only a small revolver, a twenty-two. But he'd better not go shooting at supposed ghosts, had he?"

"No, he certainly had not. If you hit somebody in the head or the heart, whether you mean to or not, a small revolver can kill just as effectually as a four-five that spreads your victim all over the furniture. By the Homicide Act of nineteen-fifty-seven . . ."

"Homicide, my dear? It's the other thing we're afraid of! I know it and so does Deidre, the more so because she won't say much. Mr. Barclay oughtn't to brood; this nephew does seem to mean well. States of mind like his are wild and grotesque and silly, just as the ghost is. But feelings aren't less strong because they're crazy or unreasonable. And—I can't take much more! What with one thing or another, God help us, hasn't there been enough death already?"

Fay, herself gripped by emotion, seemed deaf to the world. Supple in the blue-and-white dress, half turned from him with the remnants of sunset painting her hair and face, she made so appealing a figure that Garret wanted only to take her in his arms and tell her to forget this nonsense. But again they had an interruption.

More footsteps sounded in the corridor, approaching from the front of the train. Evidently they were the footsteps of two men seeking the restaurant-car, an impression which words confirmed an instant later.

"Anyway," cried the unmistakable voice of Nick Barclay, "I hope we can get a decent meal. And where has old Garret got to, do you think?"

"That is unlikely," said another unmistakable voice, "since the catering department of British Railways contains few *gourmets*. As for Mr. Anderson . . ."

"Easy! Damn this train!"

"Don't stumble, Nicholas; hold to the rail beside the windows. As for Mr. Anderson, the porter who brought his case said he was called back by a lady in another part of the train. A good meal, let us concede, would be an arguable miracle. But is it so unlikely that your distinguished friend should have met some acquaintance on her way to Bournemouth in June? No doubt he will be with us in good time."

Then they had passed the door. Andrew Dawlish marched first, hat off and head carried aggressively. Nick followed a pace or two behind, tending to exaggerate the sway of the train. Voices raised, looking neither left nor right, they clumped past and disappeared. Fay, who had cowered away and momentarily thrown an arm across her eyes, turned back with a deep breath of relief.

"They didn't see us! They didn't see us after all!"

"No, they did not. When people walk through a train—have you ever noticed?—they will glance into every compartment except the one at the end of the carriage."

"And they won't get another chance, believe me! Garret! Go and join them, won't you? You've had your excuse now; didn't you hear what they said? I'm an old girl-friend of yours; I *am* on my way to Bournemouth; you've just said good-bye to me. Isn't that good enough?"

"I had hoped for different things from my old girl-friend."

"Darling, I'm not joking! I'm not! Something ghastly may happen at Greengrove, something worse for both of us than any misunderstanding so far, unless we part now and meet as strangers later tonight. Won't you do this one thing for me if I beg you to? *Please?*"

Garret did not reply, though profanity wrote a fine legible hand across his brain. Still he could not make Fay's eyes meet his own. Half angry, more than a little troubled, he rolled open the sliding door, shouldered out into the corridor, and followed the other two.

Nick Barclay had not much exaggerated the lurch of the train. The door to the next carriage, caught in a draught, stuck obstinately until he wrenched at its knob. Then, hearing voices ahead, he quickened his step towards the restaurant car.

What Fay had said was probably all nonsense, yes. At the same time, there were sinister implications behind matters she had only half mentioned or not mentioned at all. The real objection to woman's intuition, or so-called intuition, was that it hit the truth more often than most people could bring themselves to admit. What *would* happen in that house at Satan's Elbow?

5

TWILIGHT had begun to smudge the sky. The car fled through it.

The car, a dark-blue Bentley saloon some five or six years old, swung left out of the station-yard into a turning call Mill Lane and skimmed up a slight rise between hedgerows. Deidre Barclay was at the wheel. Andrew Dawlish sat beside her, brief-case in lap. Her immense respect for him, no less than his obvious confidence in her, gave the solicitor an air of paternal self-importance which several times caused Nick Barclay, in the back seat with Garret, to hide a grin behind his hand.

"For the tenth time, Nicholas! . . ." Mr. Dawlish continued.

Fay Wardour had disappeared by the time Garret and his two companions returned from a meal fully as indifferent as had been predicted. Presumably Fay had hidden herself somewhere before getting out; he did not see her again. Stopping only at Winchester and Southampton Central, the train reached Brockenhurst at exactly nine-thirty-five.

On the platform, amid gathering shadows, waited a brown-haired, hazel-eyed young woman, the outdoor type of girl, in dark slacks and an orange sweater. Despite her attempt at ease, despite a straightforwardness of manner Garret could not help liking at once, she jumped a little as Nick strode up to her.

"You're Uncle Pen's wife, aren't you?"

"Yes. I'm Deidre. And after a greeting like that, there can't be much doubt about *you*."

"No doubt at all." Nick grasped the extended hand and returned her attempt at a smile. "Aunt Essie sent a picture of you; I didn't think I could be mistaken. The question is, what do I call you? I can't say, 'Mrs. Barclay,' and 'Aunt Deidre' would be a little too much. How do I address you, respected no-relation-except-by-marriage?"

"Why not just 'Deidre'? Won't that do?"

"It will do admirably, if you call me Nick."

"Thanks, Nick. I'll try to remember."

"Since introductions have been so ably managed without my assistance," Andrew Dawlish put in, 'I need only add that this other gentleman is Mr. Garret Anderson, about whom I spoke to Pennington on the telephone."

"Oh, are you really?" cried Deidre, turning from Nick almost as though with relief. "Not *the* Garret Anderson? The one who wrote——"

"If you please, Miss Deidre," the solicitor interposed again. "Mr. Anderson is responsible for *Uncle Tom's Mansion;* he is guilty of *Uncle Tom's Mansion*. But he did not *write Uncle Tom's Mansion*, as he will assure you with some fervency when you ask. Meanwhile, my dear, how are you? And how are things at Greengrove?"

"Not very pleasant, I'm afraid. Still! If young Nicholas . . . Nick, that is; I'm sorry . . . really and truly means everything you say he means . . ."

"Oh, hell's sweet bells, of course I mean it!" roared Nick. "You're much too pretty, Aunt Deidre, not to have everything on earth you want. The papers will be ready tomorrow, I'm told. What can I do to convince you until I've signed on the dotted line?"

"You've convinced me, Mr. Barclay. You've already convinced me; thanks very much. But try to believe, also," and Deidre looked him straight in the eyes, "that *I* don't want anyone's possessions: anyone's material possessions, that is. Now, will you follow me, all of you? This way, please."

With Deidre going ahead at a free stride that was almost a run, they mounted a flight of wooden stairs, crossed a bridge above another platform, and descended to the waiting Bentley in the station-yard.

Nick's suitcase and Garret's overnight bag were stowed away in the boot. Deidre, motioning Garret and Nick into the back seat, opened the left-hand front door for Andrew Dawlish. The engine throbbed to life at a touch. A grey, white, and red village fell away behind them as they swept into Mill Lane and picked up speed through open country. The lawyer had begun some oracular pronouncement when Nick interrupted.

"Now, then," he said without preamble, "what's all this guff and hoo-ha about the ghost? Who *was* Mr. Justice Wildfare, anyway? What dirty work did he do in the eighteenth century, or what did somebody do to him, that he keeps sticking his face back and revisiting the glimpses of the moon?"

"For the tenth time, Nicholas"—Mr. Dawlish craned round —"I must repeat that I know little or nothing concerning the history of the alleged ghost. Have you no comment to make, Mr. Anderson? Surely your antiquarian research can help us?"

"My antiquarian research," Garret answered, "has not gone very deeply into the records of the eighteenth century. As for Sir Horace Wildfare, I looked him up once in the *Dictionary of National Biography*."

"With what result, may I ask?"

"Nothing very informative regarding his proclivities after death. There's a fair amount about his life. Sir Horace Wildfare was that most savage and inflexible of Augustan characters: a hanging judge with bad temper."

"They were harsh times," Mr. Dawlish said sententiously, "and with harsh laws to be administered. Need it surprise us, sir, that a judge on the bench should have been infected with that same harshness?"

"Possibly not. But the great objection to this particular judge seems to have been that on one occasion he was not harsh enough."

"Well, Mr. Anderson?"

"In seventeen-sixty, shortly after Sir Horace had been raised to the bench, the son of a very wealthy landowner was haled into court on a charge of murder. It was the particularly brutal murder, by throat-cutting, of a twelve-year-old girl the landowner's son had debauched. Mr. Justice Wildfare, instead of pitching into the prisoner and the prisoner's witnesses according to his habit, went violently in the other direction. He condoled with the prisoner, raved at the prosecution, bullied their witnesses, and so cowed the jury that amid storms of hisses they returned a verdict of not guilty."

"And that, I take it," interjected Nick, "didn't go down well with anybody."

"No, it did not. George the Third had just come to the throne; the Whig-Tory battle was warming up. Sir Horace Wildfare, a Tory and king's man, had already been under heavy fire from political enemies. Now the mob hooted him in the streets, and somebody threw a dead dog into his coach. It was said he had been bribed, which was probably true; even the discreet D.N.B. admits 'strong suspicion.' Two years later, under still heavier fire but with nothing proved, he resigned from the bench and retired to Greengrove, which had just been completed and which he may or may not have built with bribe-money."

"O.K., old son. What else?"

"Officially, Nick, that's the end of the story. He died there in seventeen-eighty. But I don't know the circumstances, or anything else concerning him, or why, as you put it, he should 'keep sticking his face back' now."

"Well, *I* know a little," observed Deidre. "And if it's all the same to both of you, I wish you wouldn't harp on his face!"

"Easy, my girl!" Nick said sharply. "Gently, good-aunt-who's-not-really-an-aunt! Getting the jumps, are you?"

"I'm not a nervous person, or I never thought I was. But we've all been a little upset, you know. And—"

Deidre did not speak for a moment.

Though dusk was descending, outlines remained clear except at a distance. The car skimmed along a good road through open heath or moorland, into which intruded only vestiges of the New Forest. Forest ponies grazed at the roadside, so heedless of any passing traffic that they did not even lift their heads. Through open car-windows stirred the fragrance of dew-wet grass, and a breeze blew Deidre's hair. Then the hazel eyes turned round in an indecipherable glance. Garret reflected that she knew all about him, because Fay had told her, yet not by so much as a flicker did this healthy, hearty-seeming girl betray that she knew.

"Didn't you say, Mr. Anderson, that the judge died in seventeen-eighty?"

"Yes."

"And it's true, isn't it, that they pursued enmities very vindictively in those days?"

"It's been known to happen in our own time, Mrs. Barclay."

"Not like this, I hope. Not like this!"

"Not like what?" demanded Nick.

"Pen—my husband—found a pamphlet anonymously published in seventeen-eighty-one or seventeen-eighty-two." Deidre was still addressing Garret. "The pamphlet is called *Dead and Damned;* it sums up the judge's career; it's the most vicious attack you ever read. Sir Horace Wildfare, it says, was even worse at home than in public life. According to the pamphleteer, he died of an apoplectic seizure while he was cursing one of his sons." Here Deidre looked at Mr. Dawlish. "You talk about his being infected by harshness. Towards the end of his life, it seems, he actually *was* infected with some kind of skin disease. The pamphlet says, and quotes witnesses, this made his face so loathsome that ever afterwards, in the house, he wore a black silk face-veil with holes cut for the eyes. And wasn't this a judgment on him?"

Nick bent forward. "For taking bribes, you mean?"

"For taking bribes and—and other things," Deidre said with a cryptic inflection. "But when I think! . . ."

Suddenly she trod on the accelerator. The Bentley sprang forward, unleashing power; Andrew Dawlish uttered a remonstrance; then the capable Deidre controlled herself and controlled the car.

"Oh, I'll be good," she told Mr. Dawlish. "I'm a very sensible person, as everybody knows. It's only that I get so furious when I think of this ghost or masquerader or whatever it is: the repulsive figure in the long robe and the face-veil. When I imagine myself seeing it, though I never have seen it, I picture it following me along a passage, and overtaking me, and then pushing me into a corner before it twitches off the veil to look closely in my face and . . ."

"Whoa, Nell!" interrupted Nick. He spoke gently, putting his left hand on the back of the seat beside Deidre's left shoulder. "Apart from upsetting yourself, which you mustn't do, this is where *I* enter a protest against the tale, because it violates all good ghost-story laws and protocol. There's too much colour."

"Colour?"

"That's what I said. A long robe, eh? Does the thing have a wig too? Are you seriously trying to tell us, Deidre, that Mr. Justice Wildfare's ghost goes parading through the house in all the grandeur of its judicial scarlet and ermine?"

"No, no! Don't be silly! Of course not!"

"Then what *are* you saying?"

"The robe—this comes from the pamphlet again—was an old black robe that the judge, when he was alive, thought looked imposing when he wore it in the house. At all events, Mr. . . . at all events, Nick, that's what the figure seems to wear when it's seen now."

"Let's be practical, then. Who saw it? When?"

"Mrs. Tiffin, the cook, says she saw it one night not long after we found old Mr. Barclay's second will. She saw it in the lower hall, by moonlight. It was standing and looking at her, after which it vanished through a wall. Estelle saw it late one afternoon: also in the downstairs hall, but in another part. It started towards her in a menacing way, she claims, but turned and walked through a door that's been locked for some time. Not that I should believe everything poor Estelle says!"

Nick tapped the solicitor's arm. "All this is correct, isn't it?"

"The witnesses are honest, I am sure," said Mr. Dawlish. "They were trying, no doubt, to tell what they saw or think they saw. The evidence of confused and frightened women, however . . ."

"Yes, quite a problem. Has anybody else seen the figure, Deidre?"

"No. Not to my knowledge, anyway.

"You see, according to more malice from *Dead and*

Damned," continued Deidre, her gaze fixed on the road ahead, "the judge's ghost first appeared soon after his death because he hated the world in general and his own family in particular."

"Mr. Justice Wildfare sounds a little like my late grandfather, doesn't he?"

"Nicholas!" protested a scandalized Andrew Dawlish. "Come! I can relish a joke with anyone, but we must exercise good taste. And this is too much. It is unjust, ungenerous, and unworthy of you!"

"Why is it unjust? They were a pair of old bastards by anybody's reckoning. Though Clovis at least was honest; I'll give you that."

"My dear Nicholas, I scarcely meant——"

"*You* were saying, Deidre?"

"I was saying that the ghost, even as a ghost, doesn't seem to have been very consistent. There are numbers of books with titles like *Haunted Homes of Great Britain*. Pen has one of them, published in the eighteen-nineties and written by somebody called J. T. Eversleigh; the book belonged to old Mr. Barclay."

"Well, sweet aunt?"

"Well!" Deidre looked round briefly. "The ghost appeared towards the end of the eighteenth century. It was seen once or twice in Victorian times, as recorded by J. T. Eversleigh. And then, apparently, it lies doggo and *perdu* until all of a sudden it pops up to frighten Estelle and Mrs. Tiffin. Why should it be appearing now?"

"Now, there," Nick declared with an air of inspiration, "is exactly the question I asked old Garret when I was telling him what little I knew. The eighteenth century, the nineteenth century, and not again until . . . Hold on, though! I seem to remember my father mentioning . . ."

"Mentioning what, Nick?"

"Mentioning another appearance. Look, Blackstone!" And Nick punched his fist slowly towards the lawyer's ear. "Years ago? When both my parents were alive, and I was a very small fry, and we were all three living at Greengrove? Wasn't there one other visitation?"

"We deal with great nonsense," Mr. Dawlish replied stiffly. "Yet I am instructed to say that *something* appeared."

"When? How? To whom?"

"My dear Nicholas! I can't possibly answer that in full, especially as regards the date, without consulting my diary for whatever year it was. I keep a complete file of such diaries; they are most useful in a business sense. It was years ago, as you point out; I was a young man learning my profession under my own father's tuition; I had no cause to remember particularly and only noted it down because . . ."

"Yes, Coke and Littleton? Don't stop there!"

". . . because it was Mr. Barclay himself who saw what appeared. He telephoned and complained to my father."

"Old Mr. Barclay saw something?" Deidre cut in. "Pen never told me."

"Perhaps Pennington never knew. However! I will state what facts and circumstances I remember, corroborating them with dates and other circumstances when I have found the diary for that year.

"Mr. Barclay, though he had inherited the large library at Greengrove, scarcely ever opened a book. But he had read *Haunted Homes of Great Britain*. I need scarcely remind you, Miss Deidre, of the two full-length windows facing west in the library. Is it possible, Nicholas, that *you* can remember those windows?"

"I haven't been inside the house for nearly twenty-five years. But I think I can remember 'em, yes."

"Victorian sash-windows, like others on that side, stretching to the ground and somewhat destroying the Georgian line of the house. Opposite those windows, some sixty feet away across the lawn, there is . . . what?"

"A large and darkish garden," answered Nick, "set out in crisscross alleys of yew hedges twelve feet high. One entrance to the garden is opposite the left-hand window as you look out of the library."

"One mild evening at dusk, much as it is now," continued the lawyer, "Mr. Clovis Barclay was standing at that left-hand window. The window was open, as were most windows on fine days. All day, as he afterwards acknowledged, he had been in an uncertain temper from some cause which now escapes my memory. As he stood at the window, doubtless breathing deeply, something emerged from the garden. He would not say what shape emerged from the garden, and moved across the lawn, and then suddenly rushed at him as though bent on mischief. He would not tell us, I repeat. . . ."

"No, he wouldn't have told," blurted Nick Barclay, "but I hope it scared him. Oh, Judas, I hope it scared the pants off him!"

"And so do I," breathed Deidre. "I shouldn't admit that," she cried, "but so do I!"

"The expression you use, Nicholas," Mr. Dawlish said severely, 'is both inelegant and inexact. Endorsed by you, Miss Deidre"—and he seemed to spread protective wings—"it becomes little less than shocking. No, Nicholas, your grandfather was *not* so affected. He was much more angry than frightened, as he forcibly explained by telephone. He had retreated precipitately, it is true, and had received something of a shock. He did not believe in this ghost. But which of us shall be entirely free from fear or escape the gathered superstition of centuries? A voice whispers, 'There are more things . . .' "

"There are," agreed Nick, as the other stopped. "Let's brood on 'em, shall we, and see if we can come up with an answer. I wish a man named Gideon Fell were here to brood on 'em too. Anyway, let's do what we can."

Perhaps they all brooded, perhaps not. But they were silent for some time. Cresting a rise at a cross-roads, they swept down through the village of Beaulieu—pronounced Bewley—whose Cistercian abbey was older than Magna Charta. By another good road, with Beaulieu River glimmering on their right and on their left both the remains of Beaulieu Abbey and the very modern shape of the Montagu Motor Museum for veteran cars, they left the village for more miles under tall trees, through twilight and the sweet evening air.

Then Deidre, who had switched on the car's lights, turned abruptly to Mr. Dawlish.

"Must I *always* be on my dignity? Always and always and always?"

"It is advisable, I think."

"And I do wish Nick wouldn't go on about the ghost, or what's been written about the ghost either. *Dead and Damned. Haunted Homes of Great Britain.* I'm not much for books, really, though I do happen to be Pen's wife. Fay could tell you much more than I can. And where *is* Fay, anyhow?"

"Fay!" exclaimed Nick, sitting up straight. "That name, somehow, strikes a reminiscent note. By your leave, everybody: before we ask where Fay is, Deidre, may I ask who she is?"

"Fay Wardour. Pen's secretary. He sent her up to town today to get some books for him. I thought she'd come down by the same train as the rest of you, but she didn't."

"No, evidently she didn't. Has Miss Wardour been Uncle Pen's secretary for a long time? And is she a blonde, by any chance?"

"Yes! Fay *is* a blonde and an awfully sweet person, though she does dream so much about books and their authors. She's not been with us for so very long a time. But Fay's an old friend; I've known her for ages. As I said to her in Rome last summer . . ."

"Well, well, well!" mused Nick, carefully not looking at

Garret. "In Rome, where all roads lead. And last summer, was it? Being no gentleman but a damn good friend, I still don't ask why the lady's name strikes such a reminiscent note. . . ."

You'd better not! Garret Anderson thought with some viciousness.

"And yet, all the same, I'm inclined to wonder just where we're going?"

They had swung left at another cross-roads, past a village shop with an outside telephone-box on the right.

"This is Exbury," snapped Mr. Dawlish, indicating a metal signpost at the roadside. "At the moment—in the literal sense of your question, at least—we are going to Satan's Elbow and Greengrove."

"My question was meant to be taken literally, Friend Blackstone."

"Then we are little more than a mile from our destination. May I further suggest, Nicholas, that a continuance of the brooding silence would be both in good order and in good taste?"

Again Deidre trod on the accelerator. Open fields in which cows were still grazing, an occasional house set well back, unreeled past as though in fantasy. The road, after dipping into a hollow, climbed to the left up a low headland bowered in trees. Past that headland, past squat entrance-pillars with a sign reading "Lepe House—Private," they saw water at last.

On their right and well below them, following the curve of Lepe Beach, the Solent threw out faint gleams against a darkening sky. The breeze was fresh and westerly; waves showed white. In evening hush, above the motor's tiger-purr, they could hear the surf slap at a shingle beach. It was Andrew Dawlish himself who broke silence.

"Well, Nicholas? Do things look familiar now?"

"They're beginning to, yes." Nick swept out his arm to the right, southwards. "That's the Isle of Wight across there, isn't it?"

"That is the Isle of Wight. Three miles away, though it seems closer. And well ahead of us there, where the promontory juts out at right angles beyond the end of Lepe Beach, you can see the roof of Greengrove beyond those trees. You are nearly home."

"Yes!" Deidre said in a curious voice. "I hadn't thought about it so definitely, I suppose. But you *are* home, Nick, aren't you?"

"Home, for Pete's sake?" roared the other.

"Yes! You've said some harsh thing about old Mr. Barclay. Maybe I've said them too, or as good as said them. But you ought to be grateful to him, oughtn't you? He left you the house and everything else!"

"Home for me, my pretty, is either an apartment on East Sixty-fourth Street or the good old Willis Building on Madison at Forty-eighth. That damned dank old place up ahead of us, where draughts get down the back of your neck wherever you turn, does not belong to me and never will. How many times must I tell people I don't want it?"

"That does not in the least alter the fact, does it? It *is* yours. Whereas poor Pen! . . ."

"Come, now! Come!" Squat though he was, Mr. Dawlish seemed to tower. "May I remind you, Miss Deidre, that Pennington is not left exactly destitute in a cold world? Even apart from what our young friend so generously proposes."

"He can afford to be generous, I dare say, with something he doesn't want. But shall we accept charity and be grateful? And does he really mean it anyway? When I think of Pen . . ."

The wooded promontory loomed ahead. Deidre yanked the wheel to the right. At much reduced speed she sent the car along an ill-paved road, between stone entrance-pillars having a heraldic design atop each, and up a broad sanded drive lined with trees and rhododendrons. Rather more than a hundred yards ahead, dimly visible, rose a wide, rectangular stone house with its long façade facing north in their direction.

"I have to remember," Deidre cried, "I *am* Pen's wife after all. Poor Pen! I keep thinking of him with that twenty-two revolver of his. Walking about with the revolver in the pocket of his smoking-jacket. Brooding and brooding, as Mr. Nick Barclay," her voice poured with bitterness, "says *we* ought to do. And telling himself nobody knows what!"

"The revolver was a mistake," said Mr. Dawlish. "I should never have permitted him to buy it, still less shown him how to use it. Do you really apprehend he may do himself a mischief? Or fire a shot to frighten the supposed ghost, as he has so often threatened to do, and perhaps do a mischief to someone else? It is possible, of course. . . ."

"No, it is not!" cried Deidre. "It's not, and I know it's not! Pen is much too sensible, under that abstracted manner of his. He's not well and he does brood. But he knows what's what, more so than anybody guesses. Besides, he can't; I've taken precautions so he can't. And in any case, he won't. He'll be waiting for us in the library; you'll see! There's not the least, slightest possibility that—"

She stopped in mid-flight. The noise they all heard, though not very loud, pierced sharp and distinct through twilight.

THE HOUSE AT SATAN'S ELBOW 57

Then it was as though a nerve had jerked uncontrollably in the calf of Deidre's left leg. Her foot slipped from the clutch; the car stalled and stopped.

"Ladies and gentlemen," began Nick Barclay, "we are already encountering all the fun of the fair. Either a big blacksnake whip was cracked to amuse the customers or else somebody has just fired a twenty-two. I could give you a few other guesses, but you won't need 'em."

He flung open the rear right-hand door and paused in a crouch before jumping out. For several seconds nobody moved.

"Oh, my *God!*" Deidre said.

Nick jumped out, with Garret following. Andrew Dawlish, clutching his bowler hat, descended more sedately from the other side. The car had stopped some fifty feet from the house. Nick set off at a run but stopped again when he had emerged from under the tunnel of trees not far opposite the front door. The other two hurried to join him.

Not a light showed at the front. Two main floors, topped by a mansard roof pierced in smaller windows for a servants' floor, lifted lines of eighteenth-century windows with their frames painted white. A couple of worn stone steps led up to the front door. The sanded drive turned left, eastwards, and then stretched south past the left-hand side of the house. Old qualms, which had not touched Garret Anderson for a quarter of a century, returned to him as he looked. Nick, also studying the house, took an abrupt step backwards.

"Easy, Garret! Easy, old horse!"

"What do you mean, 'easy'? You're the one who bumped into me. And what do we do now? Charge in by the front door?"

"No, I think not. 'Waiting for us in the library,' Deidre said. Look, Garret! You visited here once, if memory serves. Can you remember anything about the place?"

"No, not much. For a second I imagined I did when somebody began talking about the long windows in the library. But it's gone."

"The library"—Nick swept his arm out—"is the last room at the end there, right-front, with its long windows just round the corner. We'll go in by 'em whether they're open or not. Anyhow, what the hell's delaying us? Come *on!*"

Once more he pounded away at a run. Garret and Mr. Dawlish hurried after him over smooth grass slippery with dew. In Nick's wake they rounded the side of the house.

Separated by the projection of a broad rough-stone chimney-stack, two ground-length sash-windows faced west towards a dark garden. The far window, whether open or shut, was curtained. But the near window stood wide open, its sash pushed up fully and its curtains drawn back. Nick, ducking his head a little, peered inside.

Westwards, towards the mouth of the Solent, a last red ember burned in the sky. Otherwise, at just past ten o'clock, there was barely enough light to see. Somewhere a wind seethed amid leaves. Garret, looking past Nick's shoulder, could just make out the figure of a man seated motionless in an easy-chair beside a big writing-table set about a dozen feet back from what must have been the fireplace, between the windows.

Then the man in the easy-chair rose to his feet. And a rich voice spoke. It sounded a trifle breathless, as though from mental or physical shock. Wrath tinged it as well. But it remained a fine voice—full, rounded, resonant—from one who knew how to employ it.

"Who's there?" the voice demanded. "Are you back at the window again?"

"Back at the window? But I've just got here! I'm Nick, Nick Barclay. Is that you, Uncle Pen? Are you all right?"

"It is indeed myself," the voice answered, "and I am as well as can be expected under the circumstances. Young Nick, did you say? Please come in; you are expected. Isn't there somebody there with you?"

"*I* am with him, Pennington," said Mr. Dawlish, pushing past, "to say nothing of others. What happened here? We heard what sounded very much like a revolver-shot."

"Andrew Dawlish? Your perspicacity never fails. It *was* a revolver-shot."

"Come, then!" said the lawyer, more shaken than he would have admitted. "Since you are at least alive and no damage has been done, what occasioned the noise? Was it you taking a pot-shot at the alleged ghost?"

"Well, no," replied Pennington Barclay. "As a matter of fact, Andrew, it was the alleged ghost taking a pot-shot at me. With a blank cartridge."

6

Relief? Or again a sense of anti-climax? Garret could not be sure.

"You said . . . *what?*" Mr. Dawlish exclaimed.

"Be not so hasty, Andrew. Lights, I think," remarked Pennington Barclay. "Lights!"

The indistinct figure moved round towards the indistinct shape of a floor-lamp at the other side of the writing-table. The soft glow which smote out from a hundred-watt bulb under layers of green silk in its shade made them all blink or turn away until eyesight adjusted. Nick had crowded after Mr. Dawlish into the library. Garret followed both.

It was a very large room, its length running east and west. In the north wall, facing front, four Georgian windows were closely curtained. The east wall, some distance opposite the way by which the visitors had entered, seemed of unusual thickness; it had an alcove with a closed door leading to some other room. On either side of this alcove massive open bookshelves in carved and scrolled oak rose almost to the ceiling. More such mausoleums of bookshelves rose against the south wall, on either side of another door which must lead to a crosspassage through the house. If a man sat behind the big writing-table in the middle, he would face towards a high rough-stone chimneypiece between the Victorian sash-windows.

The whole place had a scuffed, down-at-heel air, like its frayed carpet and worn tapestry chairs. Bleakness breathed out of it; there was a faint smell of burnt cordite. But always Garret's gaze returned to their host.

Pennington Barclay, emaciated-lean in a short marooncoloured smoking-jacket with shiny dark lapels, seemed almost too frail for that resonant voice. His face was haggard, with a big nose and a high framework of bones under thin grey-white hair whose strands shone like spun glass. But he also showed much urbanity and a good deal of virile charm.

"Enter, good nephew!" he continued, moving round from behind the table and extending his hand, which the other gripped. "I rejoice to see you, Nick, whatever anyone may say. 'Oh, come ye in peace here, or come ye in war?'"

"Not in war, that's for sure. Don't forget the rest of the quotation, though."

"'Or to dance at our bridal, young Lord Lochinvar?' But there is no question of a bridal, so far as I know! Or is there?"

"Hardly, Uncle Pen; how could there be? Your own wife met us at Brockenhurst station...."

"Yes, Miss Deidre was kind enough to do so," interposed Andrew Dawlish. "Was it your thought to send the car, Pennington? Or was it hers?"

"It was Deidre's own idea, though I encouraged it. It seemed only good manners. And speaking of good manners—"

He looked at Mr. Dawlish, but his eye strayed towards the fourth member of the group; and the solicitor, fuming at his own negligence, hastened to introduce Garret.

"You are very welcome, Mr. Anderson," their host said cordially. "All of us here are familiar with your work. And you shall be spared pointed references to an embarrassment called *Uncle Tom's Mansion*. You must already have endured so much cheap humour that I would not add to the burden."

"Thanks."

"But it is true, is it not, that to his own family the formidable Lord Macaulay actually was known as Uncle Tom?"

"To the Trevelyan children, yes."

"And it is also true, I believe, that there was no woman in the life of so full-blooded a character? No wife, no fiancée, nobody he fancied?"

"So far as proof exists, nobody at all."

"And yet, since the Victorians are now known to have been a sexually enterprising lot——"

Again Mr. Dawlish intervened.

"While we are on that subject, which seems to preoccupy you so much, may I beg you to spare a thought for your lady-wife? She drove us from Brockenhurst, as I have already remarked. And a rare fright you gave her!"

"A rare fright *I* gave her?"

"Well, something did. I am at the end of my patience. Confound it, man, what happened here?"

"There are times, Andrew, when you exceed your fancied authority. Even old friendship and the best of intentions cannot excuse *every* officious act."

"I have no wish to press you or to seem officious. But surely it is time for an explanation? Hide-and-seek in the half-dark! Ghosts firing revolvers with blank cartridges!"

"Which provides proof, if any were needed, that we deal with no ghost. Gently, Andrew! I mean no harm; I never do. And I shall be happy to explain. But at the same time," said Pennington Barclay, and a curious note of pettishness crept into the rich voice, "at the same time, can nobody spare a thought for *me?*"

"For you?"

"Yes! I have been through a most unpleasant experience." He touched the left side of his chest and winced with pain. "I have been struck by the wad from a blank cartridge: no tragedy, but a disturbing nuisance. There has been a particularly silly attempt to frighten or to kill. If Deidre cares so much for my welfare, as I honestly believe she does, why didn't she accompany the rest of you? What has happened to her? Where is she?"

The question was answered by Deidre herself, who at that moment sauntered in through the open window. She seemed much more composed, though her rather broad mouth was unsteady and a glaze of fear remained in her eyes.

"I'm here, Pen!" she said. "I did follow them round the side of the house. Then, when I heard you speak and saw you weren't hurt, I went to put the car away in the garage."

"You went to put the car away?"

"Yes. Somebody else's car is in the drive; I don't know whose. Good gracious, Pen, what would you have wanted me to do? Cry out, 'My husband'? Or scream and faint like a woman in Macaulay's time? Is that what you'd have wanted?"

"Hardly, though it would have shown the proper spirit."

"Look, Uncle Pen—" began Nick.

Above the rough-stone mantelpiece, on which now stood only one china jar with its ornate lid, hung a rectangular Venetian mirror framed in eighteenth-century gold-leaf. For some reason Mr. Dawlish gestured towards this mirror with his bowler hat.

"Yes, Pennington? We are waiting."

"Sit down, my dear," their host said to Deidre, "and I will try to explain."

He moved round the floor-lamp to the writing-table, behind which stood a swivel-chair with a cushion and at the left side of which, facing towards the mantelpiece, was the easy-chair in which he had been sitting when they first saw him. Then he addressed himself to Garret.

"I spend a good deal of time in here, Mr. Anderson. They call it my lair. You observe"—and he nodded towards the east wall, some distance opposite—"you observe that the wall there is very thick? That it contains an alcove with a door at the back?"

"Yes, Mr. Barclay?"

"The door leads to the drawing-room. The wall seems unusually thick because it is a double one. Built into the wall, on both sides of that alcove, there is a small self-contained room. My grandfather, who also introduced Victorian sash-windows, had those two little rooms built towards the end of the last century. From the position in which you are standing now, you can't see the door to either unless you crane your neck sideways. But the room on the right is a kind of book-cupboard where I keep volumes not on display here. The room on the left is a cloakroom. It contains a wash-basin with hot and cold, a locker for some clothes, even a couch. Since I spend so much time in the library, and often work late . . ."

"Did you say work?" the lawyer demanded.

"Yes, Andrew, that was the word."

"You mean this play of yours?"

"I have been preparing a drama," replied their host, "which shall explore human behaviour under stress. Work, Andrew, is not always accomplished by dashing about the countryside in your own style. Work is cerebration. It does not flap. It is *here*." He rapped his knuckles against the side of his head. "However, I will not bore any of you with that. Do I make myself clear so far, Mr. Anderson?"

"Very clear."

"In this household we employ three servants. There is Mrs. Tiffin, a cook singularly imaginative in every respect except that of preparing meals. There are two maids, Phyllis and Phoebe, whose lives seem devoted to messing about in here when they are not wanted and to never being on hand when they are. Well!"

Here he drew himself up.

"Well! After dinner this evening, about half-past eight, I came in here as usual, while others went their various ways. Deidre left for Brockenhurst in the car, allowing herself far too much time. Dr. Fortescue went upstairs. My sister, Estelle, had already departed for the music-room to insult her hi-fi by playing pop records. If she wants good music, there is plenty of that. If she wants attractive music, she has Gilbert and Sullivan. In a better world, ladies and gentlemen, pop records would meet the same fate which overtook the weasel. But this is not to our purpose!"

"Agreed," said Andrew Dawlish.

Garret glanced round the group. Deidre had sat down in another tapestry armchair placed cater-cornered in the south-west angle of the room. Beyond her rose up the left-hand Victorian window, closely muffled in dusty dull-brown curtains bearing a faint thread of green and gold. Nick Barclay fidgeted before the fireplace, a tiny bald spot at the back of his head reflected in the Venetian mirror above the mantelpiece. Mr. Dawlish stood motionless, hat in one hand and brief-case in the other, with his eye on a corner of the mirror.

"Let me repeat," their host continued, "that I came in here about half-past eight. For once Phyllis and Phoebe had not done their worst. Both those western windows were wide open, as they should have been and as in fact they still are, though the left-hand one was not then curtained as you see it now. The light was still strong and good. I sat down at the table in this swivel-chair and made some notes for a letter to the *Times Literary Supplement*. I was expecting to dictate this to my secretary, who had been in London to bring some books from Hackett's; but she did not come back to dinner, and so far as I know, she has not returned even yet."

"That's true, Pen!" Deidre assured him. "Since Fay wasn't back by the three-fifty, I felt sure she'd be on the nine-thirty-five. But she didn't take that either, as any of our guests can tell you."

"Well, well," Pennington said indulgently, "no doubt she has found a way of passing the time. Miss Wardour, Nick, is a most fetching young lady. If I myself were not so engrossed with a charming wife . . ."

"Oh, Pen, please! You don't know what you're talking about!"

"Indeed I don't, my dear; I have never investigated. However, as Andrew will be the first to point out if I don't, this is not to our purpose either. *Revenons à notre histoire*.

"By half-past nine"—he thrust out his left wrist to consult a watch—"I had finished what work I meant to do. I pushed the notes aside; they are still on the table. Shadows had begun to gather. I got up from the swivel-chair and sat down in this easy-chair to the left of the table, facing towards the left-hand window. And there, looking out across the lawn towards the garden, I sat in musing mood."

Again Pennington Barclay straightened up. A dreamy look crossed his face. As though to himself, the fine voice spoke softly.

" 'What is the real good?'
 I asked in musing mood.

"Order, said the law court;

Knowledge, said the school;
Truth, said the wise man;
Pleasure, said the fool. . . ."

He got no further.

"Really, Pennington!" said Mr. Dawlish with a kind of explosion. "I am inured to your moods, as I have to be, but that goes too far. To quote poetry at a time like this—"

"Poetry, Andrew? The mind of the Philistine is mysterious. That was verse, and very indifferent verse, though it has a certain meretricious catch. Never mind! Do you want evidence, all of you? Look there!"

"What?" cried Deidre, sitting up as though burnt. "What? Where?"

"Yes, my dear, I *was* looking at *you*. On the floor. Just beyond your left foot, but nearer to the window."

Deidre jerked back her foot. She sprang up and ran over to stand between Nick and Mr. Dawlish. Though the light from the floor-lamp beside the table did not reach too far, being muffled in several layers of green silk, its edge shone on a smallish but heavy blue-steel revolver with a hard-rubber grip.

"I see," said Mr. Dawlish, who was bending forward. "An Ives-Grant twenty-two."

"Chambered, as you have already informed me, for the twenty-two short cartridge."

"Yes, you quote the correct technical term. Is that your revolver?"

"It is. I recognized it even in somebody else's hand. But what's the matter, Andrew? You made a move as though to pick it up and then drew back. What's the matter?"

"Frankly, my dear fellow, I was thinking of fingerprints."

"There will be no fingerprints on *that*. Observe!"

Haggard-faced but intent, his hands trembling, Pennington Barclay came out from behind the table. Beside the chair in which Deidre had been sitting was another floor-lamp, this one with a buff-coloured parchment shade. Their host switched it on as he passed; it threw out bright light. Strongly illuminated, he bent down and scooped up the revolver. Then he returned to his position behind the table, where he struck an attitude like a schoolmaster or a lecturer.

"Look, Uncle Pen!" Nick burst out. "Have you got a permit for that gun?"

"A firearms-licence, you mean? Yes, of course I have. In this country, my boy, we must produce the licence in order to buy ammunition."

Here he pulled open the capacious drawer of the writing-table.

"The last time I saw this weapon before tonight, it was here in the drawer, and fully loaded with real bullets. Let's see what we have now."

Breaking open the revolver, he jabbed at a metal pin down the centre of the magazine-chamber. Six tiny brass cylinders popped out on the desk-blotter. Their host picked up and examined each.

"Six blanks, please note, one of them exploded. I can't say where they came from; I bought plenty of live ammunition but no blanks. Now, let me digress for a moment on the subject of ghosts, of fingerprints, and of an idea which *seemed* good when it occurred to me. Do you honour me with your attention?"

"Yes," said Mr. Dawlish.

"Following the demise of my late lamented father and the discovery of his second will . . ."

"About that will, Uncle Pen—" Nick began.

"Do you honour me with your attention, all of you?"

"We're right with you, Uncle Pen; go ahead!"

". . . following this, I say, the ghost of the late unlamented Sir Horace Wildfare, in its black robe and black face-veil, was twice seen in the month of April. Up to that time, so far as we know, it had not been seen by anybody for nearly a hundred years."

"But—" the lawyer broke out.

"But what, Andrew?"

"Nothing at all! Forgive the interruption."

"The supposed ghost was seen by Estelle and by Mrs. Tiffin: under circumstances, it seemed to me, which a little ingenuity could easily explain. But if someone had been playing ghost, it also seemed, then I must not be slow in playing detective.

"Now, how was I to do this? I have no practical knowledge of police work. Such information as I possess comes only from reading detective novels, of which I devour an inordinate number."

"Hear, hear, *hear,*" said Garret.

"In detective stories, as we all know, they never find fingerprints. But it might be different in real life. This library two centuries ago had been the den and spider's web of the living Sir Horace Wildfare. Here he prowled, with his raging tempers and his disfigured face. How had the face come to be disfigured? Was it a skin disease like eczema? Or a serious disease like syphilis, since he seems to have been something of an old rip with a taste for very young women...."

"Pen, *don't!*" Deidre almost screamed.

"Or was it, as we find hinted in a pamphlet of seventeen-eighty-one, because some member of his family had been feeding him poison? But you are quite right, Deidre, It doesn't matter. What did matter (or so I thought) was that a counterfeit ghost in our own day would take good care to haunt the library, and might have left flesh-and-blood prints all over the place. Afire with this notion, I procured certain things. Look here!"

From the capacious drawer he took out a series of articles, holding up each as he named it and returning all but the last to the drawer.

"This book is a learned work on fingerprints. This bottle with the chemist's label contains the 'grey powder' used in taking such prints. This is a brush for spreading the powder. This, I need hardly say, is a magnifying glass. Finally, we have here a pair of rubber gloves such as housewives use in the kitchen.

"Pursuing my investigations a month or so ago, I put on the gloves—like this." He did so. "They must be rolled on, as you see. But I found them as clumsy then as I find them now. With these on my hands, with powder and brush and magnifying glass, I began going over surfaces in this room.

"There was a fine crop of my own prints and of my secretary's. I plunged on, undaunted, in the best style of Dr. Thorndyke. It was not until I discovered Phyllis's and Phoebe's that I was suddenly struck by the futility and even the absurdity of the game I had been playing."

"Pen, what on earth *do* you mean?" cried Deidre. "The library is *your* room; all right! But everybody else comes in sometimes. What proof would it have been, what difference would it have made, no matter whose fingerprints were found here?"

"No proof or difference whatever, my dear. That was the discovery I made. Could I cry a triumphant checkmate at discovering prints where they had every right to be?"

"And this," Mr. Dalwish asked abruptly, "never occurred to you until—"

"No, it did not. Behold the fate of a man who thinks himself clever but does not stop to think. My only hope was to catch the ghost in person, robe and mask and all. But the ghost, up to this evening, showed itself singularly chary of appearing to me. And then, when it did appear . . .

"Well, we will set the stage. As one more exhibit from the

drawer, let me draw your attention to this box of Ives-Grant twenty-two short cartridges. I open the box, you see, without removing it from the drawer. Observe again!"

There was a small rattle as he swept the six little blanks from the blotter into the drawer. Somewhat clumsily in rubber-gloved hands he filled the magazine of the revolver with six rounds of live ammunition from the cardboard box.

"*Finito!*" said Pennington Barclay, shutting up the cylinder with a snap. "There is the pistol as I imagined it to be tonight. We will put it . . . no, not in the drawer. To point the drama, which is an unpleasantly painful one in its most literal sense, I put this weapon at one side of the table.

"Now, then. Imagine that it is again just before ten o'clock. I was sitting in the easy-chair beside the table here, facing towards an uncurtained left-hand window. Would anyone care to occupy the same chair now? You, Andrew?"

"Thank you, no. A full reconstruction is not necessary."

"Not necessary, I agree. And I certainly won't ask Deidre, whose placid exterior is a little misleading. Still! Shall we attempt to reproduce other conditions by turning out the lights?"

"No!" Deidre shrank towards Mr. Dawlish. "It's completely dark outside now; it's pitch-black. And it wasn't quite dark at that time, was it?"

"Not quite dark, no. I could see outlines fairly well, or could have seen them if I had been paying attention. But I was not paying attention; I dreamed. And then . . ."

"It occurs to me, Uncle Pen," said Nick, "that this is exactly like one of the times when you used to tell me ghost stories."

"The same thought, my boy, had occurred to *me*. You yourself were of no sluggish temperament in those days; I see you have not changed. Well! I sat there dreaming. The tenor of my thoughts is of no importance. I was badly depressed and shaken, let me confess. Indeed, I——"

"*Don't pick up that gun, Uncle Pen! For the love of Mike don't. . . .*"

"I beg your pardon, Nick; the movement was involuntary. My hand had not actually touched the revolver. We will put this newspaper over it, with your permission, and blot the ugly mechanism from sight.

"As I sat lost in my own thoughts, I had not heard or seen anyone approach. Nor can I say what attracted my attention. But I glanced up; I woke up. And there was something standing just inside the window looking at me."

"This is all very well, no doubt," said Mr. Dawlish. *"What* was looking at you?"

"I can tell you only that it was a figure in a black robe, with what appeared to be a dark mask or veil over the face. There may have been eye-holes, though I can't be sure."

"Well, try to be precise about the figure. Tall or short? Fat or thin? What?"

"The only word that occurs to me is 'medium.' And I am not making bad puns about ghosts. It also occurs to me," said Pennington Barclay with a struggling kind of gesture, "I have been adopting rather a lofty or contemptuous attitude towards our visitant. Such was not the case, believe me, when I saw it. I knew this figure to be human; I felt it to be human. And yet, if I said that I felt *no* jump or start, that I did not, in fact, experience the shock of my life, I should be only what Nick's Yankee speech would describe as a cockeyed liar.

"A worse shock was to come. I yelled at the visitant, I fear. I said, 'Who are you?' or 'What do you want?' or something else I can't remember. That was when I heard in the distance the sound of a car coming up the drive. I knew Deidre was returning from Brockenhurst. And I reach the one part of the story where I can be precise.

"My visitor seemed to have some sort of pocket in the right side of the robe. He—or she, or whoever it was—put a gloved hand into the pocket and took out a revolver. Don't ask me how I knew it was my revolver! Don't ask me, even, how I could be sure about the glove! But as God is my judge, Andrew, I *was* sure."

"What sort of glove was this? A rubber glove like the ones you're wearing?"

"No: the colour was different, anyway. And it was no kid or suede glove such as we usually wear. I should call it a thin, close-fitting glove of grey nylon; my visitor's finger never fumbled in going through the trigger-guard. What that visitor did was lift the revolver and fire straight at me from a distance of about a dozen feet away.

"A flash, a report, a hard blow in the region of the heart. My thoughts, if I had any thoughts, were only: 'This is it, then; he came to kill me.' The visitor never spoke a word. He dropped the revolver on the carpet. He backed out through the window, pulling the curtains together as he went."

"And presumably," struck in Mr. Dawlish, "ducking his head under the open sashes? Since we agree this was no ghost, he must have done that?"

"Andrew, Andrew!"

"Well?"

"Yes! I suppose he must have done that, unless it was a small person after all. I can't remember seeing him duck his head. But in those windows there's a good foot or eighteen inches between the line of the curtains and the actual window-glass. All I can testify is that he went inside the curtains and closed them."

"What did *you* do?"

Their host's left hand flew to the left side of his chest. A spasm crossed his face.

"I was dumbfounded to find myself still sitting there: shocked, upset, but alive and breathing. Something had fallen into the chair beside my left hand. I recognized this as soon as I touched it. It was the paper wad from a blank cartridge; when I was a boy we used blank cartridges on Bonfire Night. This shot was fired from too far away for powder-burns or even for powder-grains to cut my smoking-jacket. But the wad hit me like a spent bullet."

"Forgive my insistence; I have a reason for asking. What did you actually *do*?"

"I got up; I walked to the right-hand window over there; I threw that accursed paper wad out on the lawn."

"To the *right*-hand window? Not the left? Didn't it occur to you to set up an alarm or give chase?"

"No, it did not. First, I was too shocked, angry, and (let me confess it) in a funk. Second, I had heard the car stop; I heard loud voices, and after a delay, more voices and running feet. I wanted no fuss or uproar; I detest fuss and uproar, as I detest all mess. I returned to my chair, sat down, and awaited you."

It was Nick Barclay who spoke then. Leaving his position by the fireplace, Nick strode to the left-hand window, flung back the long curtains, and turned round.

"Uncle Pen, for God's sake! Is this the window he went out of?"

"It is."

"But the window's closed! Look here!"

"My visitor—or visitant—could have closed it as he went. Those windows slide easily in their grooves, and the rest of you were making a good deal of noise."

"Uncle Pen, look! Couldn't this joker have hidden behind the curtains, and waited a moment or so, and then slipped away through the room when you weren't looking?"

"No, Nick, he could not! Please accept my word for that. It's hard to describe the impression of sheer *malice* that figure conveyed. I awaited its possible return; I even feared its return. What's the matter with you?"

Nick took a step towards him.

"I'll tell you what's the matter. Either you were dreaming, Uncle Pen, or we've walked into the screwiest thing I ever met in all my newspaper experience." Then Nick turned back. "This window is locked on the inside."

7

"I WAS NOT dreaming, on my oath! And I was not—" Pennington Barclay stopped.

"Locked, I'm telling you!" repeated Nick. He pointed to the metal-and-porcelain catch, which was turned outwards in its locked position and firmly secured the two leaves of the window. "A friend of mine out in Westchester has a house that was built in the early eighteen-seventies with windows like this on the ground floor. You can't mess with 'em, as we discovered once when we tried to play a joke on him. If you're outside a window of this kind, you damn well can't leave it locked on the inside."

Here he turned to Garret Anderson.

"Look, Garret. I don't know whether a ghost—if there are such things—can walk through a wall or a locked door as the old judge's spook is supposed to have done for Aunt Essie and Mrs. Tiffin. But I do know a living man who's just fired a gun can't melt through solid glass and window-frames or leave 'em fastened behind him when he's just skipped out. It's a flat impossibility; off the stage and without props, no magician on earth has ever done it."

"What's the matter with you, Nick?" demanded his uncle. "What's the matter with all of you?"

A change had come over Pennington Barclay. Hitherto rapt, carried away, hypnotic of eye and voice, he had dominated the room and towered there. Now there welled up through his voice the same strange note of pettishness they had heard once before, as of a child's feelings raging in an adult mind and heart.

"Why am *I* always in the wrong?" he said. "Why must *I* forever defend myself against some charge or other? I tell you, or try to tell you, a perfectly straight story which also happens to be a true story. And yet . . ."

"Easy, Uncle Pen! Nobody's calling you a liar!"

"No, Nick?"

"Absolutely not, on *my* oath," Nick assured him. "There's an explanation, that's all, and we're going to find it. I'm not here to make trouble; that's the very last thing I want, though you must excuse my manners. It's hardly decent, is it, to come charging into somebody else's house and create a lot of difficulties as I seem to be doing?"

"You're forgetting again, Nick," Deidre said in a clear voice, "that you're no outsider and this is not somebody else's house. It's *your* house, nephew, and has been since your grandfather's will fell out of the tobacco-jar. Don't be backward, Nick! A man in your position is entitled to make all the difficulties he likes."

"You know, Aunt Deidre," said Nick, "you shock me. For the first time, my hearty-and-pretty, you honestly and truly shock me. As for the house: embarrassing though it is, I have already tried my damnedest to talk about the house, but Uncle Pen wouldn't let me get a word in edgeways."

"Ah, the house!" Pennington Barclay had regained all his ease and suavity. "Come, Nick! Steady the Buffs! I was depressed this evening; I have admitted it. And yet there is a very simple solution to all our difficulties."

"What difficulties?" demanded Nick.

"What solution?" asked Andrew Dawlish.

Dominant again, their host began to pace back and forth behind the table. The others crowded round him.

"A very simple solution, I say. What a pity it has only just occurred to me! I will buy the place from you, Nick. A fair price shall be set by any good firm of auctioneers at Lymington or Lyndhurst, and I will buy it from you at whatever figure they name. That's fair, is it not?"

"No, it is not," howled Nick as though completely outraged. "I'm *giving* you the damn house, Uncle Pen. As a matter of fact, to all intents and purposes I've already given it. You can't stop me from giving you the place, now can you?"

"Being no lawyer, I don't know. What you choose to give, no doubt, is your own affair. On the other hand, as six of one and half a dozen of the other, you can hardly refuse the free gift of remuneration for the favour. Observe also," said Pennington Barclay, "how the man of law looks at me. Aroint ye, Andrew! And don't stand there and preen, I beg! You have rather a fine head, for all your unimpressive figure. But don't stand and preen like Macaulay come to judgment. What do *you* say to all this?"

Mr. Dawlish, in fact, had been watching him with a steady, concentrated eye of interest.

"I was wondering," he replied. "This suggestion of buying the house, you tell us, is still another thing which has only just occurred to you?"

"Yes, it is. Don't you believe me?"

"I have not said that. Yet this evening, it appears, you were so depressed and in such low spirits that you almost . . ."

"Almost what?" the other shot back.

"That question, Pennington, is one for you yourself to answer. Have you nothing else to tell us?"

"What should he have to tell us?" asked Deidre. The fixed glaze remained in her eyes, as of unshed tears. "But he mustn't go upsetting himself, you know. Pen, Pen! All this excitement has been very bad for you. Your heart . . ."

"My heart, Deidre, will stand almost anything."

"But it's no joke to be shot at, even with a blank cartridge! Hadn't Dr. Fortescue better have a look at you?"

"It gratifies me, my dear," breathed her husband, "that you show womanly sympathy at last. There is a bruise, I believe. Yes, Ned Fortescue must certainly have a look at me. In the meantime, something is troubling Andrew more than circumstances would warrant."

Mr. Dawlish had bustled up to the wide-open drawer of the writing-table.

"It is extraordinary, Pennington, what a magpie's collection of articles you keep in this drawer. Most of them you have already displayed: the fingerprint-powder, the brush, the magnifying glass. And here, beside the box of cartridges, is a tube of glue."

"Will you be good enough to tell me," yelled their host, "just what the devil a tube of glue has to do with this business?"

"Nothing at all, my dear fellow; don't lose your temper. I was thinking of cartridges."

"Cartridges?"

"The cartridge fired by the phantom figure"—and Mr. Dawlish frowned—"was a blank. It was fired, true, from a distance of at least a dozen feet. At the same time—" He hesitated, ruminating again. "What happened to the paper wad from that cartridge? Where is it now?"

"I have already informed you, it seems to me, that I threw it out on the lawn. We shall find it there in the morning. Or if the matter is of such earth-shaking importance, we can take

THE HOUSE AT SATAN'S ELBOW

an electric torch and look for it now. *Is* it of such importance?"

"No, hardly. But I still wonder: what steps do we take with regard to the pistol-carrying attacker from the grave? Do we inform the police?"

"Police?" Pennington Barclay addressed the ceiling. "Great Scott, no!"

"It is best to be wise in these matters. Are you sure you have nothing to tell us?"

"'Phantom figure,' 'Attacker from the grave.' I have to tell you," said the other, "that I am growing unutterably weary of the constant implication which makes me out no more than a pointless liar. Observe once more—and for the last time!"

Moving out from behind the table, he strode to the left-hand window. With the heel of his hand he struck the metal-and-porcelain catch, driving it sideways into a flat position. With both hands on the inner sash, fingers above and thumbs below, he sent the sash rolling softly upwards so that the window was now wide open.

"There!" he added. "Whether you credit me or not, that is how the window looked when my visitor appeared. For this happened; I can only swear it happened. We must now devote our wits to devising an explanation; Nick will agree there is one. And why am *I* always the culprit? Why will they believe everybody except *me?* If Estelle may have a black-robed spectre melting through a locked door, is it so difficult to imagine some malicious human being contriving his way through a locked window?"

"What's this?" interrupted a new voice. "What's this, what's this, what's this?"

All of them whirled round.

From the east side of the room, at a kind of diffident run, hurried a middle-sized, middle-aged woman with a kittenish manner and voluminous hair rather obviously tinted red. Though not at all ill-looking; if somewhat scrawny-faced and staring of eye, she wore an embroidered blue house-coat and brilliant tartan slacks which would better have suited the figure of Deidre Barclay or Fay Wardour. From her left wrist dangled a tapestry knitting-bag, and in her right hand, at a flourish, she carried a glass jar nearly full of what the label described as "Best Orley Farm Honey."

"Is that you, Estelle?" Pennington Barclay said in no very cordial tone. "Well, come in and shed the light of your presence. Have you been hiding again?"

"Hiding?" echoed Estelle Barclay. "Pennington, you silly fellow, there's no need at all to be unkind. Isn't it a shame—

isn't it a great, devastating, devouring shame—that poor Father's no longer here to keep you in order and teach you your place?"

"At least you are still eating, I see."

"Eating, did you say?" It was as though Estelle would have scorned this too. "But I *need* vitamin B; Dr. Fortescue says I need vitamin B; and honey's *full* of vitamin B. Besides! It's ten-thirty, probably later. In half an hour or even less we shall be holding my birthday-reception in the dining-room. And you wouldn't prevent that, would you?"

"On the contrary, Estelle: I shall be happy to preside at your birthday-reception and to wish you many happy returns."

"Thanks, Pennington. You *can* be kind when you're determined to be." Then her eyelids fluttered as though with tears. "Hiding, though!" she said.

It was Deidre who answered.

"You were in the cloakroom, weren't you?" asked Deidre, nodding towards the alcove on the east side, then towards the door at the left of the alcove, and finally at the mirror behind her over the fireplace. "Weren't you in the cloakroom, Estelle?"

"You mean you saw me in that mirror when I came out?"

"And when you went in, about ten minutes ago."

"Oh, Deidre dear, is there any reason why your poor, useless sister-in-law *shouldn't* be on hand when she wants to be?"

"Good heavens, no! I only said——"

"And don't you say anything either, my lofty Pennington! I didn't come to the library to see *you!*"

"Then, without the slightest objection to your presence in the library, or the cloakroom, or anywhere else that suits your maiden fancy, may the lofty Pennington ask why you are here?"

"It's Nick!" cried Estelle. "It's little Nick!"

"Hullo, Aunt Essie," said little Nick, towering above her.

"Hul-*lo*, dear! If you're too grown up to have a kiss for your old aunt, Nicky, your aunt's not too old to have a kiss for you. Come here!"

Slipping round his neck the left arm, from which dangled her knitting-bag, Estelle stood on tiptoe to kiss him first on one cheek and then on the other.

"There, that's better! And I'm not so old or so unattractive either, am I? I even flatter myself that I'm with it. Do you know, Nicky, this isn't the first time in the past half-hour I've seen the charming girl who has become your other aunt?"

"It isn't?"

"No, it isn't! I happened to be in the kitchen when she put

the car away in the garage, and I couldn't resist running out there. It's wonderful to have you home again, Nicky! This dear girl said all sorts of complimentary things about you, though I won't embarrass you by repeating them."

"Really, Estelle," exclaimed Deidre, "I never spoke one word of opinion, complimentary or otherwise. All I said——"

"But you *looked,* my dear; and atmospheres can be eloquent, can't they? If you were Pennington, Nicky, would *you* let a handsome young wife go off on her own for holidays abroad? To Italy last year, to Switzerland in sixty-one, to North Africa the year before that? Of course there was no harm in it, mind! She stayed with such *pleasant* friends, including the Contesa da Carpi in Rome and Lady Banks in Lucerne. And speaking of friends, Deidre also told me . . ."

"Miss Estelle Barclay," Deidre said loudly, "may I present Mr. Garret Anderson?"

"Well, really, now!" cried Estelle, doing a complete pirouette with the jar of honey held aloft. "This is a great pleasure! Aren't you the Garret Anderson who paid us a visit early in the summer of thirty-nine? Aren't you that same young man?"

"The pleasure is mine, Miss Barclay. I'm the same person, at any rate."

"He's been here before, has he?" asked Pennington, emerging from abstraction. "I'm afraid I didn't remember; sorry."

But Estelle would have none of this.

"*I* remember, though. I never forget anything. And fancy meeting him again, now that he's all grown up and writing musical shows and everything! I'll just say hello to you, Garret, and then I'll go on to other matters. Because for once poor Essie is going to be taken seriously.

"My brother has been asking me," she continued, "what I want in his dismal, silly library. I wanted to welcome Nicky, of course! But that's not all. It's enough, for anybody with a memory or a true heart, but it's not all. I've made a great discovery; I must speak to Andrew Dawlish; and I won't let Pen distract me, either. Tell me, Andrew! When poor dear Father died, weren't you supposed to go through all the papers he left?"

"To the best of my knowledge, Estelle," replied a long-suffering solicitor. "I did go through all his papers."

"You couldn't have seen the ones *I* mean. You know the room he used to use as a study? Across the passage"—Estelle gestured violently but vaguely in a south-easterly direction—"beside what used to be the housekeeper's room and the butler's pantry? The room with the big rolltop desk? Yes, yes, you're familiar with all that. But did you know there's a secret compartment in the desk?"

"A secret compartment?"

"Well, no more did *I* know it. And it's not a very mysterious kind of secret compartment, though Father loved things like that. But Providence does help us sometimes, doesn't it?

"After dinner," she went on with extraordinary intensity, "I was in the music-room playing pop records; we must move with the times, Andrew. But I couldn't concentrate on the Roysterers or the Upbeats. Something seemed to be calling me or summoning me. 'Go to the study and look,' it seemed to be saying; go to the study and look.'"

"Probably I'm psychic; other things have shown that, haven't they? But after a time I did go to the study. Nothing was locked there; nothing's ever been locked. The lowest drawer on the right-hand side of the desk has a false bottom. You just push one end of it, which slides back. And inside, Andrew, was a great thick bundle of papers, some of them in Father's handwriting."

"Just one moment, Estelle!" Mr. Dawlish was growing bedevilled. "Did you go through these papers? Did you find anything significant or relevant?"

"Oh, how should *I* know what's relevant? That's a man's work; that's your work. I didn't even *read* most of them."

"What did you do, then?"

"I just gathered up the whole bundle; I took them with me to the kitchen. I was in the kitchen when I heard Deidre putting the car away. She didn't come back through the house. She walked away without saying where she was going, but I knew it was to the library. I knew you were *all* in the library. So I came in by the drawing-room door." Estelle gestured towards it. "You were all so engrossed in what Pen was saying that nobody even looked round. I ducked into the little cloakroom; I didn't quite close the door. And I heard what you were saying, Pen; don't think I didn't!"

Pennington Barclay, who had stopped pacing, regarded her with an indecipherable stare.

"The situation, such as it is, becomes a little clearer. You were not hiding, Estelle. You were only waiting and listening."

"Well, Pen," retorted his sister, "I'm sure you'll twist things up as you always do. Who cares about that? *I* don't. The important thing is that bundle of papers, which I put down on the couch in the cloakroom. Oughtn't you to take charge of them, Andrew, in case there's something poor Father wanted us to know? And you *can* take them away with you, can't you? I tried to get them into my knitting-bag, and the bundle was too big. But that brief-case of yours doesn't look any too well-filled."

Mr. Dawlish deposited his hat on the table.

"There is nothing in this brief-case," he answered, unfastening its catch and holding it open, "except the toothbrush, comb, and shaving-tackle I took for a forty-eight-hour journey to London. I can take the papers and examine them tonight. That is, if Pennington thinks—"

"I think you had better," Pennington said testily, "or Estelle will give none of us any peace until you do. But I can't imagine you will find anything important."

"Nor can I. However!"

Mr. Dawlish marched to the little room opening off at the left of the alcove. Estelle fluttered after him, waving the knitting-bag from one wrist and the jar of honey in her other hand. Still bedevilled, though with a smile to mitigate discourtesy, he went inside and closed the door in her face. But he emerged after a very short interval, fastening the catch of a stuffed and bulging case from which only one article of its contents—a rather crumpled piece of paper with typewritten lines on it—projected from one side of the case. Estelle ran at him and snatched away this piece of paper with her left hand.

"My clumsiness is well-known, I'm afraid," cried Estelle. She tried to smooth out the paper with both hands and almost dropped the jar of honey. "But I'm only trying to help, aren't I?"

"After the fuss and uproar you have already made about these papers," said Mr. Dawlish, tapping the brief-case, "such behaviour is not calculated to help very much. Will you be good enough to return what you have just taken, please?

"But this," exclaimed Estelle with a remark which to Garret Anderson made no sense whatever, "this is only a receipted bill for the pin-ball machines! It's only a receipted bill for the pin-ball machines!"

"Whatever it is, will you be good enough to return it?"

"Yes, yes! *Everything's* important, isn't it?" She handed him the paper, which he put in his pocket. "Ordinarily, dear Andrew, I should *insist* you stay on for my birthday-reception at eleven o'clock. But you'll want to get home and look at those, won't you? And your car is here, you know.

"Yes, don't look so surprised!" Estelle went on, as though new energy flowered into her. "Your son brought the car over; it's in the drive now. Hugh came to the front door when I was just going from the music-room to Father's study. He was on his way to see some friends at Lepe House. Hugh said he'd leave the car for you, because his friends would drive him home. He also said he wanted to see you about the Lammas case and that it was most urgent."

"The Lammas case?" interjected Pennington. "What's the Lammas case?"

Mr. Dawlish lifted his fist.

"A young fool of that name has got himself into trouble. Dawlish and Dawlish aren't merely family solicitors, you know. What with taxes and living-costs in these days, we must even touch criminal work when it seems urgent or justified. Yes, Estelle," he added sharply, "I am going! But don't be so precipitate, I beg of you. Don't run at me as though you would hurl me out bodily. I am going, of course, but in good time and in good order. Meanwhile . . ."

"Meanwhile, we can see, you are just *wasting* time. I *know* those papers are important! Poor dear Father——"

"And again," said Pennington, "we have 'poor dear Father.' With Estelle, I fear, it is still poor dear Father. After the incident of the second will in the tobacco-jar, I hoped we had heard the last of poor dear Father."

"You will never hear the last of him, Pen Barclay," Estelle almost screamed, "as long as there's any kindness left in this world and none at all left in *you*."

"Meaning what?"

"Meaning just what I say. The things *I* could tell them about you if I had no heart either! But I don't really need to tell them. You condemn yourself out of your own mouth. This silly tale of a blank cartridge being fired in here . . ."

"Hang it, woman, *somebody* took a shot at me! Don't you even believe that?"

"I believe it if the others say so, though I didn't hear anything. How could I, at the back of the house and with these walls so thick? But you always have the delusion——"

She never completed the sentence. The door in the south wall of books, which Garret had believed must lead to a cross-passage, did in fact lead to such a passage. He had a brief glimpse of it, dimly lighted, as the door opened and closed behind a rather shambling-looking man in tweeds.

"Forgive this intrusion," said the newcomer, his eye going instantly to Pennington Barclay. "Nothing wrong, is there?"

"Come in, Ned!" their host said with a kind of nervous heartiness. "There is no patient demanding attention, it's true. What we have is another crisis, *contretemps,* or what you will. . . . For those of you who don't know him—Nick? Mr. Anderson?—this is Dr. Edward Fortescue."

"Very happy," the newcomer proclaimed in his husky voice. He did not sound happy.

"The fact is," pursued Pennington Barclay, "that at about ten o'clock, just as these good people were arriving, a figure in a black robe—no ghost, but a malicious joker of flesh and blood—fired a blank cartridge at me from my own revolver. He then backed out of the window there and in some fashion left it locked behind him."

"That window?" inquired Dr. Fortescue, following the direction of the other's nod. "It's open now, isn't it?"

"It is open now because I myself raised it a few minutes ago. *We* found it shut and locked behind closed curtains. Estelle, who heard no shot, refuses to believe me. She seems to insist I was drunk or lying."

Dr. Fortescue drew the air through a hollow tooth.

"*I* heard no shot," he said. "But I hope subsequent investigation will not bring similar charges against me too. After all, I saw the figure myself."

"You saw it?"

"My dear Barclay, there's no need to be so thunderstruck at corroboration. Would you mind telling me exactly what happened?"

After a formal introduction of Nick and Garret, Pennington Barclay gave a brief, vivid summary of the story he had already told.

Dr. Fortescue listened, shifting from one foot to the other. A tallish, loose-limbed man in his late forties, he had a long head on which the patchy brown hair had retreated beyond the arch of the skull and pale-blue ruminant eyes surrounded by wrinkles.

"Well!" he observed when the recital was finished. "Well! A form of the locked-room problem, eh?" His gaze had never left their host. "But it's not the only interesting matter at hand."

"How so, Ned? How so?"

"I'm a comparative newcomer here." Dr. Fortescue addressed the company in general. "I was called in as—what shall I say?—resident physician only after the death of the old gentleman in March. If I were fanciful, which I'm not, I should call this an unhealthy house. Not for medical reasons; it's far less damp than it seems. And it has all the creature-comforts to which I'm much inclined. A well-stocked wine-cellar! Bathrooms positively sybaritic! Hot and cold laid on in every bedroom, together with an outlet for plugging in an electric razor. There are those who like it very much. You, sir"—he looked at Nick—"are the heir from America about whom there's been so much talk?"

"I was *supposed* to be the heir, yes."

"Have family differences been settled? Your uncle wasn't sure they could be, though he's too polite to have said so to your face. Still! If family differences were on the agenda and did come up, I hope they've been settled in an amicable way?"

"They have," answered Nick.

"And 'amicable,' Doctor," Deidre said with a swashbuckling gesture, "isn't even the word for it! Their only difference has been trying to outdo each other in giving things away. You never saw two people get on so well as my husband and Nick. It's been pie every step of the way."

"Has it, Mrs. Barclay? Perhaps I'd better investigate."

Despite his casual and shambling air, despite a husky, throaty voice which seemed to hover round a subject rather than swoop straight at it, Dr. Fortescue advanced so purposefully that Pennington Barclay retreated several steps, throwing up a hand as though to ward off attack.

"Investigate?" he repeated. "What's all this? What are you at? What do you want?"

"With your permission, I want a look at you. Specifically, I want your wrist and your pulse. As resident physician I may sometimes neglect my duties; maybe I don't badger you enough. But I won't have them think me as imperceptive as Dr. John H. Watson himself. The look on your face, my boy, would alarm even a nonmedical eye. There is also the fact that——"

"One moment," said Pennington Barclay.

Before this blast Dr. Fortescue halted. Impatiently their host lifted a bare right hand and inspected the fingers. Then he lifted a left hand in which he clutched a rolled-up pair of rubber gloves.

"There are times," he declared, "when I am quite as woolly-minded as Estelle herself. Will someone kindly tell me when I removed these accursed gloves? I put them on for some demonstration or other, and then I forgot them. Andrew, when did I take them off?"

"Frankly, I don't remember," said Mr. Dawlish. "We have been milling about a good deal, more so than is seemly. (Gently, Miss Deidre!) But I saw no occasion for particular alertness; I'm afraid I don't remember."

"Can *you* help, Nick? When did I remove the gloves?"

"Look, Uncle Pen!" Nick waved his arms. "You'd been griping about how clumsy the gloves were. I've got a sort of impression you stripped 'em off, keeping 'em in your left hand, just before you went charging at the window and opened it. But that's only an impression; I can't swear to it. Garret?"

"I agree with Mr. Dawlish that I don't remember," Garret answered, "though what you say seems correct."

"And it's all very well," pursued Pennington Barclay, "for Ned Fortescue to speak of creature-comforts. There are not nearly as many creature-comforts as there ought to be, and as there will be if I remain master. Up to the time the military occupied this district during the war—they took over Lepe House, if they didn't take over Greengrove—there was not even an electric-cable to the coast."

"Excuse me, Uncle Pen," Nick objected with fiery earnestness, "but aren't you really getting all mixed up now? There was electric light in the old days, wasn't there?"

"I did not say there was no electric light. I said we had no power-cable for the company's electricity."

Here he thrust the rubber gloves into the left-hand pocket of his smoking-jacket, as though to get them out of the way for good.

"In point of fact, Nick, we had a private power-plant: which, if you remember, was always going wrong and plunging the house into darkness at inconvenient moments. Then it had to be repaired. Your grandfather could manage these repairs if no servant were available. *I* couldn't manage the repairs, which gave him sound excuse to sneer at me. And I mention this because . . ."

"Because you want to distract me, don't you?" cried Estelle with the effect of a pounce. "You don't want me to say what I must say, what I'm bound to say, what I'm *going* to say however you try to stop me!"

"Control yourself, Estelle. I mention this, ladies and gentlemen, because it has a bearing on our problem."

"Yes?" prompted his sister, raising both knitting-bag and honey-jar. "Yes, yes, *yes?*"

"I could do no electrical repair-work, I say. My one practical talent lay in the ability to pick locks. Given a piece of bent wire or even a straightened-out paper-clip"—Pennington

Barclay seemed to be counting to himself as he looked at Estelle—"and I can still pick almost any lock you show me. As for your own one talent, Estelle, we won't discuss that because so far you have not seen fit to employ it. Now, look here!"

He strode to the left-hand window, gestured out into the night, and swung round.

"The intruder in the mask and robe went out through this window, leaving it locked on the inside. How did he do this? If it were a question of tampering with some lock, I might contrive to show you. But no lock confronts us. Here, as has been pointed out, we have a solid metal catch securely twisted into place at that time. Therefore . . ."

"I'll ask you again, Uncle Pen," said Nick. "Now that you've studied the window and know the difficulties, are you sure this fellow couldn't have hidden behind the curtains and slipped back through the room when you weren't looking?"

"Am I sure? Am I entirely sure? That, Nick, is a tall order for any question in the cosmos. I don't think it happened, no. Yet at the same time . . ."

"Oh, rubbish and rubbish and more than rubbish!" pounced Estelle. "All you're saying, really, is that you can't help in any way and only want us to swallow this silly tale without asking you any questions."

"Is it a silly tale? Since Ned Fortescue appears to confirm it . . ."

"Ah, but does he confirm it? If dear Dr. Fortescue swears to something"—Estelle breathed hard—"I might believe it even though I couldn't believe it, if you see what I mean. But what *does* he say?"

"Well, there he is. Why don't you ask him?"

"Well!" observed Dr. Fortescue. "Well!"

Shambling, loose-jointed in his old tweeds, he ran a hand down across his face as though massaging it. Then he spoke alternately to Nick and Garret.

"Miss Barclay flatters me, gentlemen. I have never been sure of too many things in this world. And my faults are many and varied, though I try to make up for them. I drink too much, as you will soon hear if you have not heard it already. But I am seldom affected and never incapacitated. Miss Barclay herself will bear witness that I had drunk nothing this evening.

"After dinner, as you may or may not have been told, we all separated and went our various ways. My bedroom, though much smaller than this library, is directly above the library at the extreme western end. It has two windows facing north towards the front and one window facing west. I went up to my bedroom, I should think, about half-past eight. At the end of dinner my friend Barclay had handed me an excellent cigar, and I had a good deal of reading to do."

"Professional reading, no doubt?" Andrew Dawlish spoke as one pompous man to another. "You were deep in the *British Medical Journal?*"

"Well, no. Not the B.M.J. In my profession, sir, we are seldom such gluttons for work as the doctors you see on television. As a matter of fact, I was reading a detective novel."

Again his gaze travelled between Nick and Garret.

"This now seems very appropriate, though nothing lethal has happened or (let's hope, anyway!) is likely to happen. And yet, as I sat in that bedroom finishing my cigar and progressing towards chapter five, I can't say I was altogether happy. At dinner there had been a suggestion—or an atmosphere, perhaps, rather than a suggestion—that there would be ructions when the new heir arrived. What sort of ructions, nobody stated; I was not confided in, as why should I have been?

"There was one unimportant interruption. My cigar was finished, the fictional crime had been committed and was being investigated, when I thought I heard a car coming up the drive. 'Surely,' I thought, 'that can't be Mrs. Barclay returning?' The time, as a glance at my travelling-clock showed, was only a quarter past nine; Mrs. Barclay could not yet have met the train.

"But I had enough curiosity to look out of a front window. It *was* a car. It proved to be young Hugh Dawlish, the son of our friend here. He exchanged some words with Miss Barclay, who herself answered the front door; he drove the car round the side of the house and then left on foot.

"Afterwards . . ."

"Afterwards," continued Dr. Fortsecue, rumpling up what remained of his patchy hair, "I closed the windows, drew the curtains shut, and turned on the lights. It was not so much that I wanted to exclude daylight, which was dwindling. But it turns chilly here beside the Solent, and as you may judge from my clothing, I feel the cold.

"Well! I sat down to read again, but I had trouble in following the story. I could think only of Mrs. Barclay returning from Brockenhurst with the others. And who was I? If it came to that, *what* was I? A dependent, a hanger-on: kindly dealt with, it's true, and even treated with a measure of respect, but still a dependent and hanger-on at Maecenas's table."

Pennington Barclay straightened up.

"My dear fellow," he protested, "this is utter and absolute nonsense! I had no idea you felt like that! If you think you're not wanted here . . ."

Let's face it, though; there are times when we must all face the truth."

"And if you insist on saying all this—"

"I do insist. Now, what, on the soberest consideration," inquired Dr. Fortescue, "was my function in this house? It was to fulfill my duties and to keep myself presentable. I could and did fulfill by duties; but *was* I presentable? At that moment I doubted it.

"It must have been close on ten o'clock when I got up from my chair. I put out all lights except the little light over the wash-basin in my bedroom. I plugged in my electric razor beside the wash-basin. And I gave myself the shave I thought I needed. Now, tell me." He looked straight at Nick. "When you and the others drove up to this house—and, shortly afterwards, ran past it—did you see any lights on the floor above this."

"Not a light anywhere," Nick told him.

"You, Mr. Anderson? Anything to add?"

"Nothing whatever. I thought there were no lights at all."

"You could have seen no lights. The curtains in my bedroom, as Miss Barclay will tell you, are of heavy blackout material left over from wartime days. And you would have seen no lights afterwards. Let me conclude a foolish story.

"I finished shaving. I had heard nothing; or, if any suggestion of sound penetrated through closed and blacked-out windows to a man with an electric razor going beside his ear, it registered only in my subconscious mind. When I had put aside the razor, I can't say what impulse made me switch off the one light above the wash-bowl and grope my way in darkness to the western window, where I drew back the curtains and looked out.

"Opposite the western end of this house, gentlemen, their is a large garden laid out in walks or alleys of very high yew hedges and surrounded by a yew-hedge wall. The garden has four entrances, an entrance at each point of the compass. One of them—you could see it now if you went to either window—faces directly towards the left-hand window of this library.

"Very well! I looked out of my own window from a point between those two and above. It was not yet quite dark. Between me and the garden lay some sixty feet of smooth grass. And there, gentlemen, *I* saw something. I saw . . ."

"Yes?" prompted Pennington Barclay. "Don't stop there, Ned. You saw what?"

"I saw a figure in a black robe," replied Dr. Fortescue.

There was a pause.

"No description will be attempted," the doctor went on, "especially since the figure's back was turned. It was moving rather slowly from the direction of the house towards the entrance to the garden and had almost reached the garden when I looked. At this point I caught the faint sound of a voice from somewhere below and out of sight. It seemed to me the voice shouted, 'Come on!'"

"Yes, you heard it." Nick Barclay edged forward. "We delayed a good deal, for one reason or another, before we ran round the side of the house. But I was the one who yelled, 'Come on.' What next, Doctor?"

"Can't you guess? I opened my window, which is a casement-window swinging out like a little door. It made almost no noise; in any case you were too preoccupied. Three people —yourself, Mr. Anderson, our friend Dawlish—came racing round below. From the subsequent sound of voices, including that of our good host, which would have made his fortune on the stage or in films, I gathered nothing could be seriously wrong. And yet . . .

"I closed the window; I drew the curtains; I turned on the light. Then I sat down and worried. No, nothing could be seriously wrong; and yet . . . I waited for what seemed to me a respectable and decent interval, allowing the minutes to stretch out as long as possible, after which (as you are now aware) I came downstairs to ask what had happened.

"Actually, gentlemen, there is very little more. I will add only one thing: it concerns the figure in the black robe, which I last saw at the entrance to the garden. In Barclay's own account he has stressed what seemed to him the *malice* of the visitor. I can't speak as to that; I must not be fanciful; fancy wrecks our lives. I give only an impression; it's probably a wrong impression. But it did seem to me that as the three of you ran up and young Mr. Barclay went to that right-hand window, the black-robed figure raised its arm in a kind of caper, like a triumphant little dance-step, and then darted away into the garden. That's all."

"If you ask me," declared Nick, raising his own arm as though to take an oath, "if you ask me, good people, it's quite enough. You may not be fanciful, Dr. Fortescue, but you do pretty well. 'The ghosts they are coming, oho, oho!' Well, Aunt Essie? What do you say to Uncle Pen's adventure now?"

"Stuff and nonsense, Nicky! I don't believe one word of it!"

"You don't believe Dr. Fortescue?"

"I don't believe anything *Pen* says. We've got only his word for it that *anybody* shot at him! If he invented all this just to scare us and fired the revolver himself to make his story sound reasonable . . ."

"The objection to such a charge, Estelle," her brother pointed out, "is that my story sounds reasonable to nobody, not even to me. And where did the blank cartridges come from? The pistol was filled with blanks, although I myself never bought any."

"You say you didn't, you say you didn't! How do we know what you bought or didn't buy? Listen to me, all of you," begged Estelle. Slowly she waved the jar of honey as though conducting an orchestra. "I'm psychic, you know. I'm not clever, but I'm psychic, and I think *I* can tell you what happened.

"Pen invented all this, of course. But poetic justice is always waiting for us, isn't it? He didn't see anything; he's lying! He didn't *think* a supernatural presence could come back. And yet, all the time, something had come back and was watching him. Don't you *know* that's what Dr. Fortescue saw on the lawn out there?"

The harassed doctor massaged his face in desperation.

"Madam," he said, "I saw somebody wearing a black robe. That's all I saw or tell you I saw. This ridiculous talk of ghosts, not for the first time——"

"You *think* you're of the earth, earthy. But you're not really that at all. You're the sort who *can* see things hidden from other eyes. You said you felt the cold, didn't you? I felt the cold (we always do) when *I* saw the old judge's presence myself. And there's a horrible cold air about us now."

Hesitating only for a moment, Estelle ran straight at the right-hand window, which had been open all evening. Though impeded by knitting-bag and honey-jar, she pulled down its lower sash, locked the window, and swept its curtains together. Then she turned to the left and hurried across in front of the fireplace towards the place where Pennington stood in front of the left-hand window.

"Let me pass, Pen, and I'll close the other one."

"No, you will not. Stand back, Estelle! Don't touch that window!"

"But what if it's still out there? Take care, Pen! It may come in and get you even yet. For the last time, will you let me pass?"

"For the last time, I will not. We have had quite enough of this nonsense."

"Nonsense, eh? *You* talk of nonsense?"

"I do. I will not stand idly by while you call spirits from the vasty deep, and, as with Glendower, they don't come."

"Oh, you *silly* fellow! You silly, brutal, *insensitive* fellow!"

"But in all your maundering, Estelle, it may be that there is one microscopic gleam of reason. Let us use our own reason to determine this. Whatever may be happening here, it had its origin in the past."

Whereupon restraint, logic, sense itself went up the spout in hysteria as brother and sister faced each other beside the fireplace.

"The past!" Estelle screamed. "That's all you care about, isn't it? This house! Your books! That's all you care about, I mean, except when a pretty-faced young girl catches your eye. This secretary of yours may be a nice enough girl; I'm sure she is, if Deidre vouches for her. But do you think *we* don't see how you look at her and what you'd like to do?"

"That's a lie," Pennington Barclay said clearly. "Are you comparing me with Sir Horace Wildfare?"

"I'm not comparing you with anybody!"

"Not with *him*, it's to be hoped. I am old enough, God knows, and of this world a little weary. I have none of his other qualities, including the malice. And yet the clue to what is happening in this house may be found two hundred years ago. There is no ghost. But there is an atmosphere, as in many houses, infecting people's minds as palpably as a whisper in the ear. A certain other pamphlet—unread by you, or by Deidre, or even by poor Miss Wardour, whom you insist on slandering—indicates that some member of the judge's family had fed him poison. It has left a mental poison which remains to this day."

"And you told still another lie, didn't you?"

"Still another lie?" yelled her brother. "What in hell's name are you talking about?"

"Yes," gabbled Estelle, "you may well say in hell's name. Many times you've told people that the ghost has never been seen since Victorian times until Mrs. Tiffin and I saw it this very year. But somebody else saw it. Dear *Father* saw it, years ago; you must have known he saw it. So you lied about that too, didn't you? If only you weren't so unkind to me! . . ."

"I am trying to be kind to you, Estelle. *God knows I am trying to be kind to you.* I was never aware our sainted father had seen the judge's ghost or anybody's ghost; in that case, surely, he would have cursed it back across the Styx? As for the matter of being unkind . . ."

"And all this"—Estelle flew into tragedy—"must come and bedevil me at the very time things should be so *nice!* We're within fifteen minutes of my birthday-reception, when we gather round the cake in the dining-room, and it's a time for joy and family affection!"

"Tonight, Estelle, you have shown me the immense extent of your affection."

"But I do have affection for you! I do!"

"Then let me beg you, sweet sister, to restrain your tears and not explode with them. Above all things, I beg you, stop waving that jar of honey as though you would brain somebody with it. Take care, Estelle! Take care that—"

And then, grotesquely, the smash occurred.

The glass jar, perhaps whirled too blindly, struck sideways against the rough stone of the mantelpiece. The mouth of the jar broke to fragments; an ounce or two of thick honey, sluggish but hurled with catapult-force, flew out across the left breast of Pennington Barclay's smoking-jacket and began sluggishly to crawl down.

Their host stood motionless, haggard-faced but impassive.

"Mess and stickiness!" he said. "Mess and stickiness!" Still impassive, he closed his eyes. "One, two, three, four. Five, six, seven, eight!"

Estelle remained undaunted. On the ledge of the mantelpiece she put what remained of the jar, cracked but otherwise intact. Then she kicked frantically at glass-fragments on the hearthstone.

"Oh, Pen, don't be silly! I am so sorry, you know; but it's your own fault, isn't it? Surely you have several other smoking-jackets in the cloakroom? You have at least one?"

"In point of fact, I have two others."

"Then go and change at once, dear, and don't make so much fuss! You *will* preside at my birthday-celebration, won't you? Unless you've forgotten your promise or never meant it at all?"

"No, I have not forgotten." From his right-hand pocket he took out a handkerchief and swabbed at the honey-stain on his chest, but after a moment gave up in repulsion and returned the handkerchief to his pocket. The honey was soaking into the fabric; though unsightly, it had ceased to drip.

"I have not forgotten, I say. Your estimate of time, Estelle, is badly out. The time"—and he consulted his wrist-watch—"is not quite twenty minutes to eleven. But I have not forgotten; I will preside at these carefree festivities. And even if I don't . . ."

"Even if you don't?"

"If a bogle from the eighteenth century, according to your prophecy, should swoop through this window and carry me away . . ."

"Pen, *don't!*"

"You will still have Nick, the proper head of the family, to preside in my place. And now, ladies and gentlemen, I am going to change. Unduly fastidious though it may appear, I detest being seen in this condition; I feel as though I had been not only smeared with honey but covered with insects too. Also, unduly discourteous though *this* may appear, I propose to turn you all out of the library. I have one last remark for my sister's ear, after which we must part until eleven o'clock."

"No, Pen, I have a question to ask you instead." Estelle's voice, a powerful contralto as her brother's was a bass-baritone, rang in the big library. "Answer it, for my peace of mind and your own! What do you really mean to do about this fair-haired secretary? Is it marriage, Pen? Is it as bad as that? Will you turn away your own wedded wife and marry this girl instead?"

"You are entirely wrong, Estelle. Miss Wardour means nothing to me. God knows I mean nothing to her. There is another matter gnawing at my mind. It gnaws deeply; it gnaws fiercely; it will not cease or go away."

"Oh? And what's that?"

"Poison!" said Pennington Barclay. "Who poisoned the old sinner in his own household? And would it help us to know the truth now?"

That was the point at which Garret Anderson looked up.

A latch had clicked across the room. The door to the east-west cross-passage, the same door by which Dr. Fortescue had entered, was again partway open. In the aperture stood Fay Wardour; and on her face, for some reason, was a look of sheer horror.

Exactly as he had first seen her in the train that evening— blue-and-white dress, no stockings, blue shoes—she was again fumbling with a tortoise-shell cigarette-case. Fay jerked back; history repeated itself. But this time no cigarette popped out. The whole case itself slipped from her hand. It fell open on the carpet, disclosing a line of tipped cigarettes held in place by a little strip of brass. She turned and ran, slamming the door after her.

"Fay!" cried Deidre Barclay. "What can . . . whatever is . . ."

Then Deidre acted. She ran out after the other girl, also slamming the door. And Garret moved too.

The image of Fay, the knowledge of all she meant to him, swallowed up every other consideration. He no longer cared whether they went through the farce of meeting as strangers. He knew only that he had been provided with an excuse for following her now.

Inanely Garret called, "You dropped your cigarette-case! You dropped—"

It was no good elaborating. He picked up the case and closed it. He looked round, meeting the sardonic eye of Nick, and then bolted out into the passage after the other two.

9

THE PASSAGE, broad and deep-carpeted though with very dim lights, stretched west to another full-length window closely curtained. The north side of this wing seemed to contain only two long rooms, library and drawing-room, set in a line. Facing Garret as he emerged from the library were three closed doors. Presumably they led to three rooms on the south of the passage taking up the same corresponding space as drawing-room and library.

Deidre Barclay, tense and anxious, stood in front of the middle door across the passage. She stood with her hand on the knob, as though guarding it. Garret ran up to her.

"Fay!" he said. "Where's Fay?"

"She's in here. This is the billiard-room."

Deidre's hazel eyes no longer seemed so level or so straightforward. Almost in a panic, she first clutched at Garret's arm and then spoke as rapidly as Estelle had done.

"There are three rooms on this side, as you see. The one on my left, nearest the window at the end of the passage, is the music-room. The one on my right was old Mr. Barclay's study. Beyond there"—Deidre gestured eastwards—"beyond there, as you see, the passage opens into a central hall through the house. Beyond that, still east, there's another passage like this one: morning-room and dining-room at the front, butler's pantry and housekeeper's room and something else at the back, though there hasn't been a butler or a housekeeper here since World War One. Anyway, that doesn't matter. Garret—do you mind if I call you Garret?"

"No, of course not!"

"You're Nick's great friend, aren't you?"

"I am; but how did you know that?"

"And you're Fay's— But that doesn't matter either. Anyway, this behind me is the billiard-room. And it's not only the billiard-room. Old Mr. Barclay had two pin-ball tables put in there."

"*Old Clovis* had two pin-ball tables put in?"

"Yes! He was fond of them; except for an occasional hundred-up at billiards, he didn't seem to like anything else. He ordered them, the real commercial machines, from a place that supplies amusement-arcades in London. And he had them set up, with a bowl of pennies beside each so that anybody could play. I never saw him laugh, but he did smile sometimes when he was putting pennies in the slot and ringing up scores on the pin-ball machines."

"About Fay: you were saying?"

"She ran in just now. She couldn't lock the door; there's no key. You don't know Fay's story, do you? You don't know what happened to her?"

"No, I don't."

"Well, you'll have to know now. All sorts of accidents have been happening; it was the worst kind of brutal accident that my husband used those words when he did. But—oh, I don't know! Maybe it'll be good for her to tell you; I think *you'll* be good for her. Go after her; talk to her; be as gentle as you know how. You *will* be nice to Fay, won't you?"

"I'll try."

And then everything seemed to happen at once.

Another female voice said, "Please, ma'am?" From the direction of the central hall appeared a trim, rather pretty if stolid-looking girl of eighteen or nineteen. Deidre, herself sturdy and more than trim in her dark slacks and orange sweater, swung round as the girl approached.

"Yes, Phyllis?"

"Please, ma'am, there are two gentlemen at the front door."

"At this time of night, Phyllis? Who are they? What do they want?"

"Well, ma'am! answered the flustered maid. "One of 'em is a great big stout gentlemen, all bulging out like a spinnaker with the wind behind it. He says his name is Fell."

"Fell?" exclaimed Garret, who felt that things were happening much too fast. "Gideon Fell? *Dr.* Gideon Fell?"

"Yes, sir, that's it." Then Phyllis gabbled at Deidre. "The other gentleman is younger and not fat. I went back and whistled at Phoebe, who's in the passage to the kitchen. And Phoebe said, 'That's no gentleman; that's a p'leeceman in plain clothes.' And I'm sure *I* don't know, ma'am! I think the second one is Scotch, though he don't talk like it."

"Phyllis," said Garret, "is his name Elliot? Deputy Commander Elliot?"

"Elliot! I knew he was Scotch! But I didn't know what to say, ma'am! I told the stout gentleman, I said there was nobody ill here, and we'd got a doctor anyway. But he said he wasn't that kind of a doctor, ma'am. He said Mr. Pen sent for him."

"Mr. Pen sent for him?" repeated Deidre.

There was another interruption. Phyllis had scarcely made her appearance when the door to the library was thrown open. A pause had ensued, as of people listening; and then, at Deidre's last words, there was a general exodus from the library.

First came Dr. Fortescue, who shambled across the passage and disappeared into what Deidre had indicated as the music-room, at the rear south-western angle of the house. Next hurried Estelle, sideways like a cat, but pausing beside Deidre and Garret at the door to the billiard-room. She was followed by Andrew Dawlish and Nick, who closed the door to the library.

"Forgive me, Estelle"—Deidre raised her voice—"but did Pen really send for a Dr. Gideon Fell?"

"Well, really! Whether he did or he didn't, my dear, *I* want to see Dr. Fell. Where are these two men, Phyllis?"

"Please, Miss Estelle, they're at the front door. I told them, I said——"

"You should have shown them into the drawing-room. Never mind; I'll do it. You see, dear," Estelle continued to Deidre, "Pen has some slight acquaintance with the good doctor. At least they've corresponded; oh, these literary subjects! Dr. Fell is at the Polygon Hotel in Southampton; there was an item about him in yesterday's *Echo*. Somebody has presented to William Rufus College, Southampton University, what purports to be the original manuscript of Sheridan's *The Rivals*, and Dr. Fell is here to decide whether it's genuine. *The Rivals*, of course! That's the eighteenth century again, isn't it?"

"It is indeed," agreed Mr. Dawlish, bustling up beside her. "Sooner or later, with luck, we shall get away from the eighteenth century for good. Meanwhile, since you are so insistent on my examining these papers, I had better get on home. The car's in the drive, you said?"

"It's just outside the garage. Hugh insisted on leaving a mackintosh for you, though I *told* him it wouldn't rain. And now I must welcome Dr. Fell; I must tell him . . ."

"Yes," boomed Nick, "but you're not the only one, Aunt Essie. Uncle Pen kicks us out of the library; all right! I'm the fellow who's roaring to see Dr. Fell; he's the one man on earth who can help us with this business. Ask Garret if he's not! Garret's a close friend of his; Garret can introduce us. Come along, old horse; we're going to——"

"No, *we're* not," Garret interrupted, with Fay's image blotting out every other thought. "Just go along and introduce yourself; he'll be glad to see you. But you've got to excuse me for the moment; there's something else to be seen to."

"Go on, Garret!" Deidre's whisper was low and fierce. "Go on in there! I'll hold the fort if it's necessary; I'll give that poor girl some peace from bad jokes and knowing remarks. Go on!"

Garret twisted the knob, slipped inside, closed the door behind him—and stopped short.

It was a fair-sized room: oak-panelled, carpeted in rubber matting. Three Georgian casement-windows, closed but uncurtained, looked out across lawn, trees, and a flight of stone steps leading down through shrubbery to Lepe Beach. Above the white edges of surf, glimmering and coiling against darkness, rose a watery half-moon that presaged rain.

Here in the room itself, shut and stuffy, lights burned inside a muffled canopy above its covered billiard-table. The only other illumination—vague, varicoloured—shone faintly from behind the upright glass panel of a pin-ball machine pushed against the left-hand wall. Fay, her shoulders eloquent, stood beside the pin-table and would not look at it. For a moment she would not look at Garret either. Then she turned towards him, raising her head and eyes. The stuffiness of the room caught at Garret's lungs; Fay's expression caught at his heart.

"Fay . . ."

"You followed me, didn't you? You deliberately followed me!"

"Of course I followed you. Don't you know I will always follow you?"

"For a second I thought I wanted you to. And now I wish you hadn't. It's no good, Garret! It's no earthly good in this world!"

"It's no good, certainly, to think the world's come to an end. Nick would say, 'Come off it, my pretty; enough of this ranny-gazoo.' I can't talk like that, though I wish I could. Shall we try the pin-ball machine?"

"No!"

"Let's try it, all the same. Look here!"

Across the upright panel ran the red letters "African Safari." The figure of a hunter in white sun-helmet and khaki shirt was raising his rifle towards a patch of yellow-green vegetation evidently meant to be jungle. Beside the pin-table stood a tabouret bearing an earthenware bowl full of pennies. Garret picked up a penny, dropped it into the slot, and drew the handle partway back on its spring. The spring released six small but heavy metal balls, forcing one of them into a runway at the side of the table.

Garret pulled back the handle to its fullest extent.

"In the old days, before tobacco was taxed out of sight, you could win five cigarettes for a score of twenty-five thousand or thereabouts. Let's see what happens now."

There was a loud snap as he released the handle.

The ball shot up the runway and spun round; the whole table twitched to metallic life. Phantom figures flickered wildly across its screen: a lion appeared from jungle, charged, and took a bullet in mid-spring as the ball whirled and thumped to a maniacal dinging of bells and flashing of coloured lights. The ball vanished. Garret inspected a first-score in red figures at the foot of the panel.

"Six thousand," he said. "We got the lion, anyhow. There's a rhinoceros to come, and a crocodile in the river. Shall we bag those too, or shall we apply the same method to your own blue-devils?"

"It's no *good,* I tell you!" Fay retreated two steps, her handbag under her arm. "I said it was sordid, but you don't know how sordid. You think, from reading those stories, you could understand what it would be like. But you can't understand, Garret! Nobody can understand, nobody in this world, who hasn't been touched by it and dragged down by it."

"Touched by what? Dragged down by what?"

"Murder," answered Fay.

She retreated still further, pressing her handbag against her side.

"It wasn't murder, of course. But some people thought it was; they thought I did it; they may arrest me even yet. And speaking of other people, tonight I walked up the drive just behind them."

"Look here, my dear: what are you talking about *now?* You walked up the drive behind whom?"

"Dr. Fell and Mr. Elliot! They left their car at the entrance to the drive. I got out of the bus from Southampton and walked on the grass so they wouldn't hear me and sneaked in the back door. Mr. Elliot is third in command at the C.I.D., next only to the Commander and the Assistant Commissioner. Dr. Fell—well I think I could tell *him* anything, but in a way he frightens me even more.

"Once I could have sworn Mr. Elliot turned round and looked straight at me. I don't think he's seen me before, but he may have seen a photograph. The point is that they're here; it'll all come out, and you'll be involved in the mess. It's bound to come out anyway, because in some fashion Mr. Barclay's learned about me, and *he* knows. Didn't you hear what he said in the library? 'Poison!' he said. 'Who poisoned the old man in his own household? Would it help us to learn the truth now?' Or words to that effect; I can't remember very well. Do you know what he was talking about, Garret?"

"Yes, I know. He was talking about Sir Horace Wildfare, the eighteenth-century judge who's played such havoc with everybody here."

"But he can't have been! He can't have been! He meant old Mr. Justin Mayhew, of Deepdene House near Barnstow in Somerset."

"Fay, my sweet idiot, you're as mad as a coot. And who the hell is Mr. Justin Mayhew, of What's-its-name House in Somerset? Whoever he is, Pennington Barclay never meant him or said one word about him."

"Maybe I *am* mad; I've sometimes wondered. All I know is that it'll come out, it's bound to come out, and you'll be mixed up in the beastliness along with me!"

By this time she had retreated almost to the line of the windows. The moon above the Solent was behind her. Fay's physical nearness—the dark-blue eyes wide-spaced under thin-arched brows, the line of her arms and shoulders—reminded him too vividly of the same moon at another time and place and the scenes it had lighted then.

"Do you honestly think I could be troubled by anything in which you were concerned as well? By the way, have I mentioned that I love you?"

"Oh, I wish you *could* tell me that! I wish you could tell me and tell me and tell me. But you mustn't. And don't touch me, please! I might do something silly, and that would make it even worse. Listen, Garret! Stand still and listen!"

"Yes?"

"My name, before I changed it legally by deed-poll, was Sutton: Fay Sutton. That was more than a year ago, in March of sixty-three. Can you guess how common a name Sutton is?"

"I shouldn't have thought it was very common, no."

"Then you'd be wrong. There are four columns of Suttons in the London telephone-book—from Sutton, A., in Torrington Park to Sutton-Vane in Stanhope Gardens and Suttonfish of Great Portland Street. For all I know . . ."

"There's Suttonyen in Camberwell and Sutton-Zug at Colney Hatch? Why don't you laugh, Fay? That'll be better: go on and laugh!"

"Darling, this is not funny."

"All right! Let's agree we don't split our sides or roll in the aisles just because somebody is called Sutton. It's a damn good name, I should think. Now, then, what's it all about?"

Emotions were going up to a mighty pitch. Fay broke away from him. She stalked to the billiard-table, threw her handbag on it, and turned a face of desperate seriousness.

"Under the name of Sutton, early in sixty-two, I answered an advertisement and went as secretary to Mr. Mayhew, a retired stockbroker. Barnstow is a little village in the West Country, about six miles from Bath. Mr. Mayhew was older than Mr. Barclay and not much like him, although *he* tended to brood too. Mr. Mayhew and I got on pretty well. In the summer he asked me to marry him."

"You got on pretty well, you say. Were you his . . . were you and he? . . ."

"No!" Fay's eyes opened in horror. "I'm no Puritan, as I told you; I've never pretended to be. But the answer is no, no, no!"

"What did you say when he asked you to marry him?"

"I said no, of course. Mr. Mayhew's wife was dead; he had a grown son and daughter. But it wasn't so much his age. He was rather peculiar; I didn't like him much; he frightened me, and marriage has always frightened me, because I've made a living for myself. He just seemed to brush aside everything I tried to tell him. He said I'd better marry him because he'd made a will in my favour. Things weren't easy in that house. And then, one morning in October, he was found dead from an overdose of sleeping-tablets."

Fay's tone did not change when she added: "Mr. Mayhew had cancer, you see. We learned that at the inquest. His doctor had told him; he'd agreed to try surgery, which might have saved him, though he preferred to kill himself. He *had* made a will in my favour. But he hadn't signed it. What people said was that I didn't know he hadn't signed it. Worst of all, they were *my* sleeping-tablets, from a bottle in my room. Oh, Garret, do you begin to see where this is leading?"

"Yes."

Now Fay's voice rose passionately.

"The talk! The awful, interminable whispering and buzzing! The police-inspector in charge! 'Now, miss, if you'd just tell me again—' The coroner at the inquest! 'Surely, Miss Sutton—' "

"What was the verdict at the inquest?"

"Suicide while the balance of his mind was disturbed. But do you think that helped? 'Well, miss, it's only a coroner's verdict; we can always set it aside when we find evidence of something different.' And the son and daughter too! 'Why are you still here, then? If you turned the old man down, why didn't you leave his employ?' To go where? To do what?"

"Gently, Fay!"

" 'You thought you could jolly him out of it, eh? You thought he'd forget he proposed to you? You *didn't* know he never signed that will?' And everywhere I turned, the press taking photographs of me. There was an awful splash in the press. Didn't you see anything of it, Garret?"

"In October of sixty-two? I wasn't in England, if you remember. I was in New York watching an atrocity called *Uncle Tom's Mansion*."

"Or maybe there wasn't so big a splash as I fancied; we're always terrified of what we're afraid to see. I thought I was going out of my mind; I almost did. The only thing that saved my reason, if anything saved it, was that I'm not photogenic."

"Not photogenic? If you mean—"

"Don't say nice things; *please* don't say nice things! All I mean is that I don't photograph well. Or else, as usual, they published the worst and awfullest pictures they took. And yet, in case anyone should recognize me, it's left me as camera-shy as a woman who's poisoned half the neighbourhood.

"I'm not going on with my tragedies, Garret. You can see what happened afterwards. I told you in Paris an aunt of mine had died and left me a very small legacy, which was perfectly true. My mother's maiden name was Wardour; the aunt was her sister. And I was to receive the legacy provided I changed my name to Wardour."

Standing sideways against the covered billiard-table, Fay walked her fingers with concentration along its edge. The lights above the table shone on her sleek hair and brought out the warm colours of her skin. Well beyond her, against the billiard-room's west wall, had been pushed another (unlighted) pin-ball machine. Fay did not glance in that direction, but swung back again towards Garret.

"Of course I wanted to accept the legacy," she told him. "What scared me were the public proceedings of changing one's name by deed-poll. And the press! They say they don't mean any harm, but they can be absolutely merciless when they think they've got a story. I was terrified they'd connect the Fay Sutton who wanted her name changed with the Fay Sutton, late of Deepdene House at Barnstow, whom the police wanted—and still want—to arrest for murder."

"You didn't do it, you know. Since there's no actual evidence, the police can't hurt you."

"Oh, who cares for actual evidence? It's what thinking about it can do to a person's life."

Fay ran towards him. He touched her hands briefly as she extended them, and then she ran back to the table.

"Well, apparently I was alarming myself unnecessarily. Either the legacy was too small to attract the press's attention or else they just missed the story. No cameras, no flashbulbs, nothing! In May I went abroad. I met you. For ten days I was happier than I had ever been. But even then, when we were together in Paris, it was still with me. Before I went abroad, you see, Deidre had got me the job as Mr. Barclay's secretary, to begin after———"

"Fay, this has got to stop! You've been through a very bad time, my dear. But it's over now; we can forget it."

"It's not over; it'll never be over! Garret, what's been going on here tonight?"

"I wish I knew the truth."

"Yes, but what's been *happening?* I walked up the drive, as I told you, behind Dr. Fell and Mr. Elliot. They were saying something about ghosts and walking through walls. I crept in by the back door. Then I went to the library to tell Mr. Barclay I'd got the books he wanted and left them on the table in the main hall. I could have sworn he didn't know one single thing about me. The only newspaper he ever sees is the *Times* or the *Daily Telegraph* or maybe the Southampton *Echo*, but he seldom glances even at those. And yet, as soon as I opened the door . . ."

"He doesn't know anything about you! Those words were sheer accident, as Deidre said."

"Deidre said something else too. I ran out of there; I made a dreadful spectacle of myself, I know. Deidre ran after me. Just before I dodged in here to hide, *she* was blurting something about walking through walls and—and blank cartridges.

Darling, you've got to tell me!" Suddenly Fay stiffened. She raised her hand, whipping in the direction of the west wall. "And what is it now, Garret? What's that noise?"

10

GARRET POINTED at the west wall.

"Next door, Deidre mentioned, we have the music-room. There's a hi-fi belonging to Nick's Aunt Essie. When the whole crowd tumbled out of the library a little while ago, Dr. Fortescue went across to the music-room."

"Dr. Fortescue, was it? Then what we're hearing? . . ."

"What we're hearing, Fay, is a Gilbert-and-Sullivan medley on a long-playing record. It began a minute or two ago with *H.M.S. Pinafore;* it's now going on to *The Mikado,* and probably something else too. That's a powerful hi-fi, and he's got it turned up. It shakes the room, doesn't it? But the doors are closed; the walls are thick; you can barely hear the singers' words."

"Oh, well. Gilbert and Sullivan can't hurt us. But what happened tonight, Garret? Aren't you going to tell me?"

"If it will do any good to tell you."

"I'm bound to hear sooner or later. And I'd rather hear it from you than from anybody else, whatever it is. Please, Garret, don't be cruel. You of all people mustn't be cruel. Tell me!"

The stuffiness of the room continued to oppress his throat. He went to one of the southern windows and set it open. A clean breeze blew through; he could hear the pounce and slap of waves at a shingle beach. The story he had to tell seemed less clean. He made it as brief as possible, beginning with their arrival at Brockenhurst. He touched only lightly on any point at which Fay's name had been mentioned. But it took time; even a long-playing record had reached its thunderous, cymbal-clash climax well before he concluded.

Fay listened intently, sometimes running towards him and then retreating again.

"One last point, Garret. Does anything in the whole business strike you particularly?"

"Well, yes. If we believe Pennington Barclay's account of the intruder with the revolver, and against all reason I do believe it . . ."

"If we believe that, what?"

"Granted somebody was playing ghost and fired a blank cartridge, what did the intruder think he was trying to do? When you pick up a revolver without taking out the cartridges to examine 'em," argued Garret, "a gun loaded with blanks looks exactly like a gun loaded with real bullets."

"All right; what if it does?"

"Was the 'ghost' just trying to warn or scare his victim with a revolver he knew to be loaded with blanks? Or was he really trying to shoot Uncle Pen through the heart? What's the meaning of those blanks, and who put them there? If it wasn't Mr. Barclay himself——"

"It wasn't." Fay's intensity had grown greater. "*I* can tell you that, though I can't tell you anything else. Deidre herself bought the blanks and put them there."

"Deidre did?"

"Of course she did. For some time he's been in such a state (don't we know it already?) she's been horribly afraid he would kill himself. She didn't have the nerve just to steal the revolver and dispose of it, which is what I'd have done. She didn't tell me that, but I know Deidre. If the revolver simply disappeared, he might have begun brooding on gas-ovens or p-poison or heaven knows what. So she substituted blanks for real bullets."

"Come to think of it"—Garret stared at the past—"she did say she'd taken certain precautions so that he couldn't shoot himself or anybody else. She didn't say what precautions. But she said it the instant before we heard that shot and thought it was all up."

Fay had come over to stand in front of him near the windows. Once more, as always, he became conscious of the faint perfume she wore.

"Garret, listen! A tragedy didn't happen, but it might have happened and there may be one even yet. I asked you whether anything in this business especially struck you. And you answered—forgive me!—with some detective-story point a man *would* seize on. But that wasn't what I meant. You must have seen it; you're not stupid; you must have seen it!"

"Seen what?"

"A year ago," replied Fay, running her hand up the lapel of his coat, "I came here as secretary to a man not very much unlike Mr. Mayhew himself. Another well-to-do recluse with a tendency to brood on his troubles! Another place in the country more full of dissensions than Deepdene House ever was! Haven't you asked yourself about history repeating itself? Haven't you wondered, in your heart, if it mightn't be the same business all over again?"

"Only in one respect. Is there anything between you and Pennington Barclay?"

"No, no, and a thousand times no! Even if I liked him more than I do, which isn't a great deal, he's much too wrapped up in Deidre when he isn't wrapped up in himself. And I think he's a hypochondriac; I don't believe there's anything really wrong with his heart."

"Then he hasn't asked you to marry him?"

"Oh, never in this world! If he'd even so much as indicated an interest, I should have run out of this house as though old Sir Horace Wildfare were after me. Doesn't it look sordid, though? Since you seem to have heard the suggestions that dreadful woman has been making . . ."

"You mean Aunt Essie?"

"Yes, of course I mean Miss Barclay! In the train this evening I wondered if you'd guess anything about her from what I *didn't* say. She has only one talent; she can take a pen and imitate somebody's handwriting so that he'd swear he wrote it himself. Maybe she doesn't mean any harm; maybe her interfering is only a way of attracting attention to herself. But never mind her! She's not exactly a personality, whereas Mr. Barclay is. What did you make of *him?*"

"I liked him, I thoroughly liked him, until he first dragged your name into the conversation with a kind of tolerant leer. Afterwards he had to defend himself against Aunt Essie, which he did with a good deal of dignity. Though neither of them made much sense, the balance was restored and he seemed a very good sort again. But at first, damn his eyes! . . ."

"Garret! Don't tell me you're jealous!"

"You know I'm jealous. I could cheerfully strangle any man you looked at—or who looked at you, for that matter. It can't be helped; that's the effect you have. They may call me Old Sobersides . . ."

"Garret, Garret, whoever called *you* Old Sobersides? *I* could tell them something different, couldn't I?"

"In that case——"

"No, don't! Let me go; we mustn't!"

"Why mustn't we, when you can return a kiss like that?"

"Because you won't see it! You refuse to see it!"

This time Fay retreated to the nearer pin-ball machine, backing against it with her colour high and her breast heaving. From the music-room next door arose a strengthening swell of sound. It seemed evident that Dr. Fortescue, unsatisfied by his first try at Gilbert and Sullivan, had started the same record all over again. But Fay paid no attention to this.

"Garret, stop and think! When you talked about this person in the mask and the black robe, you kept using the word 'intruder.' That's the wrong word; it's the worst possible word. Because this wasn't an intruder, and we both know it. Four of you—yourself, Deidre, Nick Barclay, and Mr. Dawlish—drove from Brockenhurst in the Bentley. Whoever the intruder may have been, it couldn't have been any of you four. Am I right?"

"Yes, I can take my oath to that much!"

"Then who was it? If we can't really believe it was the cook or one of the maids, there are only three people left. It must have been Miss Barclay, it must have been Dr. Foretscue, or it must have been me. And you know who they'll say it was, don't you? They'll say it was me. Don't tell me how ridiculous that is; they'll say it was me! I wasn't even here; I missed one bus and had to take a later one, but who's to prove that? When the police pitch in——"

"What do you mean, when the police pitch in? The police weren't called!"

"Darling, they're already here. That Mr. Elliot is here. I've told you what's worried me sick already. Can they still have something against me for what happened in Somerset? Can they still be after me?

"It worried Deidre too; Deidre's been a good friend. Both she and Mr. Barclay are acquainted with the chief detective-superintendent of the Hampshire C.I.D.: Superintendent Wick, I think his name is. Deidre said she wanted to find out what my position actually was. And I said, 'Dee, are you clean out of your mind? You'd not go to the police; you'd *never* go near the police?' She said she wouldn't and later swore she hadn't, and I believe her.

"But what happened tonight changes everything. It's all back again, the mess and the sordidness and the awful interminable *suspicion*. It's not what a person really is; it's what they think she is. You can guess what almost anybody will think of me now. I might have been—what's the word they use on television—I might have been set up for this, mightn't I? But I'm sorry, Garret; do forgive me! I don't want to bore you with my silly little troubles."

"Your troubles, whatever they are, mean just as much to me as they can possibly mean to you. I happen to be in love with you, my sugar-candy witch. But I tell you again you're worrying without cause. If the matter should ever come up, which it won't, there's a bus-conductor to prove where you were at any given time. As for the past, that's past and forgotten."

"And I tell *you* again," cried Fay, "it's not forgotten and never will be. They'll all guess something now; they're bound to guess. Your friend Nick will guess if he's as intelligent as you seem to think."

"What is it," demanded another voice, "his friend Nick will guess or won't guess?"

The door to the passage stood open. Nick Barclay, somewhat rumpled-looking, stood in the aperture and studied them.

"Look, you two!" he added.

Fay, instantly poised, went to the billiard-table and picked up her handbag.

"You're Mr. Nicholas Barclay, aren't you? Yes, Garret and I have met before. I understand he's told you that, just as I've told a friend of mine, under conditions of the most absolute secrecy. As things stand, though, I don't see how I can deny it to anybody."

"Oh, you're the mysterious Miss X? Yes, I thought you must be." Nick looked at Garret. "Congratulations, old horse; may I say your predilection for blondes is fully justified? But I want a word with you, young fella-me-lad, about something you seem to have been concealing."

"And I want a word with you," retorted Garret, "about something you definitely have been concealing."

"Well, both of us——" Nick stopped. "What the hell's that row next door?"

"Dr. Fortescue is having his second go at a Gilbert-and-Sullivan medley. It begins with *Pinafore,* as you can hear now; it goes on to *The Mikado* and ends in a wallop with the Constabulary Chorus from——"

"Well, both of us will have to wait." Nick turned towards the west wall. "Shut that damn thing off," he yelled.

No doubt Dr. Fortescue couldn't hear. Above the swell of music a voice sang vaguely but lustily that its owner, being captain of the *Pin-a-fore,* was a model of propriety who never used a big, big D. Nick, a small blue vein beating at his temple, evidently gave up in despair.

"Our questions will have to wait, I was saying. I've just finished telling Dr. Fell everything, and he's the man they keep to crack impossibilities. But look, Garret: it's eleven o'clock! Aunt Essie is howling her head off about the birthday-party, whereas Uncle Pen . . . can't you rally round and lend a hand?"

"Lend a hand with what?" asked Garret, following him back to the door.

The passage under its dim lights stretched deserted from the curtained window at the west end through the central hall and beyond to its termination in a second curtained window at the east end. Nick, after glancing up and down it, pointed at the closed door of the library a little way down on their left.

"When Uncle Pen kicked us out of there at twenty minutes to eleven, I closed that door. He bolted it. Just a minute, now!"

Nick hurried across to the library door, where he laid hold of the knob.

"Uncle Pen!" he called, leaving the knob to rap sharply with his knuckles. "I also remember," he added over his shoulder, "there are two bolts on this: one near the top and one near the bottom. I deduce, brilliantly, that he's still there because he hasn't come out. But where is he? Uncle Pen!"

The passage was no longer deserted. In addition to Nick, with Garret standing at the entrance to the billiard-room and Fay beside Garret, the door to the music-room had opened. Dr. Fortescue, loose of limb as well as rather stoop-shouldered, took one step out and hesitated. Melody flowed past him, filling the passage. But it had lost its nautical tempo; compressed, as though coiling energy for a new surge, the music also hesitated in a momentary dreaminess before it soared.

> On a tree by a river a little tom-tit
> Sang, "Willow, titwillow, titwillow. . . ."

And at the same moment, far down in the eastern passage, Deidre Barclay emerged from what had been pointed out to Garret as the dining-room.

"What is happening, please?" she called. "Where is my husband?"

"I don't know," Nick yelled back. "If it comes to that, where's Aunt Essie? Is she still howling her head off?"

"I can't say what she's doing because she's not doing it here. She seems to have disappeared."

"She—*what?*"

"I said she disappeared." Deidre advanced closer. "After you used your right as lord of the manor to turn her out of the drawing-room, Estelle didn't seem at all herself."

"Hell, woman! I *didn't*——"

"But you did; you turned her out of the drawing-room so

that you could monopolize Dr. Fell. And is it really necessary to shout at the top of your lungs?"

"Forgive *me*," struck in Dr. Fortescue, massaging his forehead, "but I thought *I* heard . . . Do you object to this music, sir?"

"No, no," said Nick, "who am I to object to anything? Let's have plenty of it; keep the damn hi-fi going full blast. All the same, this business of Uncle Pen's not answering is the damnedest thing we've met yet. What's the word, Garret? Any advice?"

"No advice at all. You don't think—"

"No, I do *not* think! Besides, this is a good, solid door. The idea of doing what just occurred to me would be completely crazy."

"Probably it would. Isn't there another door, between the library and the drawing-room?"

"Yes, there is! You bet there is! Half a minute!"

As though devil-driven, his necktie flying, Nick dashed to the passage-door of the drawing-room along the wall on his right. He flung this open. Against an eighteenth-century drawing-room of dark blue picked out with white and gilt, Garret Anderson had a brief glimpse of a familiar figure: an immensely stout man with red face and bandit's moustache above several chins, and of eyeglasses on a broad black ribbon. Nick closed the door. They could hear him shouting again and the noise of a fist pounding at wood. He returned in little more than the half-minute he had promised and stood staring at Garret.

"That's done it," Nick said. "The door between the library and the drawing-room also has two bolts. Both of 'em seem to be fastened on the library side. What's the word now?"

Music and massed voices smote together:

"Behold the Lord High Ex-e-cutioner! . . ."

"And don't go on at me like that," Nick bawled at Garret, who had not said a word. "Don't be so impatient, for God's sake! What's the good of telling me to break down a door when there are two full-length windows giving on the lawn? One of 'em was closed and locked—Aunt Essie locked it—but the other was wide open when we left. Come on, old son. You'd better come too, Dr. Fortescue. You may not be needed, but on the other hand you may be needed at any minute. What's delaying us? Come on!"

He raced down to the passage-window at the western end, which would give him access to the lawn. Garret, waiting only long enough to press Fay's hand as she cowered against him, hurried after Nick. Dr. Fortescue was immediately behind both. Nick swept back the curtains of the long window, finding it closed but unfastened, and pushed up the sash. All three of them dodged out on the lawn and turned to their right towards the library.

A damp breeze blew at them. The half-moon rode in a cloud-fretted sky. Everywhere here, Garret thought, you had a feeling that thick shrubbery brushed against you, though in actual fact there was no shrubbery near the house.

What had been the left-hand window of the library as you stood inside the room looking out had now become the right-hand window as you stood outside looking in. Garret had last seen it open and uncurtained. It was still uncurtained. But it had been closed and locked; they could see the catch solidly turned into place.

"The other window, the one Aunt Essie locked." Nick was bellowing almost into Garret's ear. "Is that still fastened too?" Have a look-see, will you?"

Garret darted round the chimney-stack. The moon provided comparatively little light. But there was enough to show, against a background of closed curtains, another window closed and locked. Garret did not linger there but hurried back to the others beside the first window. One glimpse into the library had been enough.

More than a dozen feet back from the window, beside the easy-chair in which he had been sitting when they first saw him that evening, Pennington Barclay lay face upwards on the carpet. The light of the two floor-lamps shone on him. He was bleeding badly from a wound at the left side of the chest. The fingers of his right hand clawed feebly at the carpet; his own revolver lay near his left foot.

"It certainly seems—" Dr. Fortescue began.

"It does," snarled Nick.

A blown leaf touched Nick's face; he flinched as though under attack but did not hesitate. Whipping off his sports-coat, he wrapped the coat round his right fist and drove his fist through the window just underneath the catch. A crash of glass exploded; pieces flew and fell. With his right hand, still protected by the coat, he groped through the smashed aperture. He found and turned the catch, and from outside he sent the window sliding upwards. All three of them ducked through.

"Garret! See if there's anybody hiding here; see whether the doors really are bolted. Because *if* they're bolted . . . if nobody's hiding . . . oh, God's teeth!"

There could be no doubt of this. Both on the door to the passage and the door to the drawing-room in the alcove, small and tight-fitting bolts were securely fastened. Garret reported the fact as Nick and Dr. Fortescue bent over the limp figure of their host.

In the alcove, on the right as you faced the drawing-room, a smaller door opened into a little room, hardly more than a cupboard, windowless and lined with books on dusty shelves. Garret found a hanging electric-bulb, switched it on, and saw only more books piled on the floor.

The cloakroom on the left, though larger than a cupboard, was big enough to contain only a wash-basin fitted to the outer wall, a couch with pillow and blankets, and a metal locker, door closed and tiny key in lock, of the sort to be found in gymnasiums.

"There's nobody hiding," Garret said, "but no window of any kind either in the cloakroom or the book-cupboard."

Nick had straightened up. Dr. Fortescue, who in an emergency seemed capable and unflurried, was still kneeling beside Pennington Barclay. Their host's right hand had ceased to twitch.

"In short," declared Nick, "no way out except ways we know to have been locked." Then he drew a shuddering breath. "Oh, God's teeth! Poor Uncle Pen! Poor old . . . he's gone, I suppose?"

"Well, no." Dr. Fortescue looked up sharply. "He's not dead; and granting a little luck, we should pull him through without undue trouble. There is too much blood."

"*Too much* blood?"

"Too much, I mean, for a direct heart-wound. He has fainted from shock and loss of blood. It is no trifle, of course, but——"

"He *did* change his smoking-jacket!" Nick roared. "That's not the same one Aunt Essie spilled honey on. It looks a little the same, same heavy red material and black facings, but there's frogging on this one, and——"

"No, it is not the same. If you will allow me to finish, Mr. Barclay, I can say what I think and then we must take action. You will find no honey here, but there *are* powder-burns. This was very nearly a contact wound, with the weapon held almost directly against his chest. The heart is higher up than most people think it is. Unless, course, he did it himself. . . ."

"Did it himself?" Nick echoed with hollow incredulity. "Holy cow, Doctor, did he strike you as being in a suicidal mood?"

"No, not at all. But let's not speculate, shall we?"

"O.K.; what do we do? Ring a hospital?"

"That won't be necessary. If you will take his feet while I take his shoulders, we can get him up to his bedroom. Gently, young man! Mr. Anderson, will you unbolt the door to the passage?"

Garret did so, drawing the bolts gingerly with the crook of his little finger. He opened the door and came face to face with Deputy Commander Elliot. Elliot, a lean and wiry man in his middle fifties, had a hard jaw but a not unsympathetic eye.

"Telephone," he said to Garret. "Never mind the formalities! Is there a telephone here?"

"If that's the Scotland Yard man," yelled Nick, "there's a 'phone—or used to be—out in the main hall. Look, Lestrade: somebody took another shot at Uncle Pen. But how did he do it? How the hell did he do it?"

They did not hear the other's reply, if in fact he made one. Elliot had turned away. Rather awkwardly Nick and Dr. Fortescue hoisted up the dead weight of Pennington Barclay. With doors open to night stillness, music and voices rose in crescendo as the record neared its end:

> When the felon's not engaged in his employment,
>   Or maturing his felonious little plans,
> His capacity for innocent enjoyment
>   Is just as great as any honest man's.
> Our feelings we with difficulty smother
>   When constabulary duty's to be done—
> Ah, take one consideration with another,
>   A policeman's lot is not a happy one.

11

"Ahem!" said Dr. Gideon Fell.

Except that electric candles had been substituted for wax tapers in its carved, gilded wooden chandelier, the drawing-room—dark blue and white and gold—could have seen little change in two centuries. Its carpet seemed less worn than the more modern carpet in the library. The furniture was ornate Chinese Chippendale. A long-case eighteenth-century clock, loudly ticking, indicated the time as ten minutes to one in the morning.

Deidre Barclay paced restlessly, sometimes bumping into Deputy Commander Elliot, who also paced. At opposite sides of an eighteenth-century card table, cumbersome by modern standards, Fay Wardour and Garret Anderson sat with furtive glances at each other. Nick Barclay and Dr. Foretscue occupied chairs nearby. His back to the white marble mantelpiece, a vast swaying figure with a half-smoked cigar between the fingers of his right hand, stood Dr. Gideon Fell.

His big mop of hair, years ago only grey-streaked but latterly a dull grey-white, had tumbled over one ear. His bandit's moustache curved down above several chins. The red face shone behind the eyeglasses. Untidy in black alpaca, his other hand on the handle of a crutch-headed stick, he stood swaying like a tethered elephant. Yet even that drugged hour of the morning could not lessen his spiritual kinship with Father Christmas or Old King Cole.

"Ahem!" repeated Dr. Fell, clearing his throat. He gestured towards the clock. "Observe the time, ladies and gentlemen, which even for one of my reprehensible habits would appear unreasonably late. Elliot and I must shortly make our apologies and be off. Meanwhile, let us recapitulate."

"Recapitulate, eh?" began Elliot with the air of a man bent on oratory, but Dr. Fell, whose specialty was oratory desired or undesired, cut him off.

"We arrive here," Dr. Fell continued in his rumbling voice, "at not quite twenty minutes to eleven. After being held in play by a damsel named Phyllis, we are greeted in something of a rush by three persons—a somewhat self-important solicitor, who speaks much but says little, by Miss Estelle Barclay, and by Mr. Nicholas Barclay there."

"May *I* speak?" asked Garret.

"Oh, ah; by all means. About what?"

"About your mission in two places. William Rufus College at Southampton University, we heard, has been presented with what may or may not be the original manuscript of Sheridan's *The Rivals*. You were asked to determine the authenticity of the manuscript. Is that correct?"

"It is."

"Well! *Is* the thing genuine?"

"My dear Anderson," replied Dr. Fell, even managing to cough amiably on cigar-smoke, "you should be better acquainted with the habits of the academic mind. I have been given no opportunity to decide on the manuscript's authenticity, since I have not seen the manuscript. Somebody has lost it."

"The other part of your mission, then—"

"Our ill-mannered intrusion here? Oh, ah! Faced this afternoon with news that the senior tutor could not remember whether he had left the manuscript in his desk or inadvertently dropped it somewhere else, I received a short note from Mr. Pennington Barclay begging my presence here on what was described as 'a matter of life and death.' Now, this in itself seemed curious."

"Why?"

"My only acquaintance with Mr. Barclay," said Dr. Fell, "has been through correspondence. Most of his letters have been dictated to his secretary and typed. I believe that is so, Miss Wardour?"

"Yes!" Fay gave a nervous start, her eye on Elliot rather than Dr. Fell. "Mr. Barclay is always writing letters, mostly dictated. But sometimes he does write in his own hand."

"This one was only the second hand-written communication I had received. It would not do, it would not do at all," Dr. Fell said argumentatively, "to maintain I was greatly suspicious of it, though it contained one or two phrases which hardly seemed characteristic. And, by thunder, it was justified!

"Let us recapitulate, I say. We arrive here to be greeted by the three persons already described. The lawyer, Mr. Dawlish, pours out a smoke-screen of words. He then dons a mackintosh left for him by his son and departs in his car for Lymington to examine, quote, 'a great mass of papers.' And then? Miss Estelle Barclay, until stopped by her nephew with the polite intimation that she is somewhat off base, begins pouring out an incoherent story——"

"She ran away, you remember?" cried Deidre. "Estelle's locked herself in her room and still won't come out. She's hysterical. Sometimes I wonder . . ."

"Yes, Mrs. Barclay?" Elliot prompted sharply. "You wonder what?"

"I don't know." Deidre lifted her shoulders. "It has been such a perfectly horrible evening—won't everybody agree?—that I honestly don't know what to think about anything."

"It is therefore all the more necessary," said Dr. Fell, "to decide what it is we do know. With your permission, all, I will drop the present tense. Miss Barclay's tale was taken up, not incoherently and in much detail, by Mr. Nicholas Barclay. We heard family history. We heard of a ghost, or of someone masquerading as a ghost. We heard of the attack on Mr.

Pennington Barclay, or the alleged attack, by means of a blank cartridge fired from his own revolver." Here Dr. Fell looked at Nick. "While you were describing all this——"

Nick, who had lighted a cigarette, rose to his feet and interrupted.

"While I was telling you," he supplied, "I wanted Garret's corroboration about something or other. Garret had gone to the billiard-room to be with—— Garret had gone to the billiard-room. There was another reason why I went to haul him out. It was eleven o'clock; Aunt Essie, before she rushed out of here, had been yelling about starting her birthday-party on time."

"The birthday-party has not begun"—Dr. Fell blew out a great cloud of smoke—"and it may never again. No sooner had you gone, both to find our friend Anderson and to round up birthday celebrants, than a Gilbert-and-Sullivan record was played for the second time in twenty minutes.

"Since nobody in the house or outside it heard a second revolver-shot—a real bullet this time, fired at Mr. Pennington Barclay from very close range—it seems plain that it was fired at some time during the playing of the record. We can't be certain of this; we can't be certain of anything. If I were to hazard a guess according to the nature of the evidence, I should say it was fired during the first playing of the record."

"And so should I say it," agreed Dr. Fortescue, rising to his feet as Nick had done. "The amount of bleeding would be consonant with the time. But am *I* to blame for that, sir?" He made a vague, harassed gesture. "I am to blame for much, I suppose. But because I bent in absorption over a hi-fi and our would-be murderer chose this time for his stroke, am I to blame for that too?"

"No, sir, you are not." Dr. Fell, wheezing gently, threw his cigar into the empty fireplace. "The point is mentioned, believe me, only to emphasize the cloud of obfuscation in which we have landed. What happened, permit me to ask? We examined that library, or Elliot did; we studied a room locked up like a fortress. Here in the drawing-room, for nearly two mortal hours, we have questioned witnesses and belaboured the obvious. If we are ever to discover where we stand . . ."

"I'll tell you where *I* stand," interposed Elliot. "In fact, Maestro, I've been trying to tell you for a long time."

Elliot lowered his sandy head as though about to butt with it, and then, remembering dignity, he straightened up.

"I have no authority here," he added, "and no business here either. When Mr. Pennington Barclay was shot, either because a black-robed ghost went after him or because somebody else did, I took the only course I could have taken. I 'phoned Detective Chief Superintendent Wick of Southampton, whom I know very well. And what did I find?

"The rest of you had better hear too. I found Wick in bed and nearly speechless with summer flu. He promised to be here himself no later than tomorrow afternoon. Meanwhile, he's got half a dozen good men he could have put in charge. But would he do that? No, he would not. As a special favour to him, nothing would serve but that *I* must take over, *I* must do his donkey-work until he arrived. I had to 'phone London for special permission; I almost didn't get it.

"And can you guess," pursued Elliot, striding up and down, "can you guess why he was so insistent? It had nothing to do with me. It's because he'd heard Dr. Fell was here, and this sort of thing is the maestro's meat and drink. I've known Dr. Fell for thirty years, or as good as. I've admired him sometimes and cursed him often. But he has one special talent: not very often useful to the police, though invaluable when it's needed. For the ordinary criminal case, of course . . ."

"For the ordinary case," interrupted Nick Barclay with an air of dazzling inspiration, "he'd be no earthly good at all. It's the hundredth instance where he scores. I never met him until tonight, but I've heard all about him. He's the cross-eyed marksman who hits the game without aiming at it; he's the scatterbrained diver you send into murky waters. His special talent is useful only in a case so crazy that nobody else can understand it."

"Oh, archons of Athens!" groaned Dr. Fell.

Then, with a long sniff, he drew himself up for majestic utterance.

"Sir," he said to Nick, "you overwhelm me. Nor can I consider your metaphors entirely well-chosen. If you will picture my corporeal shape poised at the end of a diving-board, you must think these waters very murky indeed. Cross-eyed I frequently am, not to say cockeyed too. But if on occasion"—here, with hideous effect, he literally turned both eyes inwards—"if on occasion my eyes are shown crossed in this fasion . . ."

"Yes?" demanded Elliot.

"It is from following my nose."

"Well? Where does your nose lead you now? Do you see any light in this business here?"

"I will not say," replied Dr. Fell, "that the landscape seems altogether dark. There are two lines of inquiry, both of which must be followed to find the point at which they converge. The first might be described as its Peter Pan aspect."

"As its *what?*"

"As the aspect of Peter Pan, that somewhat irritating boy who refused to grow up. The second, to avoid irritating *you* with what must seem mumbo-jumbo, I will not describe as the Captain Hook aspect. In plain words, there is one person here who seems too impractical for this world. There is another person who seems too practical and too clever by half. Have these two a meeting-point? We have much information already, but we need more information. In this case, as it happens, the victim himself can testify; sooner or later he will do so. Pennington Barclay is still alive, and if he remains alive——"

"Excuse *me*," Deidre Barclay burst out, "but isn't this bad enough without your suggesting worse? What do you mean, 'if' he remains alive? There's no question of my husband's dying, is there? Dr. Fortescue said——"

"I said, Mrs. Barclay, I had every hope." Dr. Fortescue looked still more harassed. "These things are sometimes chancy, you know; he is not responding as well as we might have liked. On the other hand, I have given him a sedative; he is resting as comfortably as can be expected."

"But they all said——"

"*If* you please, madam! Don't be alarmed; the chances are ten to one in favour of recovery. What Dr. Fell really meant, I think, was something different."

"Something different?"

"Something very different," the resident physician assured her. "A murderous attack was made on Mr. Barclay. If the revolver had been held a little higher, he would have been shot through the heart."

"You see, Mrs. Barclay," put in Elliot, "we can't take the chance of somebody trying it again. At Superintendent Wick's suggestion a police-constable has been stationed in your husband's bedroom. A constable will be on duty there until Mr. Barclay is up and about or until we make some sense of what has been going on. Don't you agree with the precaution?"

"Oh, I agree! But——"

"But what?"

"I thought I was *helping*," cried Deidre. "I've told you everything. And in the statement I made here a while ago, I've admitted I bought blanks and put them into Pen's revolver. The second attempt on his life, the one with the real bullet that almost succeeded—are you absolutely sure *it* couldn't have been suicide?"

"Why should it have been, Mrs. Barclay? If earlier in the evening he may have thought he had reason to do something foolish, he had none at all when he met the new heir and heard for certain he wasn't to lose his house."

"Oh, I know! But I thought I was helping. And yet everything seems to have worked just the wrong way. It's as though the whole business were all my fault."

Fay Wardour rose up from the card-table.

"You know, Dee," she said, "this isn't like you. You're the one who's being ridiculous now, and you really must stop it. He wasn't hurt with a blank cartridge, dear; he was hurt with a real bullet, *and he's going to get well*. That's why you've got to stop brooding, Dee. It wasn't your fault; how could it be your fault?"

"Well!" Deidre straightened her shoulders. "I didn't say what it actually was, Fay; I only mentioned what it seemed to my conscience. Have you any more questions to ask me, Mr. Elliot? Or you, Dr. Fell? If not, would you mind if I excused myself and said good night? This has been quite a day."

"It has, Mrs. Barclay," agreed Elliot, "and I don't think we need detain you any longer. Dr. Fell and I will have a last look at the library, I think; then we must be going until tomorrow."

Dr. Edward Fortescue also made his appeal.

"If you have no further use for me either, Deputy Commander, may I beg the same privilege of retiring?"

He looked at Elliot, who nodded. Then the tall, loose-limbed physician shambled towards Deidre in the doorway.

"I want to sleep," he added. "The French have a proverb, haven't they, which says *Qui dort, dine*? On occasions like this it might be amended to *Qui dort, oublie*."

"Sir," demanded Dr. Fell, rearing up, "do you find sleep and forgetting vital necessities to welfare on the occasion? Is there so very much on your own conscience?"

"There is nothing at all on my conscience, sir, though usually much on my mind. After all, I am a fugitive from the National Health. But I don't mean to sleep too seriously, Mrs. Barclay; I shall look in on the patient several times before morning. Good night, madam. Good night, all."

He nodded and was gone. Deidre, as though torn between several emotions, still hesitated in the doorway.

"As for our guests and their bedrooms," she said, "please don't forget that Nick Barclay is in the Green Room. In case you've forgotten, Nick, that's upstairs on the south-east corner at the back. Mr. Anderson is next door, in what's called the Red Room or the Judge's Room from you-know-who. Your bags have been put in each. I'm not showing up well as a hostess, I'm afraid, but the unusual circumstances must plead for me. Mr. Elliot! Dr. Fell! The servants are in bed; do you mind letting yourselves out when you go? We never lock doors in this part of the country. And now *I'm* off. Coming Fay?"

"Well, no." It was Elliot who spoke. "Miss Wardour—it is Miss Wardour, isn't it?—had better remain for a little. She and I may have something to say to each other. Will you sit down again, Miss Wardour?"

"Of course, if you insist"—Fay was at her most guileless—"but I really don't see how else I can help you. I wasn't here, remember? I had been in London to bring some books; I was delayed by an errand in Southampton and only got here at the same time you and Dr. Fell did. What else can I say?"

"Sit down, please."

The long-case clock struck one. It was only Garret's fancy that the lights seemed to dim or darken a little, as though with a late-night power-cut. But it was no fancy that a shriller wind blew from the east.

"And now, while Dr. Fell and I pick up a few bits and pieces in the library"—Elliot looked at Garret—"our friend Anderson might care to come with us. Would you like to go too, Mr. Barclay?"

"You bet I'd like to go," said Nick. "This business has got me chewing nails and dancing on a hot-plate. But look: seriously now! I never knew the cops in this country were so broad-minded about letting witnesses tag along to the scene of a crime. Aren't you supposed to be suspicious of everybody?"

"I *am* suspicious of everybody, and I tell you so frankly."

"Well?"

"But there's one person I don't seriously suspect: Garret Anderson, a man I've known for some time, who had no conceivable interest in shooting at your uncle either with a blank cartridge or a live one. And there's one person I can't suspect: yourself. *You* had no interest in killing your uncle either; but that's not the point. At any time he might have been shot, so far as the evidence indicates, you were here in the drawing-room with Dr. Fell and me. If you want an alibi, you might call on us to provide it."

"Look, Lestrade, I'm not calling on *anybody* for an alibi. To hell with that! I only said——"

"And as for going to the library." cried Fay. "you can't want *me* there, can you?"

"Well, no." Elliot took out his notebook. "If the idea upsets you, Miss Wardour, there's no reason why you should accompany us. But don't go away; stay within call."

"For what, please?"

"For your own good; we'll come to that soon. And now, Maestro . . ."

"Oh, ah?" said Dr. Fell.

Wheezing, groaning, muttering to himself with cross-eyed concentration, Dr. Fell had produced a pigskin cigar-case. He extracted a cigar, bit off its end, spat the end in a majestic arc at the fireplace, and lumbered round again in precarious balance on his crutch-headed stick.

"Let me understand this, Elliot. We are going to the library, if I heard aright, to 'pick up bits and pieces' of the near-murder. Very well; will you accept a further suggestion?"

"If it's a sensible one. What's the suggestion?"

"Having done that," returned Dr. Fell, "let's forget the near-murder, shall we? As Mr. Barclay here has just aptly said, to hell with the near-murder. Out upon it! You want to concentrate on looking in the right direction, do you?"

"It's usually advisable."

"In this case, Elliot, I wonder. Having once done our duty in the right direction, let's turn to look very hard in the wrong direction. And by looking hard enough in the wrong direction," rumbled Dr. Fell, "it is possible that our squint eyes may discern truth. Archons of Athens! Which way to the library?"

12

FOUR OF THEM—Dr. Fell, Elliot, Nick, and Garret—gathered round the big writing-table in the library. The two floor-lamps threw their crossing lights between one side of the table and the corner of the left-hand window. There were ugly stains on the carpet, though must of the blood had soaked into Pennington Barclay's clothes. On the table's blotter, surrounded by a clutter of articles from the still-open drawer, lay the Ives-Grant twenty-two revolver.

Elliot, notebook in hand, had grown more than a little testy.

"Because the victim's not dead," he explained, "Superintendent Wick wouldn't order the full treatment: photographs, sketches, fingerprint-tests by a squad of the proper people, as he might have done. Oh, no! *I* must mess about myself, which I already have. This revolver, for instance. Note the traces of 'grey powder' from the bottle in the drawer I spread with the brush here. There are no prints on the gun except those of Pennington Barclay himself."

Nick Barclay reached out as though to touch the pistol but instantly drew back.

"Were you referring," Nick asked, "to Uncle Pen's suggestion that the original black-robed figure wore nylon gloves? Is that what you mean?"

"No, it is not. A gun-butt like this, even gripped with the bare hand, will show no marks but smudges. In New York years ago they proved you never get prints from a revolver or an automatic unless it's been handled by the barrel or the magazine, and any wide'un knows better than to do that. Now, then!"

Here Elliot looked very hard at Nick.

"You quote your uncle as saying—everybody else quotes him too—that he himself took a number of fingerprint-tests some time ago. And so he did. In this drawer is a batch of unglazed cards, each with the fingerprints of somebody's right hand in an impression made from an ink-pad, and each labelled in your uncle's handwriting. Damn it," snapped Elliot, as though somebody had doubted this, "it's the same handwriting as his notes for a proposed letter to the *Times Literary Supplement,* and his wife's identified it. One fingerprint card is labelled 'Mine,' one 'Miss Wardour,' one 'Estelle,' and two more respectively 'Phyllis' and 'Phoebe.' "

"Yes?" prompted Dr. Fell, who seemed much less crosseyed as he studied the table.

"The card labelled 'Mine' has the prints of both right and left hand. Those same prints—Pennington Barclay's own—are all over the magazine and the barrel of his revolver; he loaded it with real bullets under the eyes of four or five people. He put it down on the table under this copy of the *Southern Evening Echo.* Anybody who could get into the room could have picked it up and shot him. Or else, in some momentary brainstorm, he could have turned it on himself. I swore to Mrs. Barclay this wasn't likely to have been suicide. And yet, so far as actual evidence goes, how do we *know?*"

"We don't know," said Dr. Fell, "except to be very certain it was no suicide. As for the fingerprints . . ."

"Oh, the fingerprints?" Elliot was almost raving. "Everybody's prints are all over the place; you can see it by the traces I left in pursuit of 'em. But as Mr. Barclay also said, that proves nothing. Anyway, most of 'em are very old prints and smudges. Aside from Miss Estelle Barclay's prints on the right-hand window—no concealment at all—there's only one set of fresh, clear prints anywhere away from this table. It brings us to the question I want to ask. Who closed and locked that left-hand window?"

"Eh?"

"Who closed and locked the window there's been so much fuss about? Look here!"

The lower leaf of the famous window, with a great hole shattered in it where Nick had driven his fist through, gaped to the night-breeze. Notebook in one hand and magnifying glass in the other, Elliot strode to it over fallen fragments and used the magnifying glass as a pointer.

"Here (see the powder-traces?) are Pennington Barclay's dabs again. A clear, sharp set from both hands—fingers above, thumbs below—on the middle sash at either side of the catch. The housekeeping in this place is pretty slovenly; you could have seen those prints in the dust without having to use powder. Did Pennington Barclay close the window himself either before or after the attacker got him? And if so . . ."

"That won't do at all," objected Nick, lifting both fists. "You're way out in left field; you've got it all goosed up. Look, Gregson—"

"Just one moment!" Elliot said with steely restraint. "I don't in the least mind being called Lestrade or Gregson or Athelney Jones, as you've been doing for well over two hours. I like it better, in fact, than I think your solicitor-friend liked Blackstone and Sir Edward Coke. But don't carry it too far, Mr. Barclay. Don't let your sense of humour run away with you."

"Sense of humour?" howled Nick. "Sense of humour, did you say? God's teeth, man, I was never more serious in my life."

"Then what do you want to testify?"

"I've already testified! Are you following me?"

"Yes?"

"Uncle Pen didn't close that window. He *opened* it, with his hands just in the position of those prints, when we pulled the curtains back and saw the window was already closed and locked. You didn't find any prints on the catch, did you?"

"No prints; only smudges."

"No, you bet you didn't! He hit the catch open with the side of his fist. And it's all in your notebook. Uncle Pen did that some time before the real bullet was fired; I told you so in the drawing-room after we found him lying here. Look it up, can't you?"

Elliot leafed back through the notebook. Garret Anderson

THE HOUSE AT SATAN'S ELBOW 119

listened carefully while the Deputy Commander repeated the substance of Nick's account. Though Garret had not heard Nick testify in the drawing-room, since each witness was examined separately, it was exactly the same thing Nick had said in the library at an earlier time.

"I see," Elliot commented. "Your uncle took off a pair of rubber gloves he'd been wearing and couldn't remember when he took 'em off. He ran at the window; with his bare hands he opened it—here's the evidence he did—and refused to let your aunt touch the window afterwards. Correct?"

"That's my impression, anyway. How many times have I got to repeat it?"

A Gargantuan and half-witted expression of distress had crossed the face of Dr. Gideon Fell.

"I say, Elliot!" Dr. Fell looked still more half-witted. "The fingerprints are very clear, are they? Not blurred in any way? What about smudges in the dust?"

"Well! Also on the sash, well out from these prints, there are some finger-smudges, as though somebody had handled the window with gloves."

"No broad smudges anywhere? Nothing much wider than the smudges of individual fingers in gloves? Almost as though the sash had been wiped?"

"No, nothing like that. Come and see for yourself!"

Dr. Fell lumbered over, took the magnifying glass, and blinked in myopic fashion at the window. His distress had increased when he lifted his head.

"Clear prints," he said in a strangled voice. "Clear prints, a lot of dust, and yet no broad smudging at all. O Lord! O Bacchus! Don't we see, Elliot, the conclusion we must draw here?"

"Suppose you draw it?" Elliot snatched back the magnifying glass. "I'm not having any, thanks, because it leaves us worse off than we were before."

"How does it leave us worse off?"

"Maestro, *somebody* closed and locked the window. It *could* have been done by a would-be murderer in gloves; but how did he turn the catch from outside? Or is it possible the window had nothing to do with this? Is it possible the murderer—ruling out suicide and allowing a murderer—got in and out through a door fastened with bolts both at top and bottom? I tell you, it's getting to be too much for any rational brain. The more I think of this whole ruddy mess . . ."

"Elliot, don't!"

"Don't what?"

"May I beg you, my dear fellow, not to complicate matters

by going off the deep end yourself? More and more, as the years advance, you are beginning to sound like Superintendent Hadley before he retired."

"Maybe I am; maybe I've got reason to. I understand Hadley now; I know what he had to put up with in the way of mumbo-jumbo. Will you draw the conclusions, sir, or will you take refuge in Delphic mutterings? If it's to be the latter (and I see it is), can anybody else offer a suggestion of any kind? Mr. Barclay? Anderson?"

Garret, who had been pacing the floor and trying to keep Fay from his thoughts, stopped beside the ranks of bookshelves along the south wall.

"The notion that occurred to me," he said, "is a little too wild and wool-gathering to be seriously discussed."

"Well, everybody else's ideas are wild too. Don't let that stop you. What's the notion?"

"I've heard somebody remark that these locked-room cases mostly conform to one of three possible explanations: the time was wrong, the place was wrong, or the victim was entirely alone. Suppose, in this affair, there is something wrong with our conception of the time?"

"The time?"

"The time, that is, at which Pennington Barclay was shot? What if the real bullet hit him in the chest at an hour earlier than we think: ten o'clock, say? For some reason he refused to admit this. In some way (God know how) he concealed the blood. He walked about, he talked to us, and it was only long afterwards that he collapsed. This sounds wild, I know . . ."

Elliot, it was evident, only just resisted an impulse to hurl his notebook on the floor.

"It sounds wild," he retorted, "and it *is* wild. Hiding all that blood—to say nothing of shock, physical hurt, or any other factor—would have been more impossible than tampering with a door or a window. We've learned tricks with doors and windows; the other thing is out of the question. All evidence rules it out. The victim changed smoking-jackets, remember, between twenty minutes to eleven and eleven o'clock. The jacket he wore when he was shot at close range, the one with the powder-burns and the blood, is in his bedroom now. The one he wore when he talked to you earlier, the jacket with the honey-daub and the pair of rubber gloves in its pocket, is hanging up over there in the cloakroom. There's the revolver, a single bullet fired, on the table in front of us. What do *you* say, Dr. Fell? Are we to have more Delphic mutterings, or do you agree Anderson's notion is clean daft?"

"Not daft," said Dr. Fell, "merely mistaken. It did not

happen like that, I agree; Pennington Barclay, as we have thought all along, met his near-quietus towards eleven o'clock. But have you asked yourself what else happened here?"

"What *else* happened here?"

"Yes! I have been accused—unjustly, I venture to think—of mumbo-jumbo and Delphic mutterings. However this may appear, pray believe I am doing my best not to confuse you. And therefore, Elliot, I redirect your attention. About midnight, while employed in questioning witnesses in the drawing-room, we wandered back here for a first look at the library. Well, let's note what we saw then!"

Dr. Fell, who had at last managed to get his cigar lighted, marched massively into the alcove between library and drawing-room. The others hastened after him. The door to the little cloakroom still stood wide open; the light was burning inside. Dr. Fell, turning a fierily argumentative face, pointed with his stick.

"As you say, Elliot! . . ."

The metal locker, which Garret had last seen with its little door closed, was now open. In the locker, neatly on a wire hanger beside two empty hangers, was suspended a maroon-coloured jacket messily daubed with honey-stains. From this Garret's gaze moved to the wash-basin, to the couch bearing pillow and blankets, and back again to the locker.

"As you say, Elliot!" Dr. Fell repeated. "There is the jacket, badly smeared with honey, he was wearing when he spoke to his guests from shortly past ten o'clock until twenty minutes to eleven. Upstairs, as you also point out, we have the burnt, powder-singed jacket with the bullet hole in it. Very well; things are straightforward so far. But where is the third smoking-jacket?"

"The *third* smoking-jacket?"

"By thunder, yes! All witnesses quote Barclay as saying he owned three such jackets: the one he was wearing and two others. His wife later confirmed this. They were very similar though not identical, she said; they were kept in the locker there; and you observe two empty hangers. Unless we think both Barclay and his wife were telling a pointless lie, we must believe that too."

"All right; I accept it. But where's the third jacket, then?"

"It's been stolen."

"Stolen?"

"Indeed, I rather expected it to be stolen. In sanity's name, Elliot," begged Dr. Fell, "consider the state of affairs as presented to us by the evidence at our disposal.

"Estelle Barclay, Nick Barclay, Andrew Dawlish, and Dr. Fortescue were somewhat unceremoniously chucked from here. We know this to be true. Pennington Barclay bolted both doors and changed his smoking-jacket. We know *this* to be true. But what followed, according to the evidence? At some subsequent time a would-be murderer entered the library, shot his victim, and then, pausing only long enough to pinch a third smoking-jacket from the locker, made his exit for the last time."

"Leaving doors *and* windows locked as they are now?"

"Oh, yes. Yet with some care I have used the words 'according to the evidence.' Therefore, if this is what evidence tells us, there is something wrong either with the evidence itself or with our interpretation of it."

"Hang it all, Maestro, you don't have to remind me of that! I'll accept it without a struggle, even if it leads straight to the lunatic-asylum. But where does it leave us? What do we look for now?"

"For the ghost," answered Dr. Fell, "or the pretended ghost. One moment! I do not refer to this night's work; I refer to earlier occurences. Will you accompany me, please?"

Breathing smoke and sparks like the Spirit of the Volcano, he lumbered towards the door to the passage, hesitated long enough to glance at its bolts, and went out with the others after him. Then the four of them stood and looked at each other in that dimly lighted passage, stretching to its tall window at the western end.

"Once upon a time," pursued Dr. Fell, "here walked the bitter old judge of whom we have heard so much. In the present century, previous to this evening, three witnesses are said to have seen the veiled figure in the black robe. One of these witnesses was old Clovis Barclay himself. We can't question old Clovis; he is beyond our grasp, and it happened long ago. But Andrew Dawlish, as I understand it, has promised to look up the matter in an old diary and tell us when this visitation occurred?"

"Yes," agreed Nick, who seemed to be labouring under an even greater excitement. "He promised, and he'll tell us. That's water under the bridge, though. Do you think it's important at this late date?"

"Nothing is water under the bridge," said Dr. Fell, "when its tide still threatens to swamp us. Yes, sir, I consider it very important, as related to certain other dates you yourself have mentioned. For the moment, however, let us forget Clovis. Much more recently—in the month of April, following the old gentleman's death and the finding of the second will—both Estelle Barclay and Mrs. Tiffin, the cook, are alleged to have seen the ghost too. What a pity we have not had a first-hand account from either! But perhaps, Elliot, *you* consider this unimportant and too much of a look in the wrong direction?"

"No," Elliot retorted. "I don't think it's unimportant or a look in the wrong direction. And I'll tell you why.

"What we want is one solid piece of evidence that won't come apart in our hands. We can't seem to get any line on who fired that shot. Tomorrow, Dr. Fortescue says, we should be able to question Pennington Barclay."

"And if he himself can't tell who tried to kill him?"

"We'll hope he can; we'll meet that difficulty when we come to it. Meanwhile . . ."

"Oh, ah? Meanwhile?"

"You've already said it. To adopt your own conversational style, Dr. Fell, the only solid thing in this case seems to be the ghost. Somebody—black robe, face-veil, and all—has been playing merry hell with the people here. The stage-props are real, anyway; somebody wore 'em; they're in the house, and I only wish I could take the place to pieces and find 'em."

"With a search-warrant, you mean?"

"I could get a search-warrant, of course. That's what an old-fashioned copper would do. But these are influential people. What's the good of starting an unholy row and antagonizing everybody before there's any need to do it? Tomorrow morning, I'll bet you anything you like, Pennington Barclay will give permission for a thorough search. Meanwhile, answering your question, I've taken at least one step. Mrs. Tiffin is supposed to have gone to bed long ago. She didn't go to bed; I had a private word with her. All right; let's see. Follow *me* this time, will you?"

Facing them across the passage were the three doors in the southern part of this wing: to the music-room, to the billiard-room, and to the room which old Clovis Barclay had once used as a study.

Elliot, paying no attention to these, led his three companions eastward along the passage to the square central hall which stretched through the depth of the house. Its furniture was of the early nineteenth century; a few smoky-looking portraits adorned panelled walls; at the back rose a massive staircase. But Elliot did not linger in this hall. Instead, gesturing towards the eastern continuance of the cross-passage, he led his companions into the cross-passage.

"You see?" he continued. "At the front, corresponding to drawing-room and library in the other wing, we have first what the Victorians called a morning-room and then the dining-room. Across the passage from these . . ."

Garret Anderson turned and looked.

Across the passage, instead of the three rooms on the southern side of the other wing, there were only two rooms separated by a broad corridor stretching to the rear of the house. Elliot pointed.

"The room on your left, at the south-eastern angle on the ground floor, was once a butler's pantry. The room on your right, next to the central hall there, was once the housekeeper's room. There has been no butler or housekeeper for many years, as we've heard. But the housekeeper's room is still used by the cook, who acts as a kind of unofficial housekeeper in keeping an eye on the maids." Then Elliot knocked at the door of the housekeeper's room and raised his voice. "Yes, Mrs. Tiffin? Will you come out and join us, please?"

Instantly, as though somebody listened just inside, the door was opened by an elderly woman, short but massively broad, with an air of intense respectability and audibly clicking dentures. Strands of grey hair floated out as her breath blew upwards.

"Yes, sir? You were saying, sir?"

"I'm sorry to have kept you up so late, Mrs. Tiffin."

"Oh, that's all right, sir! Don't you fret about *that*. But I did bake such a lovely cake, and not one of 'em as much as looked at it!"

"You're the cook, I believe?"

"I'll not deceive you, sir. I *am* the cook, though maybe Mr. Pen thinks I oughtn't to be."

"Have you been with the family a long time, Mrs. Tiffin?"

"Eighteen years, it'll be now. I come at the end of the last war. Old Mr. Clovis, he was a proper gentleman! And I try to take some of the work off Miss Deidre's shoulders, as I used to try to take it off Miss Estelle's."

"You and Miss Barclay, they tell us, are the only ones who have seen this alleged ghost?"

"As to what Miss Estelle may have seen, sir"—again the dentures clicked—"I'm sure *I* can't say. I'm not even sure what I saw meself. But if you ask Miss Estelle . . ."

"We needn't trouble her tonight, Mrs. Tiffin. And I'll not detain *you* much longer. I have only a few questions to ask you and a few things to say to a certain young lady. And then——"

Both Nick Barclay and Garret Anderson jumped; even Dr. Fell started a little. Clearly, through night stillness, above a rustle in wind-tugged trees, rose the click-clack noise of someone in flat-heeled shoes running down a hardwood staircase. Garret glanced to his right across the central hall and into the western passage beyond. The door to the music-room was wide open. Fay Wardour, whom he had called a sugar-candy witch and who now had every appearance of being one, stood motionless with her hand on the knob.

But it was not Fay who had made that wooden-sounding noise. Into view, from the hall and the direction of the staircase, hurried Estelle Barclay. Her red hair seemed to stream out. Her costume was the same, house-coat and slacks, except that she now wore heavy sandals. The eyes had a strained fixity between tear-swollen lids.

"I heard you," Estelle cried. "*I* heard you, Mr. Elliot! If you have any questions to ask me, you'd better ask them now. And who, please, is the young lady you have something important to say to? It's Deidre, isn't it? It's nobody else but Deidre, I imagine?"

13

"I HEARD YOU," Estelle repeated. Her look had become something like a glare. "I meant to turn in hours and hours ago; I went to my room. Then, at past eleven, Dr. Fortescue tapped on the door and told me what happened to poor Pen. I—I tried to see Pen, but they wouldn't let me."

"Nobody may see him just yet, Miss Barclay." Elliot betrayed a certain impatience. "Tomorrow, with luck, he can tell us the whole story."

"I didn't know what to do, you see. I felt, being psychic—did I tell you I was psychic?—you might want me. But I didn't know *what* to do. So I hesitated, between staying in my room and sitting on the stairs, until I heard you saying to these gentlemen (hullo, Nicky!) what you've been saying in the past five or ten minutes. And dear Dr. Fell says it's a pity you've not heard from me.

"If you want to search the house, Mr. Elliot, please do search it. Pen may or may not give you permission. But *I* can give you permission; I'm Father's daughter, aren't I? You may find things to suggest somebody's been playing ghost, which would be horrid. And yet it won't in the least alter the fact that there's a true evil spirit here, a real ghost. That's what *I* saw, and I'm ready to tell you. But won't you please answer my question too? If you have some things to say to a certain young lady, who is it? It *is* Deidre, surely?"

"No, madam, it is not Mrs. Barclay. Why should you imagine it is Mrs. Barclay?"

"Well, I'll tell you," Estelle went on in a rush. "Deidre's a dear girl, and nobody's nicer; but she's so *unthinking*. She never dreams what effect she has on nearly every man she meets. Even Andrew Dawlish, who's a stodgy old square if one ever existed, clucks over her like a hen with a brood of chicks. My brother—dear, silly Pen!—fell violently in love with her when he'd met her only once. Pen has never done anything like that since nearly forty years ago he met a little actress named Mavis Gregg and set her up in a house at Brighton. With Deidre, of course, it was a very different thing!"

"I'm sure it was, Miss Barclay, and I'm sure you want to help. But what exactly are you suggesting?"

"Mr. Elliot, Mr. Elliot! Even apart from the question of the ghost, *awful* things have been going on here. Mightn't Deidre —quite unintentionally, of course, and quite without knowing it—mightn't Deidre have been the inspiration which made somebody do everything that's been done? Have you any comment to make, Mr. Elliot?"

"Only the comment that I still don't know what you're trying to say."

"Oh, how do I know *what* I'm trying to say? I feel things; I don't reason them out."

"Then since you're not sure of that"—Elliot produced his notebook—"let's go on to something you say you are sure of. You and Mrs. Tiffin are supposed to have seen the ghost. When did you have this experience, Miss Barclay?"

"Yes, Annie and I saw it," agreed Estelle, nodding towards the cook. "You'd better go first, Annie; you saw it first."

"Anything you say, Miss Estelle."

Mrs. Tiffin, immensely dignified despite the strands of grey hair floating round her head when she breathed, lifted her shoulders and looked up at Elliot.

"Old Mr. Clovis," she continued, "died on the eighteenth of March. And what a fine gentleman *he* was, even if he did have a short temper! This new will they talk about was found less'n a month later, though I can't just remember when that was."

"Let me assist your memory, Annie." Estelle also stood

much on her dignity. "The new will, leaving everything to Nicky without any qualifying codicil, was found on Friday, April tenth."

"Ah!" breathed Mrs. Tiffin, her dentures clicking. "Then I *can* tell you, sir, when I saw what I did see. It was the night just a week later, which would be the seventeenth. And I'm dead sure of that—'cos why? 'Cos there was to be another birthday-celebration, Mr. Pen's, on the next day, which was Saturday.

" 'Course," added Mrs. Tiffin, squaring herself again, "Mr. Pen's birthday's on the nineteenth. But bringing in the cake and all the rest of it is always at eleven o'clock on the night before the birthday. And so, on the Friday night, I had to be thinking of the cake I would bake Saturday morning.

"Thinks I to meself, 'Let's give Mr. Pen something he likes. What about a cake with coconut icing, because he likes that?' But a cake with coconut icing didn't seem hardly right for a birthday. It's not easy to stick in those holder-things for the candles, and you can't write a message on the icing. I always want to please Mr. Pen, though Mr. Pen thinks I don't. He thinks I get at him with what I say, taking advantage of my position as an old servant; and he thinks I won't serve the dishes he likes. But I wanted to please him, and what was I going to do?

"I couldn't sleep that night. My bedroom's on the top floor, next door to Phyllis and Phoebe. And I couldn't sleep; sometimes I can't. It mighta been midnight or maybe half-past when I thought I'd come downstairs and look at the kitchen —just *look* at it—and maybe look at the dining-room too. And then it might be I could decide. Now, sir! And you too, sir!"

Nodding first at Elliot and then towards Dr. Fell, Mrs. Tiffin swept her hand out towards the corridor stretching south to the back of the house between the butler's pantry on the left and the housekeeper's room on the right. The only light that fell into it came from the passage in which they were all standing. At its far end, where there was an uncurtained casement window through which showed the edge of a blurred half-moon, the corridor branched left and right too.

"You see, sir?" insisted Mrs. Tiffin. "If you turn left at the end of it, there's a passage with the back stairs going up and a door to the kitchen, and also, as there would be, a second door to the butler's pantry besides the door we can see now. If you turn right, the passage leads to the back of the central hall. Well, howsobeit! I come down here, as I say . . ."

Elliot held her eye. "That would have been between midnight and half-past twelve?"

"As near as I can remember, sir; I can't swear to it no closer!"

"Never mind; it's close enough. What happened?"

"There were no lights anywhere, and I didn't turn 'em on. I know the house so well I didn't need none. Anyway, I had a pencil torch and there was bright moonlight."

"Yes, we understand; go on!"

Mrs. Tiffin tossed her head.

"Well! I stopped awhile in the kitchen, thinking-like. After that I come down this corridor and across to the dining-room, only flashing my torch once or twice. I stopped only a few minutes in the dining-room. That's where I decided: *not* a coconut-icing cake, but the usual kind of cake with white icing and 'Happy Birthday' in red letters. That was that, I thought. So I walked back into the corridor here, not needing my torch at all. There was moonlight through the window at the end there, a good deal brighter than it is now. I was on the way to the back stairs and the top floor. And near the end of the corridor I saw . . ."

"You saw the ghost, didn't you?" demanded Estelle. "Speak up, Annie! If it was a being out of another world—and there are such things, whatever scoffers say—don't be frightened to tell us now."

"As God sees me, Miss Estelle, I can't say no more than what's true!"

"Oh, Annie! . . ."

"Miss Estelle," cried the cook, "it was a man or somebody in a long black robe and a mask with eye-holes. It was standing towards the end of the corridor, near the right-hand wall of the housekeeper's room, with the moonlight down the side where it hadn't got a face, and looking at me sideways.

"Then it turned round towards the wall of the housekeeper's room. I was some distance away, here at the beginning of the corridor. What I thought at the time was that it just melted through the panelling and disappeared, like you'd expect a ghost to do. As I say, this is what I thought at the time. . . ."

"You 'thought,' did you?" screamed Estelle. "You only *thought?* Oh, Annie, Annie! Can't you do better than that?"

"No, Miss Estelle, I can't," Mrs. Tiffin screamed back. "'Cos why? 'Cos it was a man or somebody; it was real; it was a human being; I seen the moonlight shine through the mask-hole on its right eye. And it didn't walk through the wall either. Being so near the turn of the passage at the back, he just walked away to the right along the passage to the main hall; and it *looked* like the other thing. That's all I can say.

"You, sir!" She appealed to Elliot. "And you, sir!" She appealed to Dr. Fell. "You're going to ask me what 'twas like. He *looked* tall and thin in the robe, but I'm short and a little overweight, and most people look like that to me. So there it is, and can I go now?"

"Yes, you may go." Elliot released his breath. "But the figure was real, was it? You'd be prepared to swear to that if it became necessary?"

"Oo-er! I'll swear to it if I've got to, but let's 'ope there's no need. And I've talked a lot about giving me notice and leaving, but I won't go 'less Mr. Pen sacks me. Whatever's been going on, it's human and wicked. It don't matter about poor old Annie; I know that. But having it happen, and having to see to them two girls with their heads stuffed with films and the telly: I say it's not *right!* Good night, sir and gentlemen. Good night, Miss Estelle. *Good* night."

Away she scuttled, trailing shreds of dignity, down the corridor and round to the left in the direction of the back staircase. Estelle Barclay, shivering all over, whirled on the others.

"This is really too bad," she said. "You're all Philistines, all of you! And I had hoped that Dr. Fell at least would be sympathetic!"

Dr. Fell, whose cigar had gone out, blinked vaguely for an ashtray and compromised by dropping the cigar-stub into his pocket.

"I may well be a Philistine, madam, from the worst of the five cities. Pray believe, however, that my sympathy is at your service. What did *you* see?"

"I saw something going into the butler's pantry there."

"A ghost in the butler's pantry?" echoed Nick Barclay, making a wild gesture. "Now look, Aunt Essie———"

"Oh, yes, to be sure! Laugh and laugh and laugh, why don't you? It's easy enough to laugh, isn't it?"

"Madam," said Dr. Fell, *"I* am not laughing."

Estelle stabbed her finger towards the closed door of the room on their left.

"In nineteen-eighteen, when we ceased to employ a butler because old Trueblood went off to war, my dear father ordered the pantry locked up. It must be kept locked except when something had to be fetched from there or the room opened every year to be cleaned and painted. Otherwise, he said, people would go in there; they would leave lights burning or a tap turned on. Father, who could be so terribly generous in most respects, would practise small economies like that. I don't remember much about the beginning, of course; I was only nine years old at the time. But that's how it began, and my dear mother agreed with him. The room must be kept locked."

"And yet not perpetually locked, by all accounts," mused Dr. Fell, "since it could be entered when necessary. How was it kept locked?"

"Oh, dear! . . ."

"By your leave, madam: *how* was it kept locked?"

"Well! The locks on these doors downstairs are all the same. A lot of the keys are missing, and we never had them replaced. But any remaining key will fit any other door too."

Dr. Fell's gaze, behind eyeglasses stuck skew-wiff on his nose, wandered round in apparent vacancy. A little way down the eastern cross-passage the door to the dining-room stood half open on darkness. There was a key in the lock of its door. With a rumbling sniff of apology, Dr. Fell lumbered over and took the key from the lock. Returning with the key, he went this time to the door of the butler's pantry, where after some concentration he fitted the key of the lock there. The door swung open on more darkness.

"Like this?" he inquired.

Estelle shrank back.

"Take care!" she begged, sidling towards Nick. "You'll pay no attention to me; nobody ever does; but do please take care! How do we know what's lurking at the wickedest hour of the night?"

"If anything is lurking, Miss Barclay," interposed Elliot's common-sense voice, "we'll try to cut off its line of retreat. Will you go on with what you saw and when you saw it?"

"It happened"—Estelle was breathing quickly—"it happened on a Thursday late in April. I'm almost sure it was the twenty-third; I *know* it was a Thursday because all three servants had their day out. Annie had left a cold dinner, which I was to serve in the evening. But it wasn't quite evening; it was late in the afternoon, about six o'clock, with a thunderstorm going on.

"I had been to the kitchen for a snack to get my vitamin B. I walked back along this corridor and had just stepped here into the cross-passage. The air went as cold as ice; you'll say it was the weather, but *I* don't think so. The rain was driving against the long window at the eastern end. I had started to turn west, meaning to go along to the music-room, when there was a great jump of lightning through the window and the rain. I couldn't help glancing round. Something told me what I was going to see.

"And there it was, standing sideways to the door of the butler's pantry. The mask and eyes were turned towards me.

Just at the shock of the thunder followed, it lifted its arms in the robe with the fingers out towards me like claws—like this —and all of a sudden ran at me.

"You never felt such an aura of evil as *I* felt. I couldn't have moved if it had caught me; I nearly fainted. But it didn't catch me. It stopped. It turned back to the door. And that door, which ought to have been locked and *was* locked, opened to the figure's touch. And it went inside and closed the door."

"Just one moment, Miss Barclay!" interrupted Elliot. "How do you know the door was locked?"

"Because it was always locked! Haven't I been telling you?"

"But . . . no, never mind. What did you do then?"

"After a minute or so, when I had stopped feeling sickish and could move at all, I moved in a hurry. I ran up the front stairs to my room. I sat down and felt sickish all over again. I *knew* I had seen Sir Horace Wildfare, just as Father saw him come in from the garden at twilight all those years ago. I didn't want to alarm the house—everybody was here, though all in different rooms, as they *would* be. But I also felt I must make certain the butler's pantry was locked up properly. It took half an hour to muster up courage, and yet I did it. I crept downstairs again. Both doors—the one here, the one at the back towards the kitchen—were still locked as they'd always been."

"Madam," Dr. Fell said softly, "are you sure?"

"*Am I sure?* Oh, don't torture me! What do you mean?"

"Are you sure that door was locked when the phantom entered? Every member of the household, except servants, was here that afternoon. But they were all in different rooms, I think you said?"

"Yes! Pen was in the library, Deidre was having a bath, Miss Wardour was typing letters in her bedroom, Dr. Fortescue was playing records on the hi-fi. *Well?*"

"Somebody, let us suppose, knows you have gone to the kitchen." Dr. Fell still spoke softly. "Somebody guesses you will return by way of the corridor. Somebody takes the key from another door, as I did a moment ago, and unlocks the pantry-door we see before us. Somebody, for the not-very-humorous prank of terrifying you, dons robe and face-veil and any other necessary thing. Somebody lies in wait for you, plays the comedy, and then locks the door and goes away. One question of Elliot's has already indicated this as probable, and I think we can lay a fiver it is what actually happened. Others besides Mrs. Tiffin have suggested the presence of human evil. Don't you believe in human evil, Miss Barclay?"

Estelle rounded on him.

"Oh, God save us, *of course* I believe in human evil. I can sense that too; I always sense it; I've said so. And that's here too. All right, Dr. Fell! You too, Mr. Elliot! Do what I asked you to; search the house; you have my full permission. Even if you find a robe and a face-veil, as I've already said, it won't prove there is no supernatural presence near us. But it will prove somebody's wickedness; it may even show the direction of the wickedness. And that reminds me.

"What was I saying? Ah, yes! There was a woman—'a young lady,' you very delicately called her—who's due for a good talking-to. I thought it was poor Deidre; I could have sworn it was Deidre, though you tell me I'm wrong as usual. Oh, dear! If it wasn't Deidre, it must have been—"

Estelle stopped abruptly. And Garret looked round to find Fay Wardour almost at his elbow. For a brief time, incredibly, he had lost sight of Fay. She must have come here from the billiard-room during the distraction of Estelle's recital. Very pale, chin up but mouth trembling, Fay now stood close enough to touch. Estelle, after one glance, did not look at her again.

"Well, Mr. Elliot, it's my turn to say good night. You're the police; get on with your work! Tomorrow morning you may learn something else. But don't ever try to tell me what's here or what's not here. I know what I know!"

And Estelle, like a kind of sleep-walker out of control, took to her heels and ran. Her sandals clacked on the hardwood floor of the main hall, thence on the main stairs and up. When the noise had faded, Nick Barclay roused himself from his own particular trance.

"Aunt Essie," he declared, "may know what she knows. Speaking for myself, not that anybody's asked me, all I know is that I don't know. Look, Deputy Commander! . . ."

"Yes?"

"We've found an explanation for two appearances of the ghost. Uncle Pen said there'd be an easy explanation, and there is. But what in hell is the explanation of that locked room?"

"At the moment, Mr. Barclay, I have no idea."

"The room's still locked, isn't it?"

"It's very much locked. Unless Dr. Fell can give us some clue to his own cryptic mutterings? . . ."

"Elliot," boomed Dr. Fell, who seemed much less benevolent with the dim light on his eyeglasses, "I will expound my cryptic mutterings soon enough. But not now, if you don't mind.

There are very strong reasons why it had better not be now. Do you follow me?"

"*I* don't follow you," said Nick, "but then I guess I'm not meant to. The party's breaking up; so am I, and I'll add to it. What I want, good friends, is a breath of fresh air. And then I'm going to hit the sack. I'll be seeing you—I hope."

Shoulders back, jaw dogged, Nick marched away. Leaving the little group gathered between the butler's pantry and the housekeeper's room, he crossed the central hall and stalked along the western passage. At its end the Victorian sash-window still stood wide open. Nick lifted one side of the curtains, ducked his head outside, and disappeared.

Somewhere upstairs a deep-voiced clock struck two. Fay's blue eyes lifted.

"Mr. Elliot," she said, "is the party really breaking up, if we want to use such an everyday name for it? Haven't you anything else to say to anyone here?"

Elliot pondered for a moment.

"Miss Wardour, you didn't go to the library with the rest of us. Among other things we did there, Dr. Fell called our attention to the cloakroom. But it wasn't the first time the maestro and I had visited the library."

"Yes?"

"On the first occasion, at about midnight, I made a thorough investigation of the cloakroom. All Dr. Fell did was get down on his knees and look under the couch. There was nothing underneath it except the carpet, as he insisted. On the second occasion, when four of us were present, he didn't even look underneath the couch. But I'd give a good deal to know what he thought might have been there."

Fay made a baffled gesture.

"Then why are you looking at *me?*" she cried. "I wasn't in the cloakroom; I wasn't even in the library; I got no farther than the door. All I know of the attack on Mr. Barclay is what you've told me. Since I can't help you in any way, why are you looking so very hard at me?"

"Because," answered Elliot, "there *is* one little point on which I'd like to have some enlightenment."

"Oh? And what's that"

"I believe, Miss Wardour, you have every legal right to the name you're using now. I also believe you're the Fay Sutton who was Justin Mayhew's secretary at Barnstow in Somerset when Mr. Mayhew died from an overdose of barbiturates in October of nineteen-sixty-two. Do you think I didn't know that?"

There was a cold crash of silence, affecting Garret Anderson like a blow behind the ear. He had been expecting this move and dreading it, but it was no easier to take when it occurred.

"Well, Miss Wardour? Do you think I didn't know that?"

"I was afraid you'd recognized me, yes. And what is it now? Is it a 'talking-to'? Or is it more like what they call a 'grilling'? You'll put me into a corner, I suppose, and hammer until I give way. Did I shoot Mr. Barclay as I'm supposed to have poisoned Mr. Mayhew, and why don't I get it over with by confessing? That's what you mean to do, isn't it?"

"Well, no," said Elliot. "It's not a talking-to, as Miss Barclay seemed to think. And it's certainly not the grilling you've got into your own head. As a matter of fact, I wanted to reassure you."

"Reassure me?"

"Look here, young lady. We know you had nothing to do with Justin Mayhew's death. Inspector Harned (remember him?) now has the statement of the housemaid who saw old Mayhew steal that bottle of Nembutal pills out of your room. He killed himself; it's been established. You can't expect the Somerset police to write you a letter saying: 'Stop worrying; we know you're innocent.' Under the circumstances, though, *I* can say it."

"But——"

"Take it easy, Miss Wardour! You're badly upset; that's fair enough, but don't take good news in the worst possible way. I've had so many unpleasant duties in my time that I'd been rather looking forward to the opposite."

"I *hope* you're not deceiving me," breathed Fay. "Oh, God, I hope and hope so! But if this is a trick, if you're only playing cat-and-mouse after all . . ."

Dr. Fell, towering up like a sombre Old King Cole, made reassuring noises over Fay's head.

"Accept my own assurance, Miss Wardour, that there are no tricks or traps. Elliot and I have already conferred on this. You are *not* the sinister adventuress luring men to their death; nobody thinks so. If you yourself will think hard for a moment, you may see how you figure in this case and why you were made to figure in it at all. Therefore, if Elliot and I might have a word with you . . ."

"You hear that, Garret? You hear what he's saying?"

"I hear it."

"And also, with no information to draw on"—Dr. Fell followed Fay's eyes—"something tells me our friend Anderson is concerned in this too."

"Just how deeply I am concerned it it," Garret began at

his most oratorical, "only Fay herself can tell you. A year ago in Paris I said to her that——"

"No, Garret, please!" Tears winked on Fay's eyelids. "They say they want a word with me; they mean a word in private, and that's best. I *want* to talk to them. I was never afraid of Dr. Fell; I'm not afraid of Mr. Elliot now, but I don't want you here when I talk to them. Follow Nick, Garret; go outside on the lawn; I'll follow as soon as they let me. Please, Garret?"

"If you really think . . ."

"Yes, I really think! I'm silly, I know, but I shall be quite incoherent if you don't go soon! It really looks better, doesn't it? It looks . . ."

"As though nothing is impossible? Quite right. I am going to the garden. If I meet anybody masquerading as a ghost, I will commit a murder by strangling and add to the tally. Meanwhile—chin up, my dear. There's a good time a-coming, *et ego in Arcadia.*"

He himself, following Nick's path, strode from the eastern passage through the western passage to the open window at its far end. A last glimpse over his shoulder he had of Fay, her gold hair glimmering and the tears trickling down her face, as he ducked his head through the window into the high, incurious night.

Garret breathed deeply.

The moon was setting, though still with an unearthly skim-milk light. All wind had died. From well below sounded the drag and slap of surf at a shingle beach. Garret sauntered across cropped turf towards the loom of a yew hedge twelve feet high, towards a garden which held little menace now.

He thought he could gauge Fay's feelings by his own, and he himself was almost light-headed with relief. Fay had been cleared; Dr. Fell said so; there was nothing more to worry about.

Despite the chessboard of cross-alleys inside the garden, there were four main avenues, one from each point of the compass, leading straight to the centre. Garret, as he entered by the avenue directly opposite a shattered, lighted window of the library, was teased by a vague memory that at the centre he would find a square opening with a sun-dial in the middle of it.

The grass underfoot, the hedges on either side, shone wet with dew. Garret hardly noticed this or anything else. He quickened his steps towards the centre; he was dreaming.

No, there was nothing to worry about now. He was no longer personally concerned in this, nor was any friend of his. The situation at Satan's Elbow could be seen as a problem—

confused, ugly, of twisted ways and emotions—but still a purely academic problem in which he had no...

Garret reached the centre and stopped suddenly.

"Oh!" cried a woman's voice.

There *was* a sun-dial here, of grey weather-worn stone. Two persons, a man and a woman, stood by the sun-dial. They were locked together in so passionate an embrace that Garret never learned what had made the woman glance round. But she did glance round, mouth dark and open in the unearthly light. She uttered a cry. She tore loose from the man's grasp and darted away into the alley leading south. The man was Nick Barclay. The woman was Deidre.

Garret heard her sob as she ran. Then he stood motionless, looking at Nick.

"Well, I'll be damned," he said.

14

YOU MIGHT HAVE COUNTED up to twenty before anyone spoke, in a damp garden black and silver under the moon.

"Look!" Nick began. "Look, old son!"

Nick's powerful voice, strained and dazed, could not quite attain its usual volume. He lifted a hand to run it through his dark hair, but a pulse jerked in his elbow, and the gesture seemed both frantic and futile.

"This looks funny," Nick said, "but it's not funny at all. Were you thinking?..."

"I was only thinking I should have put two and two together long ago."

"Two and two? What two and two?"

"For one thing, can you still pretend that you never set eyes on Deidre until you met her at Brockenhurst station this evening?"

"No! Hell's bells, of course I don't pretend it! That's what I wanted to tell you!"

"Your Aunt Essie," said Garret, "can drop useful information even when she maunders. I was thinking of Diedre's trips abroad during the summer. Deidre was in Switzerland in sixty-one and in North Africa 'the year before that.' When people refer to North Africa, they don't mean Egypt or they'd say Egypt. Usually they mean Morocco or thereabouts. You were very much in Morocco in the summer of sixty. Is that where you first met her?"

"Yes, it is. We both landed by accident at the Minzeh Hotel in Tangier, and I learned who she was. But——"

Nick strode forward. Hemmed in by high hedge-walls, shut away from the world, each faced his own problem as well as facing the other.

"Nick, how many times have you met her since then? I don't ask out of idle curiosity. I ask because it may have a vital bearing on the situation here at Greengrove. How many times have you met Deidre since then?"

"Every summer, as it happens. I was in Lucerne in sixty-one, Venice in sixty-two, and last year, because Deidre had promised to visit an old school-friend, we arranged to meet in Rome."

"You know, Nick, that takes the cokernut. You were the one in Rome having a merry old time, whereas Fay persuaded *me* . . ."

"What do you mean, a merry old time? Look, Garret!" Nick was really carried away. "I don't expect you to understand. But this is no cheap affair or sordid intrigue. This is a great love, a spiritual love, something that only happens once and sometimes never happens at all. And yet I can't blame you if you feel a little sore. You're thinking that you came clean with me, whereas I held out on you when in fact I owed you an explanation."

"Nick, you don't owe me an explanation for anything; you never did. But you needn't have tried so hard to mislead."

"Mislead?"

"Yes. At Waterloo, just before we took the train, you pretended you thought your uncle's wife might be a blonde. Yes, I know! Later you covered that up by referring very obviously to a colour-photograph Aunt Essie actually had sent. But it was still misdirection, however well done."

"For God's sake, Garret, what else *could* I have done?"

"That's hard to say, if you believed you were justified. Before that, at the Thespis Club, you'd talked about 'mysterious women'—*women*, plural—'appearing and then vanishing as though they'd never existed.' That's how I thought of Fay; no doubt it's how you thought of Deidre. And yet I never tumbled!"

Nick did a little dance in the moonlight.

"And I keep telling you, Garret, you don't understand at all. What Deidre and I feel for each other, and have felt for four long years . . . it's not the usual thing. It's different. Hell, man, it's sacred! And don't stand there looking like a stuffed oracle; can't you *say* something?"

"You want the oracle to speak?"

"If it's got anything useful to say."

"Very well. After careful consideration of this recital, judgment is hereby given that what sent you overboard was nothing more or less than plain, simple, old-fashioned sex."

"Sex?" yelled a revolted Nick. "Sex, did you say? Make one more suggestion like that, and friend or no friend, I'll clock you one and have no regrets. Deidre and I—we haven't, that's all! We've wanted to, but we never have. What's wrong with that?"

"Look, Nick! This is your Uncle Garret speaking. There's nothing wrong with it, nothing in the world. But don't take it too seriously, old son. Relish sex; enjoy what the gods offer. But keep a sense of proportion. Don't magnify a sound, healthy, biological urge into a romantic grand passion out of a Victorian novel."

"For two pins," roared Nick, "I would—" He stopped abruptly. A kind of convulsion crossed his face, and he executed another dance-step. "Wait a minute, though! Haven't we been through this conversation somewhere before?"

"Yes; at the Thespis Club on Wednesday night. The words are much the same, but you were doing the preaching and I was doing the listening. It's always different, isn't it, when the case happens to be our own?"

Nick's attitude of outrage had evaporated. He meditated for a moment. He stalked across the square at the centre of the garden and stalked back again.

"This is bad," he declared. "I'm losing all sense of proportion; that's true. And it's got to stop. Say what you like, believe what you like, but with Deidre and me it's the real thing. Can you credit that?"

"Yes, if you're sure of it."

"Oh, I'm sure of it; so is Deidre. We've been nearly crazy, both of us. The question, of course, is what's to be done?"

"I wondered if you'd already suggested it."

"Already suggested it?"

"At the Thespis Club, before any question of love-affairs had come to light, you were explaining how it wasn't decently possible to rob your Uncle Pen of his rightful inheritance. 'I can't take his beloved Greengrove away from him, even though—' 'Even though,' you must have meant to add, 'I have every intention of taking his wife.' "

"Well, what other solution is there?"

"I don't know."

"This can't go on." Nick lifted his fist. "It's intolerable; it's wrecking lives for no purpose. I want to marry Deidre; I mean to marry her; sooner or later the cards must be put face up on the table. When we first got here and Uncle Pen made that quite accidental reference to young Lochinvar, I thought I could face it. And yet I found I couldn't; I damn near died."

"You know, Nick," Garret said thoughtfully, "I suppose a great love can excuse most things. But was that quite the way to do it?"

"I don't get you. The way to do what?

"The way to break the news. Should you have told him by supplying a different end to the quotation?

" 'Oh, come ye in peace here, or come ye in war,
Or to dance at our bridal, young Lord Lochinvar?'
'I come here in peace, but, when love's at my side,
I will ride on triumphant with Uncle Pen's bride.' "

"That was a dirty one," snapped Nick.

"Sorry; no offence was intended. All the same, have you thought how *he'll* take this?"

"I still say it was a dirty one. As for Uncle Pen, I've thought of practically nothing else. Neither has Deidre; her conscience has been all over her, as you've probably noticed. I've got to tell him; what the hell else can I do? He won't take it badly; even if he did, the truth's bound to come out. Haven't you got any sense of romance at all? And what about your own great love?"

"Well, what about it?"

Nick produced a packet of cigarettes. Each accepted a cigarette, like duellists accepting swords. Nick kindled them with a pocket-lighter; the flame shone on his glazed eyes and the hollows underneath. Then he resumed a feverish pacing.

"On my Bible oath," he said wildly, "the relations between Deidre and me have been as innocent as . . . as . . . well, so help me, they've been utterly and completely innocent! But can you say the same? Now that you've found your Fay again, the little blonde with the attractions, can you say the same? Was it quite the harmless and roseate romance you've sworn it was?"

"*I'll* answer that," said Fay's voice.

The uncertain light painted shadows down her face and accentuated the molding of the blue-and-white dress against her body. Otherwise, moving silently on damp grass, she loomed up like a ghost at the eastern opening in the hedge-wall.

Nick's cigarette glowed and darkened as he whirled round.

"Did you hear what I was saying?"

"I couldn't help hearing everything, Mr. Barclay. You were shouting loudly enough to wake the house. But I'll answer your last question. And the answer is no. According to your standards or Deidre's my relations with Garret have been anything but innocent. They'll go on in the same way, I hope. But not here. Oh, not *here!* Only when we're clear of the horrors and of not knowing whose face is behind a mask. Maybe I'm a shameless hussy to say all this; now that I can't harm him just by being with him, I don't care!"

"Look, Miss Wardour! What I told Garret was meant to be in confidence."

"And do you think *I* won't hold it in confidence? There's too much on my own mind; you can call it conscience if you like. The reason I've been so elusive, Mr. Barclay, is that over two years ago I was involved in what looked like a murder case and wasn't. I've been cleared of that now, as I've been cleared of what happened tonight. It's not likely I should speak one word about Deidre or you either, and yet I can't help concentrating on the glorious fact that I'm free."

"Well, I'm not free," snapped Nick. "The whole thing gets worse and more complicated every minute. We'll keep each other's secrets, shall we? And now I'm going to say a real good night this time; I advise you and Garret to say good night too. But I doubt that I'm going to sleep. Oh, God's teeth, why has *everything* got to be so complicated?"

Brooding hard, puffing and inhaling deeply, he strode away through the eastern alley between the hedges. Garret waited until he had gone.

"Fay . . ."

"Didn't you hear what Nick said, my dear? And what I insisted on too? He's right, you know: we really *must* say good night. I'm in rather an awful emotional state, Garret."

"What with one thing or another, we all are. Still, haven't you any late news from the barricades? Dr. Fell and Elliot . . ."

"They've gone. They left ten minutes ago."

"Yes, but what was it you were so insistent on telling them that I mustn't be allowed to hear?"

"Oh, Garret! It wasn't what I said to them; all I told them was what I told you in the billiard-room. It was Dr. Fell's comments on the story."

"And what were those?"

"For the life of me I can't make him out. Most of the time he looks absent-minded or even half-witted. And then, in the middle of it, he'll rap out either with something utterly incomprehensible or else something that goes bang to the heart of the truth."

"It's a habit he has, Fay. For instance?"

"For instance! I was telling him how long ago Deidre wanted to discover whether the police could still be after me in the matter of Mr. Mayhew's death and had thought of asking Superintendent Wick. Mr. Elliot said, 'But as far as we know, she didn't ask Wick.' Dr. Fell said, 'No, and if I'm any judge of Mrs. Barclay's character, she wouldn't have asked him. But what *would* she do?' Then he answered himself, in a voice like an ack-ack gun. 'That's got it, I think,' he said; 'that's nailed it down. . . .' Nailed what down?"

"Don't ask me; it seems to be one of the incomprehensible bits. Did he say anything enlightening?"

"Yes, if he meant what I thought he meant!"

"Well?"

"Dr. Fell said, 'If you were going to commit a murder, Elliot, would *you* use a firearm? As the law stands now, you know you wouldn't. Stab your victim; poison him, strangle him, kill him in any way except with firearms; if they catch you, the worst punishment is life imprisonment, which means a dozen years. Shoot him and you'll hang. This, my lad, was attempted murder which missed only by one whistle and the grace of God.' "

Fay, less than wraith-like as she moved closer, stared up with great intentness.

" 'In order to take so devilish a risk as that,' Dr. Fell said, 'either you must prove beyond cavil the death was suicide, or else you must provide—provide what?' 'You must provide a scapegoat,' said Commander Elliot. 'And, by God, this girl was to have been the scapegoat.' He meant me, Garret; he meant *me*."

"Of course he did. But to think what it means, at this hour of the morning . . ."

"I know, dear; it's not much good, is it? I'm going in now. Please, *please* don't go with me; do you understand what I mean?"

"Yes, I understand."

"Give me a good five minutes, and then follow. If you look towards the house, you'll see I've turned out all the lights on the ground floor. Take this"—Fay pressed an electric torch into his hand—"and guide yourself upstairs. Do you remember which room was assigned to you?"

"The next to the last on the south-east side, Deidre said."

"You won't need the torch once you're at the top of the stairs. I'll put on the light in your room before I go to mine. That's all, Garret; I'll see you in the morning. And let's hope, above all things, neither of us will see a ghost on the way upstairs!"

Then, after a chaotic interval, she was gone.

The garden had turned chilly; a rain-laden breeze began to whisper at the turn of the night. Garret, having thrown away his cigarette, considered lighting another and decided against it. Five minutes later, or what he counted as five minutes, he returned to a darkened house.

See a ghost on the way upstairs? Hardly. And yet ...

He stepped in through the full-length window to the passage. He closed and locked the window. Well along the passage, on his way to the central hall and the stairs, he could have sworn he heard the shuffle of a stealthy footstep going ahead of him. The beam of his torch stabbed out, finding nothing. Either the noise had been in his imagination or some night-prowler had dodged away. But ugly ideas churned through his brain and blood; he had not yet finished with disquiet.

At the top of the stairs, on his right, a thin line of light slanted out from a partly open door. It must be his room; Fay had kept her promise about turning on a light. A robed figure stood by the door and moved towards him. It was only Dr. Edward Fortescue, wearing a dressing-gown; but momentarily that sight brought the heart into Garret's throat.

"Forgive me," Dr. Fotrescue said in his apologetic voice. "I came down here to have a word with you. The light was on, but you weren't there. Can you come with me for a moment, please?"

"Yes, of course; what is it?"

"It's Mr. Barclay, Mr. Pennington Barclay."

"How is he?"

"Not resting very easily. He keeps throwing off the effect of the sedative and opening his eyes, and at times he insists on talking. I said, 'Who did this; who shot you?' The reply was not enlightening: 'I don't know.' "

"He was face to face with the murderer, closer than I am to you now, and yet he doesn't know?"

"I can only report what he told me; it may be partly delirium. 'Arm across the face, and the headgear was different.' Or, 'the headgear was strange,' something like that. And now he wants to see you."

"To see *me?* But that can't be! I scarcely know him; I——"

"Nevertheless, he would like to see you. Will you follow me?"

"Dr. Fortescue, is this wise?"

"No, probably not; you may stay only a moment. But it's advisable, when circumstances permit, to humour the patient. This way, please."

Dying moonlight touched the passage from a window at the western end. Guided by this and by the beam of Garret's torch, Dr. Fortescue led him to a suite of rooms at the front of the house. They entered an untidy dressing-room in a central position above the front door; Dr. Fortescue, in a combination of whisper and pantomime, indicated that the rooms on the east were Deidre Barclay's and the rooms on the west her husband's. From the dressing-room they turned left into their host's bedroom.

A dim lamp, muffled round with several thicknesses of newspaper, burned on a dressing-table in one corner. A door in the west wall opened on a dark bathroom. In the immense bed, supporting a canopy on its carved posts, Pennington Barclay lay with his head propped on low pillows, his nose appearing even bigger against the haggard face and his hands snake-veined on the eiderdown. His eyes were closed; Garret thought him asleep and was about to turn away when a familiar voice spoke vacantly.

"Preparing a drama," the voice said to nobody and everybody. "Preparing a drama, preparing . . . ah, there you are!"

The man's eyes had opened. Sunken and hollow and dark brown, they rolled round under the shadow of the canopy. A stolid police-constable, helmet in lap, sat in a chair near one of the front windows and straightened up as the voice spoke. Dr. Fortescue shambled round to the other side of the bed.

"Surely," the doctor suggested, "it would be better if? . . ."

"If I were to sleep and ceased from troubling? That, no doubt, was what *somebody* thought. Patience, Ned! Patience, my dear fellow! The picture remains blurred, but it is taking shape. I shall remember soon enough who pulled that trigger. If I am still uncertain, it may be partly because the truth seems too incredible. Meanwhile, Ned, why did you lock up all my razors?"

"Good friend———" began Dr. Fortescue.

"You did, didn't you?" demanded the other, stirring and trying to sit up. "I must be the last man on earth, now my father has left us, who still shaves with a straight-bladed razor. And you locked them up; I have not always been dozing; I saw you. Was it because you think I turned the revolver on myself and might complete the job with a throat-cutting? And surely," he added, eyes and voice changing abruptly, "that's Garret Anderson standing by the door there? It *is* Garret Anderson?"

"I'm here, Mr. Barclay." Garret took a step forward. "Did you have any particular reason for wanting to see me?"

"My mind is wandering. And yet I think you are an honest man. If you are in truth an honest man, O honest biographer, don't stay too long among the people in this house. They would have driven Diogenes mad. They are addicted to lies and folly, most of them; and I, *mea culpa*"—the strong voice soared—"I am the worst and silliest of all. Then, too, there is the question of the witch-woman."

"The *what?*"

"Each man of imagination searches throughout his life for the witch-woman, the siren, the charmer who shall unite all qualities in one flesh. I think I have found mine; I could die happy if I were sure of it; and yet—who knows? Who can ever be sure? Have you searched for *your* witch-woman, sir?"

"Yes."

"Do you think you have found her?"

"I know I have."

"Whoever she is, it may be so. Shall I gainsay another's dream? But now, I think, I must let the opiate take hold. Good night, my friend; tread the ways with your sorceress, and pleasant dreams attend you as I have every hope they will attend me. Good night."

Whether or not Garret's dreams were pleasant he could never have told afterwards; he never remembered them. The room they had given him, though Deidre called it the Red Room or the Judge's Room, seemed only a dull relic of Edwardian splendour. He was exhausted, physically and spiritually; he went straight to bed; he did not wake until well into the day, Saturday.

He did not wake, in fact, until past eleven in the morning. Rain drove against the windows. Garret bathed and shaved quickly in the adjoining bathroom; by eleven-thirty he was downstairs. In the ornate dining-room, where a display of silver on the sideboard had been replaced by simmering hotplate dishes, Nick Barclay sat alone at breakfast. One glance at his face brought a return of all Garret's worry.

"What's up, Nick? How's your uncle this morning?"

"Not in very good shape, Dr. Fortescue says. He excited himself about something . . . but that's not what I'm thinking about. All hell is boiling over today."

"How?"

"Elliot and Dr. Fell are here. Elliot is rampaging round in a search for the ghost's robe and veil. Dr. Fell had a word with Uncle Pen, apparently without much result." Nick swallowed coffee the wrong way. "Grab yourself some breakfast; try the sausages and scrambled eggs. Deidre's loaned me the Bentley. Within an hour or so you and I are going to Lymington. Dr. Fell is going too."

"To Lymington? Why Lymington?"

"Look, Garret! This morning I 'phoned old Blackst—Lord Macau—I 'phoned Andy Dawlish to tell him what happened. He was having a fit and was just going to ring me."

"About what?"

"He's looked up an old diary; he knows now when the ghost first appeared to Clovis. But that's still not the point; it's not the reason why hell is popping all over the place. You remember that batch of papers he took away last night?"

"Yes; well?"

"You see," said Nick, "they've discovered still another will."

15

WHIRLING SHEETS of rain flickered like mist across the pleasant town on its hill above Lymington River. You paid a sixpenny toll when you entered or left by way of the bridge. The Bentley, with Nick at the wheel, Garret beside him, and Dr. Fell occupying almost the whole of the back seat, bowled across bridge and level-crossing; it turned left along the waterfront and right up the steep hill of a High Street, which, rain or no rain, had become one vast clutter of stalls on either side. Saturday being market-day, the whole town was as crowded as though for August Bank Holiday.

"The pub to which I referred——" intoned Dr. Fell.

"Damn the pub," said Nick, his eye on unreeling shopfronts. "Sorry, Gargantua, but forget pubs and beer too! Where *is* the place, anyway?"

"I have a note of the address." Garret consulted a slip of paper. "We want eighteen-A and eighteen-B Southampton

Road. Have you ever been here before? Where's Southampton Road?"

"Yes, I used to come here in the old days. Southampton Road, I seem vaguely to remember, turns off to the right at the top of the High Street. Blackstone and Son have their office at eighteen-A and their house at eighteen-B, or maybe the other way round; it's all one house, anyway."

"If you could be a little more informative about what he said! . . ."

"I can't be more informative; he wasn't informative with me. It's trouble, that's all I know. And I hope he's not gone to lunch or anything. Holy cow, will you look at the time?"

They had been late in leaving. At a village called Blackfield, hardly more than two miles from Satan's Elbow, it seemed Dr. Fell had already discovered a pub which entirely suited him. He insisted on discussing this for some time before he could be persuaded to move. At length, from the garage at Greengrove—past a Morris mini-car which somebody said belonged to Estelle—Nick sent the Bentley bucketing over slippery roads to their destination.

It was half-past one by the church-clock when they negotiated the crush of the High Street. Lymington, both a yachting-centre and a haven for the retired prosperous, seemed only sombre amid bustle. In Southampton Road, also sombre despite whipping traffic, a double-fronted house of white stone turned its bleak face to the street. Dr. Fell, emerging from the car in shovel-hat and a transparent oilskin waterproof as big as a tent, pointed with his stick at the brass plate beside the door on the right. Upreared for Johnsonesque utterance, he led his companions through this doorway into a dusky waiting-room severely furnished.

"This way, if you will," called Andrew Dawlish's authoritative voice.

From the waiting-room a short passage with two windows facing the street led off to the doorway of a front office. In the passage, to the left of this door, a long, blue, lightweight mackintosh dripped rainwater from a hat-and-coat stand. Along the passage-wall to the right of the door had been built a low tier of sectional bookcases, their glass doors dustier than any surface in the library at Greengrove. Mr. Dawlish himself, the corners of his mouth turned down, stood on the threshold of the office.

"Good afternoon, Nicholas. It was kind of you to come."

"Not a bit; and sorry to be late. Haven't made you miss your lunch, have I?"

"In a matter so grave as this, my boy, I would miss much more than my lunch. But—you have brought strangers, I see."

"They're not strangers, old socks. They're friends and helpers; you've met both of 'em; and they're here at my very special request. That's all right, isn't it?"

"It will have to be, if you insist." Sheer anguish tinged the lawyer's voice. "At the same time, gentlemen, I must pledge you all to secrecy concerning anything you may hear or see. I am under the impression, Dr. Fell, that you have no official connection with the police?"

"Sir," replied Dr. Fell, "your impression is quite correct."

"Will you come in, gentlemen?"

With a gesture Mr. Dawlish ushered them into a room which, while remaining severe, was not without a certain austere comfort and even opulence. Above the mantelpiece hung a golfing trophy, in the form of a polished silver plaque with Andrew Dawlish's name engraved across it. Other trophies stood on bookcases with polished glass doors. Shelves of deed-boxes stretched along the back. On the solicitor's flat-topped desk, sideways to a window fronting the street, was a bundle of papers which Garret rightly guessed to be the papers Mr. Dawlish had brought from Greengrove.

There were many chairs in the room, but as yet nobody sat down. The lawyer, standing square-shouldered behind the desk, picked up from the bundle of papers a long envelope with its top slit open. Nick, bristling a little, looked at him across the desk.

"Well, Counsellor, what's it all about?"

"It is this." Grimly the other weighed the envelope in his hand. "For the moment, however, all other considerations must give way to the shocking news of which you made brief report on the telephone. Your Uncle Pennington——"

"Uncle Pen's alive."

"'Just' alive, you said. Dr. Fell, I appeal to *you*. Can there be any doubt? . . ."

"That it was a case of attempted murder? Sir," intoned Dr. Fell, puffing as he supported himself on his stick, "in my own mind, no doubt at all. Others are not so sure. Fortescue will not give up an inner conviction that it may have been a try at suicide; Elliot himself has doubts. Barclay himself, though swearing he was attacked, either can't or won't say who attacked him. He has not quite so bad a heart-condition as he believes, or he would be dead now. But it was a great shock. A little more evidence, one way or the other——"

"Yes, that's all very well," interrupted a raging Nick, "and nobody sympathizes with Uncle Pen more than I do." Again he turned to the lawyer. "But what's all this about new troubles, as though we didn't have enough trouble already? Didn't you say something about another will?"

"No, not another will." From the long envelope Mr. Dawlish drew a folded sheet of closely written foolscap. "A codicil to the existing will. And I am at a loss, gentlemen. For once, I confess it, I am utterly at a loss. Yet I have taken certain precautions."

"Precautions?"

"This morning," continued Mr. Dawlish, his gesture indicating the dripping mackintosh in the passage, "I paid a visit to Brockenhurst. For a hundred years the Barclays have entrusted their financial affairs to the City and Provincial Bank at Brockenhurst; under my advice and guidance, they still do. The manager of that branch, a Mr. Akers, is by way of being more than an amateur graphologist and authority on handwriting. Therefore, either to dispel or to verify my suspicions . . . One moment! We have a visitor."

He broke off, looking out of the window. Nick and Garret followed his glance. A Morris mini-car, driven at too high speed for that wet day, swung round from the direction of the High Street into Southampton Road. It lurched, skidded, narrowly missed smashing into the back of the parked Bentley, and then slithered to a stop against the kerb twenty feet ahead of the other car. Out of the Morris tumbled a dishevelled-looking Estelle Barclay. With some difficulty she opened an umbrella and struggled under it across the pavement towards the house.

"If you ask me," raved Nick, "this business is getting worse and worse. What's it all about, Blackstone? Why is Aunt Essie here?"

"I sent for her. Very shortly, Nicholas, you will appreciate my quandary. I have no taste for doing what must be done. But I was given no choice."

Nor had he opportunity to go on explaining. An outer door opened and slammed. Estelle, in fashionable hat and frock, struggled to lower the umbrella as she ran along the passage and burst into the office.

"Well?" began the newcomer, hurling her umbrella into a corner. "Here I am, Andrew, all merry and bright and with it. I was right, wasn't I? You did find something important among those papers, didn't you?"

Mr. Dawlish looked at the silver plaque above the fireplace and at a bookcase on one side. Then he pushed out a chair beside his desk.

"Your instinct, Estelle, would appear to have been uncannily right. Let us consider it. Sit down, please."

Estelle flopped into the chair with something of a swashbuckling attitude despite the fixity of her gaze. The others remained standing.

"I have here," continued Mr. Dawlish, spreading out the sheet of foolscap, "what purports to be a codicil to the will of your late father. The testamentary disposition remains much the same; your nephew is still the heir. But there is an important supplement."

"Supplement?"

"Supplement or modification. That is the meaning of the word codicil. This one is irregularly drawn, and yet, if genuine, it would undoubtedly be valid. *'To my beloved daughter, Estelle Fenton Barclay, whom we have sometimes neglected or undervalued, I give, devise, and bequeath the sum of ten thousand pounds free of any tax or duty which may be laid on my estate.'*"

"It's w-wonderful to think Father didn't forget me. But I don't understand the rest of it. 'Purports to be!' 'If genuine?'"

"Yes, dear lady. Why did you do this?"

"Why did I do what?"

"Why did you forge this document and make very certain I must find it among the other papers?"

"I don't understand one word you're saying!"

"Forgive me; you understand only too well. We are all familiar with your skill at imitating the handwriting of others. If you had tried this game on anyone except me, Estelle, you would have landed in serious trouble. I know the document to be a forgery; Mr. Akers at the bank says the same. As I have been telling these gentlemen . . ."

Estelle sprang up from the chair. The glare in her eyes had grown almost maniacal.

"Oh, you've been telling them? Even if all this were true, which I don't for a minute admit, a splendid friend of the family *you* are! I though you were decent, Andrew Dawlish; but you're no better than the rest of them. You'd not only insult me; you'd bring me here and shame me in front of all these outsiders too!"

"Shame you?" roared Mr. Dawlish. "I am not trying to shame you, madam; I am trying to protect you. Last night I protected another member of your family when it became evident to any intelligence that . . . well, never mind. I will go on protecting, given half a chance. Let me destroy this ridiculous document; no more need be said to anyone. Argue with me, dispute it, go on maintaining the forgery is genuine, and you will carry yourself to a point at which nobody can help.

"Nor is that all, Estelle. This trick, which you may have thought clever, was supremely foolish. According to arrangements made by Nicholas, you are to receive three thousand a year for the rest of your life. Have you any idea what an enormous sum we must set aside to provide that income? A flat ten thousand, believe me, is insignificant beside it. If your nephew should change his mind . . ."

"It's all right, Aunt Essie!" Nick waved both arms as though to stop a train. "You nephew's not going to change his mind. We've all done some peculiar things in our time, but who cares? The income stands; it's still yours; it'll be there as long as you want it."

Tear-drops flew from Estelle's eyes.

"Oh, fiddle-dee-dee!" she screeched at Mr. Dawlish. "A girl's got to look out for her own interests, hasn't she, in a world where all the men band together against her? I don't mean *you*, Nicky. I wrote that codicil; very well! But I didn't do it for the money, really. I just wanted people to think Father hadn't *forgotten*. And I see now where everything came unstuck. I've been betrayed."

"Nobody's betrayed you, Aunt Essie! You betrayed yourself. Didn't you hear what we've been saying?"

More tear-drops flew.

"I expressed myself badly, Nicky, not being a trained journalist like you. What I mean is that there's somebody at Greengrove who hates me, spites me, and would do anything to hurt me. And I'm sure now who it is."

"Estelle," Mr. Dawlish said sharply, "have you taken leave of your senses? There is not one bit of evidence for this."

"Oh, isn't there? But I'll tell you what: I'm going home now. This very day, this very hour, I'm going to have it out with the person in question. And don't try to stop me, anybody! I'm terribly grateful to *you*, Nicky. Your old aunt doesn't show herself in the pleasantest light. But it's better to be unpleasant, isn't it, than to be cruel and mean and vicious like somebody else? Don't let *anyone* try to stop me!"

Face contorted, hair seeming to loosen under the fashionable hat, she made a dart at the umbrella she had flung into a corner. Catching it up, Estelle plunged at her stumbling run out of the office and down the passage. The outer door slammed. Through the window they saw her struggle across the pavement against rain-gusts. A moment later the mini-car roared away up Southampton Road as though headed for the open country. It slowed, hesitated, backed abruptly into somebody's drive, then slewed round and tore back towards the High Street in the direction from which it had come.

Nick turned away from the window.

"This is all right, isn't it? I mean: letting her fly off to raise hell with somebody else? It's *all right?*"

Andrew Dawlish, crumpling up the foolscap sheet with the codicil, dropped it into a large glass ashtray and set fire to it with a match.

"I venture to think," he decided, watching flame curl and shrivel; "I venture to think we have finished the business. She is not the wicked aunt of legend, you know; she will be safe enough now. The only one I worry about is poor Miss Deidre, alone in that house with—whatever else is there. And I wonder, Dr. Fell, why *you* are lost in such obscure musings?"

"The ghost!" said Dr. Fell, rousing himself and blinking round with an air of not knowing where he was. "Archons of Athens, yes! In our preoccupation with wills and other perhaps extraneous matters, we are in danger of forgetting the ghost. Will you, sir, be good enough to supply me with a date?"

"Of course, if I can. What date?"

"Many years ago, as I understand it, the alleged ghost walked out of the garden and appeared to Clovis Barclay. Also, as I understand it"—Dr. Fell gestured towards Nick—"you may be able to tell us when this occurred?"

"Yes, I can tell you." Mr. Dawlish looked at a note-pad on his desk. "The exact date was October first, nineteen-twenty-six."

"You are sure of this?"

"My diary makes very sure."

"October first, nineteen-twenty-six. October first, nineteen-twenty-six. O beauteous day," breathed Dr. Fell, puffing out his cheeks, "in which the edge of the sun shall appear in splendour! Surely, sir, you appreciate the significance of this?"

"I see at least that we have been thinking along the same lines."

"Concerning the ghost, no doubt we have. Concerning other matters there is less certainty. And now," added Dr. Fell with fiery energy, "we must take *our* leave. My young friends will cry fie at my insistence on food and drink. Both of them had a late, hearty breakfast. Whereas I . . ."

Mr. Dawlish escorted them to the door of the office.

"There are my diaries," he said, indicating the lowest tier of sectional bookcases in the passage. "If I can be of any further service, command me. You were saying?"

"Grisly!" proclaimed Dr. Fell—or this at least appeared to

be the word. "For my own part, let me repeat, I could wreak havoc on a plate of sandwiches and their accompaniment in beer. Is there any general agreement?"

"Nothing to eat for me, thanks," Garret said, "but a pint of beer would be uncommonly welcome."

"Damn the beer," said Nick. "Lead *me* to a sustaining Scotch-on-the-rocks. What's this, Maestro, about something being grisly?"

Dr. Fell did not enlighten him. But that was how, at just past two o'clock, they found themselves ensconced in the red-papered lounge-bar of a hotel a little way down Lymington High Street. Rain and market-day brawled outside the bar; Dr. Fell himself was noisy inside it. Filling a mighty chair, he had consumed a dozen ham sandwiches and was just lifting his fifth tankard.

"Most firmly," he said, "I have restrained myself from lecturing. I am very fond of lecturing on the subject of ghosts, or, in fact, anything else. But most firmly I restrained myself, and marvel at my own self-control."

"Why restrain yourself?" asked Garret. "What *is* the atmosphere in that place? You never actually see anything, or at least I don't, though late last night I thought I was going to. It happened in the western passage downstairs when I came in from the garden." He recounted the incident, without mentioning Fay or Nick or anyone else. "I could have sworn I heard somebody shuffling ahead of me. But I flashed a torch and saw nothing. Was it my imagination? Or was somebody really prowling? Or what?"

"Well, which was it?" demanded Nick. "Make up your mind, old son. Cripes, if only we could get a line on the identity of this 'ghost'! Or are we being dumb clucks, Dr. Fell?"

"Oh, no. But you are concentrating on the wrong aspect; you have confused the Peter Pan element with the Captain Hook element. If at this moment you knew the identity of the ghost, are you sure we should be much nearer a solution?"

"Yes, of course we would!"

"Not necessarily," said Dr. Fell.

He did not speak for a moment, making rumbling noises in his throat.

"I draw your attention," he continued, swirling the tankard round on the table, "to a very important piece of testimony. Only three persons are known to have seen the ghost: old Clovis Barclay, Estelle Barclay, and Mrs. Annie Tiffin. These three, though extraordinarily different in almost every respect, have at least one thing in common."

"Oh? What's that?"

"Think about it. Once you have found the link, which is not a difficult one, you will see . . . O Lord! O Bacchus! O my ancient hat!"

Dr. Fell, who had been lifting the tankard, let it down with a thump. Galvanized, puffing, and blowing, he surged to his feet.

"My scatterbrain tactics, sir, have blinded me to another obvious point. We had better drive to Greengrove; we had better go in a hurry."

"Then it *was* sense to be jittery? It *wasn't* right to let Essie go?"

"There may be nothing wrong; I sincerely hope there is not. At the same time, when I think of the link between those three witnesses . . ."

"Look, what are we waiting for? Come on!"

By some miracle they had found a parking-place not far from the hotel. Within a minute Nick was maneuvering the Bentley down the hill through rain and traffic. Once they were round Gosport Street and across the bridge, with the cluttered masts of yachts rising from the basin on their right, a touch at the accelerator sent the car flying.

Fields and forest-patches sped by. Round corners and over cattle-grids, past forest-ponies and melancholy cows, Nick drove with careless skill. Dr. Fell, in the back seat, sat with hands clasped over the head of his cane. The windscreen-wiper ticked steadily. Few words were spoken; there were no consecutive sentences, in fact, until they had flashed through Beaulieu and Exbury and were on the long curve up to Satan's Elbow.

"These hints of yours, Solon," Nick said over his shoulder, "are making me even dizzier than I was before. But can't you give us any more hints? Whatever the explanation of the ghost is, what's the explanation of the attempted murder?"

"The root of it," answered Dr. Fell, "may be found in one word. Sex."

"Sex?" yelped Nick as though he could not believe his ears. "Did you say sex?"

"And yet, sir, it plays a fairly important part in all our lives. I had not thought you immune to its influence."

"Immune? God's teeth, I've never claimed to be immune! But what's all this got to do with me?"

"In one sense, nothing whatever." Dr. Fell pondered for a moment. "Or was money the mainspring of the motive? I don't know; I can't say. And yet, if my calculations are correct, both sex and the greed for money inspired a vicious, cold-blooded plot to kill."

"Frankly, I don't like the sound of 'plot.' Is more than one culprit mixed up in this?"

"No, by thunder!"

"A straight answer?"

"A straight answer. Again, unless I am much mistaken, only one person carried out the crime or knew anything about it, though it is true that the effect of a certain woman——"

"A certain woman?" Nick yelled. "Look, Aristotle, your straight answers sound as loony as the cryptic ones. Besides—"

The car bucketed up the slope, which flattened out in sight of water. The roof and chimney-stacks of Greengrove lifted above trees on its little peninsula.

"We're nearly there"—Nick made a face—"and I hope this John Gilpin race wasn't necessary. What the hell's that noise? It sounds like an ambulance-bell."

"It *is* an ambulance-bell. Slow down for the turn; take it gently! They're in more of a hurry than we are."

Dread struck Garret Anderson like the wind off the Solent. The ambulance, a white shape with red crosses painted on its rear doors, whipped out between the entrance-pillars of the grounds. It dipped into a hollow, bell clanging, and fled away up the northern road towards Blackfield. Nick hardly decreased speed as he sent the Bentley up the drive to the house, where he brought it to an abrupt stop and jumped down. Garret climbed out at the other side.

The front door was wide open. Deidre Barclay, in blue sweater and brown tweed skirt, stood there amid blowing rain.

"Nick, Nick, I'm glad you're back. It's been rather awful. It's . . ."

"Uncle Pen? Or what?"

"No; Pen's all right. It's Estelle."

"Is it, by God? What happened?"

"She fell. You know those blind little runs of hers?"

"Yes, but what happened?"

"We don't quite know; it was an accident. She came back here in a state about something. But she didn't say a word. She put the car away and started up the main stairs as far as the first landing. Then she must have mistaken the direction she was going; she often does that. All of a sudden there was an awful crash. Dr. Fortescue, who was upstairs in his room, ran out to her. She must have pitched head down. It's not the sort of thing you can deal with at home; concussion of the brain, they're afraid of. We 'phoned the hospital at Blackfield, and Dr. Fortescue's gone with her in the ambulance."

"She fell, did she? Or did somebody? . . ." Nick flung out his hands.

"Oh, God," Deidre said wildly, "it couldn't have been anything like that. There was nobody anywhere near her. The nearest person was poor Fay, coming out of her own room; but Fay was yards and yards away and didn't even see anybody when she ran there. Nick, I can't bear much more of this. What are we to *do?*"

"Do, madam?" repeated Dr. Gideon Fell. *"Do?"*

With infinite labour Dr. Fell had wheezed his way out of the car. The rain was sluicing down on them, Nick and Garret being without hat or mackintosh. Dr. Fell stood motionless, in waterproof and shovel-hat, but he made a mighty gesture with his stick.

"At least," he said, "it is some satisfaction to think we are approaching an end. Meanwhile, we can only wait for the night."

16

WAIT FOR THE NIGHT?

But already it was growing late.

Dinner, for which Dr. Fell and Deputy Commander Elliot stayed, had been served at eight o'clock. Deidre, Fay, Nick, and Garret made what sort of meal they could. They were waited on both by Phyllis and by Phoebe, a pretty, stolid-faced brunette who might have been Phyllis's twin sister and was actually her cousin. Dr. Fortescue remained at Blackfield Hospital, from which reports were not entirely encouraging. Estelle had suffered concussion, in addition to a fractured left arm and multiple bruises. But her constitution was said to be a strong one; the prognosis might have been worse. Following dinner the group disintegrated and disappeared, going separate ways.

At some point in the afternoon Garret was introduced to a burly, moustached man of imposing aspect who had been presented as Detective Chief Superintendent Harold Wick. But he said scarcely six words. At the end of dinner Superintendent Wick showed his face again, after which *he* disappeared too.

And then?

The rain had cleared into a cloudless evening. Garret and Fay, the latter wearing the same blue-and-white dress as yesterday, went for a walk on the beach. Fay's mood veered now towards emotional intensity, now away from it. At past ten, under a strengthening moon, they returned to the house. At eleven, as the clocks were striking, they bent over a pin-ball machine in the billiard-room. It was the second pin-ball machine, against the western wall; now brightly illuminated, it rang and chattered with a gaudy motor-car race.

"Bother!" said Fay, inspecting the scoreboard. "Garret, it's no earthly *good!* That's the last ball of my try; I've scored less than six thousand; this is a stupid game anyway. If you won't discuss what's been happening here . . ."

"I'm perfectly willing to discuss anything. But——"

"I've told you over and over, I've told everybody, it really was an accident! Estelle was all alone when she pitched over. Don't you believe me?"

"Of course I believe you. But for it to happen at that particular time seems so strange a piece of fortuitousness that . . ."

"Darling, it's not strange at all! You've watched Estelle; I'm surprised something like that hasn't happened before. She's a snooper, but she's horribly clumsy; she was almost bound for trouble. Besides! That's not what I really wanted to talk about. Will you come with me now?"

"Where?"

"You'll see."

Fay was irresistible. Beckoning him out of the billiard-room, she led him a dozen steps along the passage, touched a light-switch just inside the partly open door of the room next in line, and with an air of triumph ushered him into the music-room.

In the eighteenth century, it became evident, this had been a place of some importance. On polished rosewood panelling the glow of electric wall-candles cast a dull sheen. Across its blue-sky plaster ceiling, somewhat frantically decorated by a Georgian painter, amorous gods and goddesses went cavorting in colours not much faded. There was an antique pianoforte under the line of the southern casement windows. In one corner stood a shrouded harp which nobody ever touched. But both Victorianism and modernity intruded too. The west wall contained two full-length windows, exactly like those of the library, so that you could step out on the lawn if you liked. The hi-fi was between these windows, faced by several brocaded chairs and a heavy brocaded sofa.

"You see?" continued Fay, going to look at the hi-fi. "It's all ready; somebody's left an LP record in place."

"More Gilbert and Sullivan? Or one of Estelle's pop records?"

"Neither. This is the pop music of another generation: from an operetta called *The Student Prince*. Let's try it, shall we?"

Fay adjusted the needle and touched a switch. She stood poised by the cabinet, a smile on her face but fright in her eyes. The music, first threaded through with the dreaming note of a violin, threw out fragments of tunes from the whole score and then gathered strength to shake the walls with an opening chorus.

> Come, boys, let's all be gay, boys,
> For education's only scientific play, boys! . . .

"Would you mind shutting that off?" interposed a curt voice.

It was Elliot's voice. The tumult stopped dead. Into the music-room, dusky despite its yellow-gleaming wall-candles, Deidre Barclay marched with the look of one determined to do her duty. Elliot followed, notebook in hand.

"Are we in the way?" asked Garret as Fay hurried towards him. "Do you want this room for questioning?"

"No; I've done most of the questioning I need to do." Elliot wore a grimly satisfied air. "But I need some confirmation from you."

"From me?"

"Yes. Last night—or early this morning, rather—you went out to the garden while Dr. Fell and I were talking to Miss Wardour. You came back to the house . . . when?"

"I don't remember; it must have been nearly two-thirty. You and Dr. Fell had gone."

"All right. You told the maestro this afternoon, I think, that when you returned to the house you believed you heard somebody prowling in the dark but couldn't be sure of it. Is that correct?"

"Yes."

"Well, there was somebody there. Now, Mrs. Barclay, would you mind repeating what *you* discovered this afternoon?"

Deidre hesitated. She had changed tweeds and sweater for a plain dark semi-formal dress which set off her athletic figure. She looked at Fay as though for support; she glanced up at the ceiling and hastily averted her eyes.

"Really!" Deidre said. "Dr. Fell——"

"Dr. Fell is still with your husband, Mrs. Barclay," Elliot

told her. "But I've sent for him; he'll be here in a moment. Meanwhile, if you'd begin with the preliminaries . . ."

It was unnecessary to delay. Dr. Fell himself, stumping on the crutch-headed stick, appeared in the doorway and joined them.

"Yes, Mrs. Barclay?" said Elliot.

"It's not very pleasant, you know!" Deidre appealed to Dr. Fell. "And I only heard by accident. It's Phyllis—Phyllis Latimer—one of the maids."

"Yes, Mrs. Barclay?" said Elliot.

"I knew she had a boy-friend, somebody named Harry. The rest I never dreamed until this afternoon, when there was a squabble between Phyllis and Phoebe. They're always squabbling, of course, but this was a *frightful* one. I walked into the kitchen just as Phoebe was saying . . ."

"Yes, Mrs. Barclay?"

"*Must* I tell this?"

"We're investigating an attempted murder: your husband's murder. Go on, please."

"I walked into the kitchen," Deidre cried, "just as Phoebe was saying, 'Well, at least, *I* don't sneak out and meet men on the beach in the middle of the night.' Then Annie Tiffin weighed in with some remarks about what girls did in her day, and it wasn't easy to sit in judgment.

"Really, now!" commented Deidre, drawing herself up. "We can't expect to treat servants as they were treated fifty years ago. I understand that, I approve, and I hope I'm reasonably broadminded. But it does seem to me there ought to be limits. It does seem to me——"

"Just a moment!" interrupted Elliot. He consulted his notebook and turned to Dr. Fell. "Phyllis, we now know, did go out to meet her boy-friend last night. She might have gone by the back door, but in fact she went by the open window in the passage. She didn't get back until nearly two-thirty, which is the time she almost bumped into Anderson, and would have bumped into him except that she dodged into the billiard-room just before he flashed his torch."

"Oh, that billiard-room!" exploded Fay Wardour. "All the wicked women haunt it, don't they? What wicked people haunt this room, Dee?"

"For heaven's sake, Fay, whatever is the matter with *you?* Nobody said one word . . ."

"Is there something," Dr. Fell asked Elliot, "you wished to tell *me?*"

"Yes, there is. If they'll all be quiet—*did you hear me, Miss Wardour?*—I'll try to straighten out the evidence. It doesn't

THE HOUSE AT SATAN'S ELBOW 159

matter two hoots," said Elliot, "what time Phyllis came back to the house. The important thing is the time she left it and what she saw as she was leaving. Will you enlighten us, Mrs. Barclay?"

"I see no reason"—Deidre was holding hard to her nerves—"for the inquisition to centre on me. Why don't you ask Phyllis herself?"

"I have asked her. She's not the most helpful witness when you touch on her love-life; is any woman? Perhaps I'd better tell it myself. It has no concern with Phyllis's love-life, but it very much concerns this investigation. She started to creep out, Phyllis swears, at a quarter to midnight. That was fifteen minutes before Dr. Fell and I took our first look at the library; and at a quarter to midnight, Mrs. Barclay, I seem to remember we were questioning you in the drawing-room."

"So you were," agreed Deidre.

Garret restrained Fay, who seemed about to speak.

"May I ask a question, Elliot? Phyllis saw something, you say, as she was leaving the house by the window at the end of the passage?"

"She saw something, to be exact, about twenty or thirty seconds before she left the house by that window."

"Well? What did she see?"

"She saw a man in a dressing-gown slipping out by the same window with a parcel under his arm."

"A man in a dressing-gown?" Garret stared. "But that's absurd!"

"Why absurd?"

"At a quarter to midnight? Nobody was wearing a dressing-gown then. Besides . . . do you believe this story?"

"Yes! Bear in mind," retorted Elliot, snapping his fingers to draw attention, "that the girl can speak only of an impression. It may not have been a dressing-gown, just as what he carried may not have been a parcel.

"Also bear in mind," Elliot snapped, "that Phyllis was a very long distance away. She had to leave by way of the corridor from the back stairs to the eastern passage and had just turned into the passage. She had to look along the eastern passage, across the central hall, and the full length of the western passage too. The lights were on, but they're very dim out there. The man's back was turned; she can't even estimate height. All she saw . . ."

"Does anybody suggest ghosts?" inquired Dr. Fell.

"*She* wasn't thinking about ghosts on her way to a date at the beach. They can all forget ghosts when it's convenient. All she saw was a man in what looked like a dressing-gown carrying what looked like a parcel. But who was the man? Where was he going? When did he return? Isn't it more probable—"

The C.I.D. man checked himself, whirling round to Dr. Fell.

"Isn't it probable," he added, "that this fits in exactly with the theory you and I now share?"

"It does indeed. Even apart from the supernatural, it is a grisly little vignette. And it necessitiates a conference in private."

"I think it does; come along. What did you get from Pennington Barclay?"

"Everything I hoped for. Nobody has ever been more coöperative. Elliot, we close in."

"That's possible, though it may not work. The rest of you will excuse us, won't you?"

He strode out; Dr. Fell lumbered after him; the door closed. A shaken Fay was left facing a shaken Deidre in a room whose emotional temperature had shot up several degrees.

"And so," Fay cried, "the wretched little servant-girl slipped out to her assignation. Shocking, isn't it? Other people don't behave like that, do they?"

"If they have any self-control," returned Deidre, "I feel sure they don't. But I won't argue the matter, Fay dear; I'll leave you to discuss it with Garret. Excuse *me*."

Again the door closed. Still the emotional temperature soared.

"Well?" Garret demanded. "What was the meaning of that little exchange? And what do we do now?"

"We put the record on again." Fay's look was intense and yet faraway. She darted to the hi-fi. "Listen, won't you?"

Again the music swelled, filling the room with sound as a bowl is filled with water.

"You'll hear several themes here," Fay said. "One is the fragment of a tune called 'Deep in My Heart, Dear.' Then comes the famous drinking-song. Wait for it; listen to the words. Some of them are rather revealing."

The tempo altered. A drum-beat began to pound. The words a strong solo of the young man pledging his lady-love, rose with the melody in a beat that was rousing and rollicking and yet a little sinister.

> Drink, drink, drink to eyes that are bright as stars
>   That are shining on me (on me),
> Drink, drink, drink to lips that are red and sweet
>   As the fruit on the tree (on the tree!)

> Here's the hope that those bright eyes will shine
> Tenderly, trustingly, soon into mine . . .

"You hear?" cried Fay as her companion stalked to the hi-fi. "Garret! What are you doing?"

"I'm shutting the damn thing off." He did so; silence descended like an extinguisher-cap. "Revealing, did you say? Is there something revealing about an operetta forty years old? Deidre's right, Fay: what's got into you? What's all this in aid of?"

"I was thinking about the case."

"This case?"

"Yes, of course. The near-murder."

Fay struggled to draw breath. She glanced up towards the gods and goddesses—Mars and Venus, Apollo and Daphne—at their frozen amours across the ceiling.

"'Tenderly trustingly, soon into mine.' You betrayed no confidence, Garret, when you told me what Dr. Fell said today. He said the motive was a combination of sex and money. Well, who's guilty? And which particular woman inspired it?"

"Just a minute, my girl; just a minute, and take it easy! I'm not going to have you getting hysterical again."

"Hysterical? Again?"

"Yesterday evening in the train you began spinning all sorts of wild theories. Among them was the suggestion that Nick Barclay might be an impostor, not Nick Barclay at all. It was the wildest suggestion of the lot. We know he *is* Nick Barclay, and he had nothing to do with this business. At the same time . . ."

"Yes?" Fay prompted, her eyes intent. "We know he had nothing to do with it; all that's agreed. At the same time . . . what?"

"I've been worried."

"In what way?"

"Over and over it's been repeated—Elliot himself has made the point—that Nick had no earthly reason to kill his uncle. Elliot doesn't know what you and I know. Nick and Deidre have been in love for a matter of four years: helpless under the situation, fighting against it, in a state of nerves worse than yours or mine. And that's motive."

"Then you mean? . . ."

"No, Fay. I do *not* mean." Garret paced the floor. "Even if I wondered about Nick's innocence—which I don't, knowing Nick—he of all people is the one man we can't suspect. At the time somebody fired that shot, he was with Elliot and Dr.

Fell; he's out of it; he can bring the police themselves to prove his alibi."

"But who did fire the shot? And who was the woman who, deliberately or unconsciously, inspired somebody to kill? Do you know who the woman ought to be, Garret?"

"Well?"

"It ought to be me."

"Are you crazy?"

"I hope not, but I don't know. And don't rage, please; don't go on at me." Fay clenched her fists. "I'm the suspicious one; I'm the unknown quantity. At the end, as in so many mysteries, oughtn't *I* to be the mercenary and cold-hearted virago behind everything? How does that sound?"

"Not very convincing. Unless they want to argue that I'm the murderer myself, with you supplying the alibi while I left the billiard-room to do the dirty work, it's not even feasible. Or else—what other men have you been mixed up with?"

"There isn't anyone; there isn't! I told you that before; it's true. Mr. Barclay likes me, and I think Dr. Fortescue too, in his way, but it's not what *you* mean. Since I met you, Garret, I swear to God there's been nobody else!"

"This is all imagination, is it? I thought so. You've been torturing yourself, as usual, with anything you can dream up in the middle of the night?"

"You don't understand, Garret. You haven't been through the actual nightmare of being suspected; I have. It may be mostly imagination, yes; but there may be more in it than either of us can guess.

"Last night, when they told me I was cleared of suspicion, I could have walked on air. But it didn't last. You may trust the police; I don't. Were they telling the truth? Was Dr. Fell himself telling the truth? What if there's no question of some woman inspiring a would-be murderer, but simply of a would-be murderer for whom they're setting a trap? *Anybody* could guess who that might be. 'Come off it, Fay Wardour, or Fay Sutton, or whatever you choose to call yourself; we know you; you're the one we want; why don't you be sensible and confess?' "

"Look here," said a thunderous voice, "this has got to stop."

The big door of the music-room stood wide open. Dr. Gideon Fell, looming mountainous in the aperture, shifted his stick to his left hand.

"Forgive me if I intrude," he continued in a gentler tone. "But it is time somebody intruded. Go on in this fashion, Miss Wardour, and we shall have another hospital-case on our hands. It is time somebody played Oedipus: not the Oedipus of popular fancy, who seems generally believed to have been born in a Viennese psychiatric clinic, but the Oedipus who answered the riddle. I should like, with your permission, to answer a few riddles and remove a few masks. Have I that permission, Miss Wardour?"

A desperate-seeming Fay ran to Garret and shrank against him.

"Of course you have my permission! Not that it matters a bit whether I agree, but of c-course you have it! Provided, that is . . ."

"Provided, that is, I tell no lies and set no traps? Be assured, my lady fair, there are no lies or traps for *you;* you have had quite enough of them. I ask only that you and Anderson, a deeply interested party in what concerns you, will accompany me to the library, the *fons et origo* of so many disturbances. Have no fear, I beg! This way, if you will."

Garret, his arm round Fay and her head against his shoulder, quietened her trembling as best he could. In the wake of Dr. Fell he led her across the dimly lighted passage to the door of the library. On the threshold they met a grim-faced Elliot coming out.

"It would appear," said Dr. Fell, "that there is a great silence on the house. Where is everybody?"

"After all"—and Elliot consulted his watch—"it's getting on for midnight. They've gone to bed, or said they were going to. All except Fortescue; he's still at the hospital. But the doors aren't locked; they never are; he can get in at any time he likes."

"No sign as yet?"

"None." Elliot strode away down the passage.

A great silence, as well as a certain tension, held the library too. Only one light was burning, the floor-lamp beside the writing-table. And it was much tidier. The broken window had been repaired, the papers set straight on the table, the bloodstains nearly scrubbed from the carpet. The door to the cloakroom, the door to the book-cupboard, were both tightly closed. Dr. Fell looked round at the walls of books, at tapestry chairs, at faded carpet and curtains.

"It is only fitting," he went on, fishing from his pockets a fat tobacco-pouch and a large meerschaum pipe, "that certain explanations should occur here. Not only is it the scene of the crime; viewed in another aspect, it has also been the den and lair of Pennington Barclay.

"A curious character, Pennington Barclay. You have seen him for yourselves; you have heard him described both by those who like him and by those who do not. The strain of childishness in all the Barclays, from old Clovis's love of pin-ball machines to the not-very-humorous pranks played by Estelle, is most marked in him. But shall we condemn this, with so much childishness in our own natures? He is perhaps at times not the easiest person to live with. But shall we condemn this either, having all devils in our own hearts?

"What are his outstanding characteristics, aside from his passion for the past? Sensitiveness mingled with cynicsim; good nature marred by peevish rages; a love of mystery and secrecy, from the ghost story at its most terrifying—his particular specialty—to the detective story at its most ingenious. Pennington Barclay is a romantic gone sour, a kind of intellectual Peter Pan; and let me repeat that this was his lair. Here he read. Here he dictated letters. Here he brooded. Here . . ."

"He thought about the play he was going to write?" supplied Fay.

"Miss Wardour," Dr. Fell said sharply, "did he ever tell you he was writing a play?"

"Well! Of course he did! He said . . ."

Dr. Fell, juggling pipe and tobacco-pouch, lowered himself into an immense tapestry chair with its back to the drawing-room door. Fay sat down in a smaller chair opposite, and Garret perched on its arm.

"Did he ever actually *say* that," insisted Dr. Fell, "when faced with the direct question? His words, as quoted by so many witnesses who heard him in this room last night, were that for some time he had been 'preparing a drama.'"

"'Preparing a drama,'" Garret quoted, "'which shall explore human behaviour under stress.' He seemed obsessed by it. At half-past two in the morning I looked into his sick-room; he repeated 'preparing a drama' when he was half-unconscious from the sedative."

"Well, what's the difference?" asked Fay. "It's the same thing, isn't it?"

"In this case," replied Dr. Fell, "it is a very different thing."

Dr. Fell had filled the pipe, which he lighted after whisking a kitchen match across the side of the chair.

"Please remember," he continued, "that up to today, when I had several long talks with Mr. Barclay, I had not yet met the man. To a degree I felt I knew him. We had corresponded extensively."

"And he sent for you, didn't he? He wrote you a note!"

"No, Miss Wardour, he did not send for me."

"But——"

"Though not definitely suspicious of the last hand-written

note purporting to come from him, I nevertheless felt it contained several uncharacteristic phrases. We may now decide the note was forged by Estelle Barclay, who hoped for great things from my reputation and brushed me aside in disgust when I did not produce them. Assuredly it was not written by Pennington, who has since owned as much. He did not want me here; he would never have had me here; he has owned that too."

"Well," said Garret, "why didn't he want you here?"

"Because he feared me," answered Dr. Fell. "You must remember that an old scatterbrain can be childish too."

"Feared you?"

"From the first, sir, I have been conscious of two elements, the Peter Pan element—childish and rather ugly, though not criminal—and the Captain Hook element—also childish, but more adult and most viciously clever—pulling against each other. It seemed to me that you and Elliot and Nick Barclay were making a cardinal error in your theorizing. You assumed that the person who played ghost was the same person who committed the crime."

"And that wasn't so?"

"It was not so; it has caused nearly all our confusion." Dr. Fell blew out a great cloud of smoke. "To hint at what I did believe, I stated this afternoon that the ghost has been known to appear on three occasions and to three persons: to Clovis Barclay many years ago, and to Estelle Barclay and Mrs. Tiffin during the same week this April. I asked you, in attacking the problem of the pretended ghost, what these three persons had in common."

"But I still don't see it!" protested Garret. "If you're going to answer riddles and remove masks, now is the time to do it. What *did* those three people have in common?"

"Each one, at various times and for various reasons, had been at bitter daggers drawn with Pennington Barclay."

Fay shrank back in the chair. Garret sprang to his feet.

"Dr. Fell, I'll tell you something else Uncle Pen said last night. He was fighting the world or the sedative or both. 'Don't stay too long,' he said, 'among the people in this house. They are addicted to lies and folly, most of them; and I, *mea culpa*, am the worst and silliest of all.' "

"Well, yes," agreed Dr. Fell. "He has been going on like that for half the night. He is sunk fathoms deep in an abyss of remorse, and he cries out in pain from the memory."

"Remorse?" echoed Garret. "Good God, sir, where have we got to now? Are you saying Uncle Pen is the criminal, responsible for all this dirty work?"

Dr. Fell whacked the ferrule of his stick on the floor. "No, he committed no crime." Then the big voice rose. "But it was Pennington Barclay himself who played ghost, and is the only one who has played ghost in this house."

17

"Dr. Fell, are *you* crazy?"

"I sincerely hope not."

"What about the appearances of the ghost last night?"

"My dear Anderson, *nobody* saw the ghost last night."

"But look here——"

"Sir," Dr. Fell said impatiently, "will you consider the evidence?"

He surged to his feet, ash flying from the pipe. In cross-eyed fashion he stared above his companions' heads towards the left-hand window of the library.

"The facts on which I now draw," he continued, "constitute a piece of family history given to me at some length by Nick Barclay. It is the same history, I believe, he recounted to you during dinner at the Thespis Club on Wednesday. And it will serve to begin the reconstruction.

"In spring of the year nineteen-twenty-six, when Pennington Barclay was only twenty-two and Nick himself could scarcely have been beyond his second year, Greengrove shook to a fine explosion. Young Pen Barclay, after a violent quarrel with his father as well as a row with Estelle, quietly packed a bag and left the house. When next heard from, he is found living at Brighton with a young actress whose name—supplied us years afterwards by Estelle—is Mavis Gregg.

"What happened to Miss Gregg we don't know, nor does it greatly matter. What we do know is that in September of the same year (Nick told you so) Pennington Barclay had returned here. Still quiet, facing uproar with a shrug, he seemed outwardly unaffected; he let recriminations flow off him. But on October first—mark that date—on October first *Clovis saw the ghost*.

"Towards twilight, as he stood at that window there, a shape in robe and face-veil emerged from the eastern entrance to the garden. It took form and substance as the very ghost of the house; it moved across an autumn lawn; it suddenly ran at him as though with intent to carry him off. And Clovis, the iron man, received a shock that sent him reeling.

"Now who acted that masquerade? It was unlikely to have been Clovis's down-to-earth elder son, still less likely to have been the daughter who idolized him. But Pennington? Do you begin to see?"

"Yes, I see," said Garret, "and the pieces fit together. Pennington pretended to be not much disturbed by his father's tantrums. But—"

"But wasn't he upset? Wasn't he, by thunder? And so the plan came to him. He was then a young man, even less inhibited than he is now. His stage-properties—robe, mask, whatever else he thought necessary—could easily have been bought or manufactured. *Clovis* pretended, did he, to fear no ghosts or believe in them? Well, Pennington would show him! He would attack Clovis at the one point where he suspected the tyrant of being vulnerable; he would give that old bounder the fright of a lifetime.

"And that is what he did—though he covered it up afterwards and even foolishly swore he had never heard of the incident."

Dr. Fell's pipe had gone out; he relit it, whisking a kitchen match across the seat of his trousers.

"The years rolled on, as years have a habit of doing. We can accustom ourselves to anything, even to people like Clovis Barclay, and Pennington managed it. He had used the weapon of the supernatural; he had triumphed. But he must be very chary of this in the future. Having played his trump-card once, he must not play it again on the same person lest someone suspect him of having played it. Life at times grew very unpleasant. But he had his dream-world. Art, letters, and music can console for much.

"And he had something else to console him. The young man was a young man no longer. He was getting on; he felt the cold. At a very mature age, in something of a rush, he met, fell in love with, and married the young lady we know as Deidre Barclay. And then?"

"And then?" demanded Fay.

"Things did not grow worse; if anything, they grew much better. Old Clovis liked Pennington's new wife. She has much charm, as we are aware: she seemed healthy, straightforward, uncomplicated. Pennington himself had reason to view the future with some complacency. The old man could not last forever. With that obstacle removed, the sky would be serene and the dreams carry him on to happiness.

"It seemed to work out. Clovis caught pneumonia and died. But we know what ensued: less than a month of serenity. The tobacco-jar fell and smashed; the new will was revealed; Clovis's slyness struck back from the grave. To Pennington Barclay, I must tell you for the first time, there was something worse than this."

"Worse?" repeated Fay.

"Very much worse. It was not only that he had lost everything, that a new heir was coming from America. Nick Barclay it is true, *said* he had no intention of taking the house. But could this be believed? It might have been, except for the circumstance I mentioned. Constantly at Pennington's elbow there was somebody sowing doubt, somebody whispering fear, somebody pouring poison in his ear."

"Somebody." Fay began to shiver so violently that Garret sat down again on the arm of the chair. *"Somebody*, you said?"

"Just that; think of it. But before the whispers had done their proper work, think what happened in the interval. Pennington Barclay was already in an embittered, brooding state of mind. And between the finding of the second will and the time when any decision could have been made about it, the ghost appeared twice in one week.

"Did it appear to any of those he considers his supporters and allies? Did it appear to Deidre, whom he really does love and cherish? Did it appear to you, Miss Wardour, whom he sincerely likes? Did it appear to Dr. Fortescue, whom he both likes and patronizes? No; it appeared to none of these. It appeared to Mrs. Tiffin. It appeared to Estelle Barclay.

"And those two, I submit, are in somewhat different case.

"It must now be apparent," pursued Dr. Fell, waving away smoke, "that Estelle can never meet her brother without nagging him or pitching into him. She can and does carry this to frantic lengths. He can control his temper in her presence, though with some difficulty. He could arrange to have a sizeable yearly income settled on her and would have arranged it had he remained in possession of the estate. The money means nothing to him; it never has. But does he really like her? Answer for yourself.

"Mrs. Tiffin? Concerning the cook he has done no more than hint. Mrs. Tiffin herself supplied us with a partial explanation, though I think an incorrect one. Those two don't get on. Pennington Barclay, according to Mrs. Tiffin's notion, believes she does things to spite him; *he* thinks—simply, and probably rightly—that she can't cook. He will never sack a servant of eighteen years' standing, just as he will never turn

Estelle into the cold world; under no circumstances will he disturb the status quo. But what can he do?

"Let me insist that he was already in an embittered, brooding frame of mind. As if this were not enough, sister and servant together have supplied the domestic frictions that drive him mad. They don't like him, eh? They're leagued against him, are they? By thunder, he'll show 'em; by thunder, they'll smart for *this!* And so on two occasions the ghost appears, vanishing again by mechanics we have already guessed."

Fay made a fighting gesture.

"Dr. Fell," she cried, "I'll believe this if you say so!"

"I am not the only one who maintains it, Miss Wardour."

"Who else does?"

"Pennington Barclay himself."

"I'm bound to believe, of course, if he admits it. All the same, unless he's half insane . . ."

"He is not insane at all."

"Oh, have it your own way! But what happened all those years ago is one thing; what happened this year is quite another. Mr. Barclay, of all people, carrying on like a boy playing pranks in a deserted house?"

"Just that."

"A man of his age? It's grotesque and silly! And, whatever else you say, a civilized man too?"

"Our tastes may be civilized, or so we flatter ourselves. Are our feelings always so civilized too? That age brings wisdom is a thesis contradicted by human experience; this is a matter of temperaments; and I would ask you another question. You think you could never have done anything so silly as Barclay did. Could you have confessed anything so silly once you had done it?"

"No!" Fay faltered. "I see what you mean. And I was wrong; I shouldn't have spoken as I did; forgive me! There's nothing so grotesque or so silly that *I* wouldn't have done it; who am I to judge others?"

"You yourself are something of a romantic. Conquer your own tendency to brood, I urge you. You have a gift for enjoyng life, if only you permit yourself to exercise it. Enjoy life, Miss Wardour; let Anderson help you! Meanwhile . . ."

"Meanwhile, as *you* were saying, Mr. Barclay decided on his masquerade. I know he did; I've watched him while he vas dictating or just reciting; he gets carried away. He thought himself into the spirit of the old judge. He would *play* the old judge and frighten those two women into shutting up. He didn't succeed, but that's not the point. What stage-properties did he use? Not the same ones he had nearly forty years ago?"

"No, hardly that." Dr. Fell pointed with the pipe. "The trappings—a robe, a black silk mask with eye-holes, even a pair of nylon gloves—he obtained in Bournemouth. It is not surprising that Elliot's search of the house failed to find them. Until Barclay himself told us, there was no means of telling they were in his sick-room, hidden under the mattress of the bed he was then occupying."

"The bed he was *then* occupying?" demanded Garret, putting a hand on Fay's shoulder. "Isn't he there now?"

"At present, as the phrase goes, he is sitting up and taking notice. But he is weak and much stricken by remorse."

"Remorse again?" Fay said rather contemptuously. "But for what? For frightening that virago Estelle?"

"For that," returned Dr. Fell, "among many other things. If I may return to the story, remember his bitter and depressed state of mind between April and the present day. To some extent he was fighting back by playing ghost. But the black dog was on his back; a black hypocrite was at his ear, pouring poison there. The new heir will be arriving, whispers this tormentor. Pennington Barclay will be dispossessed; he will cease to be lord of the manor; he will be driven from Greengrove forever. And so he decides . . ."

"Dr. Fell, who *was* this tormentor?"

"Surely, Miss Wardour, there is evidence to indicate it?"

"I don't know!" Fay was shivering. "At times I half think I see what you're getting at, and then it goes all cloudy. But the tormentor is also the murderer we're looking for?"

"It is."

"Then go on, please, and tell us. I won't interrupt again. Mr. Barclay decides—what does he decide?"

"He has come to an end. Black dog and blue-devils have won. As several persons fear and one person most fervently hopes, he decides to kill himself."

Again Dr. Fell's pipe had gone out; this time he did not relight it. Dropping the pipe into his pocket, he lumbered past his companions to the writing-table, where he swung round. Both Fay and Garret had risen and turned to face him. The floor-lamp threw bright light on table and blotting-pad; moonlight silvered the uncurtained windows beyond.

"He has determined to kill himself, then. In this room last night, before a group of witnesses, he as good as admitted his intent. I ask you, Anderson, to cast your mind back to last night.

"Having decided on suicide, how will he go about it? He has a revolver; he has a box of cartridges; the revolver is loaded.

But there is more to it than this. Though nerved by despair, desperately sincere, he still can't resist the dramatic setting and the dramatic touch.

"His wife, who has gone to Brockenhurst station to fetch the new heir, should return about ten o'clock. There will be others with her: including, or so he believes, the secretary whom he has dispatched on a useless errand to bring books which could have been sent by post. All will be assembled for an epic gesture. The time will soon come. As he hears the car approaching, he will stand in front of this tapestry chair beside the table; he will lift the pistol; he will fire a bullet into his own heart."

Dr. Fell, wheezing hard, stabbed with his stick at the tapestry chair.

"Imagine, Anderson," he went on, "that you are again driving up here last night. But think, instead, of what went on in *his* mind. He has spent his last evening on earth, or so he believes, making notes for a letter to the *Times Literary Supplement*. His preparations are complete; darkness is falling; he can hear the car. Holding the weapon close to his chest—not quite against it; suicides loathe hurting themselves—he grits his teeth and pulls the trigger.

"There is a report, a stunning shock, a surge of pain when ignited gases singe and burn the breast of his smoking-jacket. Then—nothing. He flops into the chair; still nothing except the horror of anti-climax. His wife has loaded the pistol with different ammunition; he has shot himself with a blank cartridge."

Fay started forward but remained silent. It was Garret who spoke.

"And than?" Garret asked. "Immediately afterwards? . . ."

"I say to you," replied Dr. Fell, "that realization of this came in an instant. What also came to him was utter revulsion at what he had done. He had gone too far; he had almost made a fool of himself. But now despair was over; he would turn and fight.

"He would *not* admit to attempted suicide; he would not admit to anything. In one flash, or so he thought, he could invent a story to explain it all. You yourself have stated—indeed, several witnesses have emphasized—that there was some considerable delay before you, Nick Barclay, and Andrew Dawlish came racing round to the library window.

"All witnesses noted the look of sheer physical pain stamped on his face, as well as the physical discomfort he showed afterwards. There was good reason for this. He had been struck by the wad from the blank cartridge; he wore a powder-burned smoking-jacket, with the attendant pain of scorched skin underneath. As for the wad from the blank, did he actually throw it out on the lawn? Subsequent heavy rain has prevented a proper search. Or, since there is no lavatory in the cloakroom, did he turn on the water and have it carried away down the drain of the washbasin? My own vote would be for the latter.

"In any event, what did occur in the interval before witnesses entered by way of the window?

"He dropped the revolver on the floor near the left-hand window. He hurried to the cloakroom. In the cloakroom locker were two jackets like the damaged coat he wore. He hung up the burned jacket in the locker, hastily donning one of the others. He returned to his chair, muscles stretched for drama. And he was ready with his story by the time you entered.

"Hitherto his attitude towards the ghost had been a paradoxical one. By swearing hard there was no ghost, he hoped certain others—Estelle and Mrs. Tiffin—would be helped to believe in it. After all, he himself had been the only ghost on the premises. And with Estelle he succeeded.

"Now, faced with the necessity of explaining a revolver-shot, he seized on that image and turned it into a malevolent masked intruder who had shot at him with the blank cartridge. Where he tripped up, of course, was in not realizing that the left-hand window remained closed and locked. Seeing the right-hand window wide open, he had fancied the other must also be open behind its drawn curtains. He told his tale well; he has a hypnotic voice and presence. But spur-of-the-moment liars are often tripped by such snags."

"In that case," Garret demanded, "there was not one word of truth in his story?"

"About the veiled intruder? Not one word."

"But Dr. Fortescue confirmed———"

"Forget that, for the moment. Concentrate on what happened here after all the witnesses entered."

In Garret's memory the scene stood out vividly.

"Dr. Fell," he flung back, "what you say rings true. I *see* Uncle Pen, tall and frail, with his gaunt face and his hypnotic eye, dominating us while he attempted to put across that story. He'd had his spectacular try at suicide; it failed. He described the visit of the ghostly intruder; that failed too, though it convinced me. And I know what he must have been feeling. Already he had walked through several different hells. . . ."

"Another hell, we can deduce, was now being prepared for him. That is why I ask you to concentrate on what occurred here between shortly past ten and shortly before eleven. Somebody else, who had been hoping and praying for the suicide, also saw the attempt fail and knew why it had failed. Somebody guessed everything. Somebody saw circumstances conspire to present a perfect opportunity for murder, in which Barclay's own lies should provide complete cover to shild the murderer. Somebody seized on those circumstances and used them. I would beg you to remember that the scene was played out before your eyes. If you concentrate on it, you will see—"

Dr. Fell paused abruptly. The passage-door of the library was opened by Deputy Commander Elliot. The passage behind him was pitch dark. Elliot, an electric torch in his hand, switched the button on and off. Dr. Fell rolled his head round.

"Now, Elliot?"

"Now," answered the other. "A few minutes ago," he added. "Steady, everybody!"

Dr. Fell made a rumbling noise in his throat.

"Very well; oh, ah! Go on; the central hall; I will join you in a moment."

Elliot disappeared towards the east, the beam of his torch flashing ahead in a dark passage. Dr. Fell blinked at Fay and Garret.

"The watchword, as you heard, is, 'Steady, everybody!'" Dr. Fell himself did not seem too steady. "However, there is no reason why you two should not stay together. If you care to see the end of this comedy . . ."

"Yes?" breathed Fay.

"Be quiet; follow me."

Tucking his stick under his left arm, Dr. Fell produced a box of matches. He reached out and switched off the floor-lamp beside the table. Except for moonlight silvering the western windows, thick darkness descended in a room which had known so much emotion. Then a match rasped. The little flame curled up, shining on Fay's eyes and mouth.

Dr. Fell held the match high. In his blundering fashion he led the way to the door. Garret followed, guiding Fay with his arm round her shoulders. Elliot had left the door wide open. Dr. Fell let it remain so. He took his companions across the passage, diagonally to the right and to the door of the music-room, which was also wide open as they had left it awhile ago. Here he stationed them just inside the music-room. The match went out; Dr. Fell cursed, struck another, and spoke in a hollow whisper.

"Something may happen," he said in his bumbling way, "or it may not. If it happens at all, it should happen within the next fifteen minutes. Stay where you are; don't stir from the door; don't sit down. You may talk for a minute or two, but don't talk longer than that; and at no time speak above a whisper. If you should see anybody go into the library . . . well! Whatever you see or hear, don't speak or move or interfere. Should nothing at all occur in the time I specify, we must end the play in different fashion. If it does occur—steady, everybody, and God help us! Now excuse me."

The tiny flame went wavering down the passage towards the central hall. Then it flickered and vanished. Dr. Fell did not strike another, but even on carpet they could hear his ponderous tread.

Moonlight entered the passage from the western window, stretching its path twelve or fifteen feet along the carpet. The old house seemed absolutely still; not even woodwork creaked. But there *was* noise of a sort. Garret held Fay tightly to keep her from trembling, and whispers flicked the darkness with their urgency.

"Garret?"

"Sh-h! Easy, now!"

"I'm not speaking loudly, am I?"

"No, but . . . what is it?"

"If we see anybody go in there, he said. But why on earth *should* anybody go into the library?"

"I may be wrong, but I don't think it's the library." Garret's imagination had begun to run riot. "I think it's that cloakroom; I think it's Uncle Pen."

"Mr. B-Barclay? What about him?"

"He's not in his room at all; Dr. Fell wouldn't answer the question. I'll give you odds he's insisted on being in his lair, and they've made him up a bed on the couch in the cloakroom."

"But, Garret, why in the name of——"

"Sh-h! For God's sake sh-h!"

"Dr. Fell *said* we could speak for a few minutes. Why in heaven's name should Mr. Barclay be in there?"

"If the murderer has another go, and they're laying a trap . . ."

"Another go? With a police-guard on the victim, as everybody knows?"

"Does everybody know it? And talking of what Dr. Fell advised . . ."

"Yes?"

" 'Stay together,' he said. 'There's no reason why you two shouldn't stay together.' Nor is there any reason why it shouldn't be for a much longer time? Miss Wardour, will you do me the honour of marrying me?"

"Oh, Garret, would it work? Could it *possibly* work?"

"Why shouldn't it work, for the love of Mike? Because you may think Deidre and Nick aren't serious; is that it?"

"No, it is not! I think———"

"It'll work, my sugar-candy witch; it's got to work!"

"Garret, Garret, who's speaking loudly now?"

"I'll speak as loudly as I damn well please. Come here."

"Darling, I *am* here. How can I g-get any closer?"

"Well . . ."

But he did not speak, loudly or otherwise; it was not necessary. They kissed at some length, while imagination ran riot in another way. How long this lasted he could not have said. A distant clock, which he identified as the long-case clock in the drawing-room, throatily struck the quarter hour past midnight. It was some time afterwards that Fay's right arm, gripped up round his neck, suddenly swept up and out as though to point. Garret—nerves jumping, the dreams struck from his eyes—stood back with a shock of scattered wits.

Somebody was shuffling along the dark passage from the direction of the central hall.

Nor could he have sworn he heard it. What caught at him seemed less an identifiable noise than an impression of movement, a displacement of air, a *sense* that someone approached with no good purpose. Whoever walked here was approaching slowly, feeling the way. The first actual noise he heard was not a footstep at all. It was a faint, light rasp, as of metal drawn slowly across a hard surface, and then drawn again.

In the doorway of the music-room, where Garret and Fay waited, there was a kind of silent struggle. In that light he could barely distinguish her face, the eyes enormous. She did not speak, but the eyes conveyed a message with almost audible clearness.

"You're not going over there?" the eyes pleaded with him. "We were told to stay here. You're not going over there, surely?"

"I must!" his own gaze said in reply. "Somebody's making for the library; somebody's nearly there; and . . ."

Then he realized.

Moonlight, swimming in through the western window, had reached a point several inches further; it just touched the western side of the doorway to the library. The prowler in darkness, no longer quite in darkness but touched briefly by an edge of moonlight, hesitated one instant as he melted through that open door. The moonlight flashed and dazzled on something he was carrying, and Garret identified that stealthy noise. The prowler, entering the library with certain designs in mind, was sharpening a straight-bladed razor on the whetstone-block in his other hand.

That did it. Garret, breaking loose from Fay as she tried to seize him, was across the passage in long strides. But he made no noise; he stopped on the threshold of the library, and his eyes searched moon-dappled gloom for the prowler ahead of him. And end of mystery and riddles! A sight of the unknown's face! For that consummation, passionately to be wished, it was worth all risks if the prowler should turn and attack.

But the prowler did not attack; the prowler did not turn; the prowler did not notice. His oiled whetstone-block, wrapped in rag or some other covering, must have gone into his pocket. From his left hand darted out the narrow beam of a pencil electric torch. He was making for the closed door of the cloakroom in the alcove. With Garret four steps behind him, he reached out for the knob. He opened the door. The pencil-beam probed inside. With his right hand, razor ready, he made an experimental sweep in the air from right to left. He took a step into the cloakroom. . . .

"Well, well, well!" said a familiar voice.

There was a sharp click. Light flooded out, momentarily blinding Garret. Yet even then, until he recovered sight a few seconds later, he retained the image of Pennington Barclay, propped up to a sitting position in his couch-bed, his back to pillows against the wall. Pennington Barclay, also momentarily blinded, had in his hand the end of a long cord attached to the hanging light-bulb. But not even complete blindness could have prevented him from addressing the prowler at the foot of the couch.

"Come in, my dear fellow," said the rich voice. "You tried it again, eh? But this time, of course, they were to think I'd cut my own throat? All right, Superintendent, you'd better take him now."

The prowler whirled round, head down as though about to charge. Behind Garret, whose sight was returning, there was a kind of explosion as the door to the book-cupboard flew open. Detective Chief Superintendent Harold Wick, moustache bristling, marched with ominous poise across the alcove.

"Stand aside, sir!" he said to Garret. "We want no interference here." To the prowler he said, "Andrew Dawlish, I arrest you for the attempted murder of Pennington Barclay. I have to warn you that anything you say will be taken down in writing and may used as evidence at your trial."

18

The pub which had so much attracted Dr. Fell was the Hampshire Yeoman at Blackfield. Beyond Blackfield, on the evening of Sunday, June 14, the fires from the oil-refinery at Fawley glowed shimmering orange against the night sky. In the lounge-bar of the Yeoman, snugly illumined by red-shaded wall-lamps, something of a modest party was in progress.

In one corner, enthroned behind a table and a tankard of ale, sat Dr. Gideon Fell. Fay sat opposite him, sipping her third champagne cocktail; Nick Barclay, at one side, communed with Scotch-and-soda; Garret Anderson, at the other side, addressed himself to Pimm's No. 1. Tobacco-smoke ascended like a benediction.

"Then it was old Coke-and-Littleton, was it?" Nick said loudly. "All right; but what made him do it? Are you telling me that from all this rampaging dirty work he hoped to get *Deidre?*"

"Yes," returned Garret, "if you'll just shut up for five minutes so that Dr. Fell *can* tell us."

"I am mum," declared Nick; "I am mum and dumb. From this moment, compared with my immutable silence, the Sphinx is a raging chatterer and Quaker meetings roar with ceaseless gossip. O.K., Solon: what's the dope?"

Dr. Fell put down his meerschaum pipe.

"If I may begin at the beginning," he said, "rather than plunge into the middle as I seem to have done, we might do worse than consider that same Andrew Dawlish.

"I first met the gentleman on Friday night, when he greeted Elliot and me with much talk but little information. He then put on the mackintosh his son had left for him; he picked up a well-filled brief-case; he dashed away (or apparently dashed away) in his car.

"Remember that mackintosh—a long, blue, lightweight raincoat which we afterwards saw hanging up in the passage outside his office. Remember the brief-case too. We shall return to both.

"It is of some interest, I submit, to compare the false face he presented to the world with the real face of the man underneath. The false face was that of a staunch, no-nonsense, rather unimaginative friend of the family. The real face, which kept peering out despite himself, showed lineaments very different. He is quick-witted and clever; it sings with a kind of jeer behind every word. He is the reverse of unimaginative; when he forgets himself, even for a moment, his manner becomes as theatrical as Pennington Barclay's own. For his outstanding characteristic is vanity. The man is stuffed with vanity. His tendency to pose and preen himself can hardly be overlooked. Pennington Barclay, I believe, commented on this very trait?"

Nick struck the table with his fist.

"Uncle Pen commented on it? You bet he did! *'Aroint ye, Andrew,'*" Nick quoted. "*'Don't stand there and preen, I beg. You have rather a fine head,'* and something else. *'But don't stand there and preen like Macaulay come to judgment.'* It was true, wasn't it?"

"It was true," agreed Dr. Fell; "it is as conspicuous a tendency as Andrew Dawlish's passion for looking at himself in mirrors."

"Mirrors!" Again Nick struck the table. "Holy cow, of course! There's a big Venetian mirror over the fireplace in the library. He kept stealing glances at himself while he stood there beside Deidre. I noticed it, yes! But I never thought . . ."

"Or, even when no mirror is available," said Dr. Fell, "there are always such surfaces as a polished silver plaque and the polished glass of a bookcase. You will find these in his office, where we visited him on Saturday.

"But I beg your pardon, ladies and gentlemen! I am getting ahead of my story, and to this story I must now return.

"At some time shortly before eleven o'clock on Friday evening, Pennington Barclay was shot through the chest. This was not the fiasco of attempted suicide with a blank cartridge, which I have already described to you; it was the true attack and the true murder-attempt.

"Already we had heard much testimony. We had heard what was said by four persons—Mrs. Barclay, Nick, Garret Anderson, Andrew Dawlish—on the car-drive between Brockenhurst and Satan's Elbow. We had heard what was said by seven persons—these same four, together with Pennington and Estelle and Dr. Fortescue—during certain significant episodes in the library before Pennington turned everybody out at twenty minutes to eleven. And from these incidents the worthy solicitor began to emerge in a very curious light."

"How?" asked Nick.

"At Waterloo, when three of you took the train, he was already insisting on the possibility of suicide. He did not hammer this too much; he drew back when he thought he had gone too far; but still he kept constantly suggesting. The burden of his plaint was that he feared suicide, and if only this could be prevented!

"Nevertheless, during the car-drive to Greengrove, what else did you learn? Pennington Barclay owned a twenty-two revolver. 'The revolver was a mistake,' said Andrew Dawlish. 'I should never have permitted him to buy it, still less shown him how to use it.' Dawlish did say that, I think?"

"His exact words," agreed Garret.

"Oh, hang it all!" Dr. Fell made a face of distress. "Dawlish is not only a family solicitor, remember. He also deals with criminal cases; he knows the police, as they know him. If he had really wanted to stop Barclay from procuring firearms, a quiet word to the police would have done the trick. Barclay would never have known, but he would have got no licence and no revolver. It could easily have been done; I can quote cases where it has been done. But Dawlish took no steps. Those hypocritical words he threw out indicated two things: that he was probably expert in the use of firearms, which we now know to be a fact; and that behind his professed friendliness to Barclay lurked the edge of an ugly snarl. His exaggerated, apparently paternal devotion to Mrs. Barclay . . ."

"It wasn't paternal at all?" asked Fay. "Late Friday night, in my hearing, Estelle made another of her wild guesses and seems to have hit the truth. She indicated he was more interested in Dee than he ought to have been. That *was* true, wasn't it?"

"It was true, Miss Wardour; Estelle's guesses went right more than once. The good Dawlish hung over Mrs. Barclay a little too much; he was too insistent on being near her and touching her; he dragged her name into the conversation even when he had no need to do so. A man of his stupendous vanity saw nothing odd in his conviction that, once her husband died, Deidre Barclay could be persuaded to fall into his arms."

"Whereas Deidre? . . ."

"I venture to think," replied Dr. Fell, "she never dreamed of this. Mrs. Barclay is warm-hearted, impulsive, perhaps inclined to be over-trustful. And she trusted Andrew Dawlish implicitly."

"So did others, if it comes to that," snapped Nick.

"Yes, your uncle trusted him too."

"I meant——"

"We know what you meant. But in more than one sense,

sir, Dawlish believed he had found a good thing. Pennington Barclay was a wealthy man; if he died, his wife would inherit. How much Dawlish was inspired by the lady herself and how much by the cash that would go with her must remain a matter for conjecture. But there, in his eyes, loomed the glorious prospect. His whispers at Barclay's ear were driving the man towards suicide. If the sowing of doubt succeeded, if Barclay took his own life, well and good. If there was no suicide . . ."

"Blackstone would have to arrange a murder?"

"He would have to arrange a murder. The suicide, as we know, very nearly occurred. Dawlish, arriving on the scene in time to hear that revolver-shot at twilight, found it had not succeeded; he must change his whole plan.

"The answer to all subsequent events will be seen in Dawlish's words and actions when you faced Pennington Barclay just after Barclay *had* tried to kill himself. Dawlish knew what had happened; as he showed by his questions, he guessed every move Barclay had made. Of course," Dr. Fell said argumentatively, "at this point, in examining the testimony on Friday night, I could not swear that my gathering suspicions of Dawlish were necessarily justified. We needed more information; we needed something to confirm these suspicions, and confirmation came later."

"Look, Solon," exclaimed Nick, standing up to attract attention. "You don't need to be so ruddy cautious at this late date. We know Uncle Pen turned the gun on himself. The suicide fizzled out in a bad shock to Uncle Pen and a badly burned smoking-jacket. He hung up the burned jacket in the locker and put on another. Blackstone and Garret and I charged in. Uncle Pen greeted us, and the others soon afterwards, with his ghost story about the intruder. And you're absolutely right: old Dawlish guessed what Uncle Pen had done. There was a kind of duel, with him half snarling at Uncle Pen to admit the suicide-try and Uncle Pen not having any. 'This evening,' Dawlish said, 'you were so depressed and in such low spirits that you almost——' Uncle Pen took him up with, 'Almost what?' and then Dawlish asked him if he hadn't anything more to tell us.

"Agreed without a struggle," Nick continued, bending across the table, "but we know that; we're already convinced of that. Some very significant things seem to have happened in the library at that time. What were they? Forget caution, Solon. What happened?"

"Well!" said Dr. Fell. "One important incident, you will remember, occurred shortly before Dawlish challenged him with those words. You yourself challenged your uncle's story by showing the left-hand window to be closed and locked on the inside. That is clear in your memory?"

"Of course it's clear! So what?"

"Your uncle was distressed and upset, as well he might have been. In a fit of wrath or humiliation at being doubted, he hurried to the left-hand window and opened it. At some previous time, I may remind you, he had put on a pair of rubber gloves.

"He had procured these gloves, or so he told you, in order to carry out experiments in taking fingerprints. He did in fact take some fingerprints, though he had no need to do so. He said he was attempting to determine the identity of the 'ghost.' Of course, as will be obvious to you, his fingerprint tests were only a blind and a smoke-screen. Since he himself was the ghost, he took those tests for the sole purpose of diverting attention from himself.

"But he did have the fingerprint-cards," pursued Dr. Fell, "and he did have the rubber gloves, which he put on in your presence. Afterwards there was some dispute as to whether he was or was not wearing those gloves when he ran over and opened the left-hand window."

"Well?" demanded Nick.

"Your uncle," said Dr. Fell, "quite honestly could not remember. *I* will supply the answer if you like. Contrary to your own impression, sir, at the time he opened the window he was still wearing those gloves."

"He . . . *what?*"

"He was still wearing the gloves, and this statement I am prepared to prove. One moment!"

With intense concentration Dr. Fell fumbled through the inside breast-pocket of his coat. From this, among many other papers, he at length found a note-sheet, which he spread out on the table as he blinked at Nick.

"Here, sir, is your own statement. You made it to the other witnesses; you made it to Elliot and me; Elliot took it down verbatim, and I, with some labour, so copied it.

"This is the answer you made to Elliot about the gloves. 'I've got a sort of impression he stripped 'em off, keeping 'em in his left hand, just before he went charging at the window and opened it. But that's only an impression; I can't swear to it.' Your reply to your uncle, you said, had been in the same words. Anderson and Dawlish replied only that they didn't remember at all; Anderson because he was honest, Dawlish because he failed to see how any kind of answer could help him. But this is what you said?"

"Yes, I said it," returned Nick. "What if I did?"

Dr. Fell replaced the note-sheet in his breast-pocket.

"At past one in the morning," he went on, "you were present in the library when Elliot and I discussed this same evidence. A complete set of Pennington Barclay's fingerprints—both hands, with fingers above and thumbs below—showed with sharp outlines in the dust of the middle sash on either side of the catch. You then repeated your testimony, saying the prints must have been made when your uncle raised the window. And it won't do, you know! It can't be at all!"

"What won't do? What can't be at all?"

"Try the experiment," insisted Dr. Fell, "of raising such a window with a pair of rubber gloves against the palm of your left hand. You may perhaps leave sharp impressions of fingers and thumbs, as these were; I say you *may*. But permit me to tell you what you won't do. You won't do this without leaving broad smudges in the dust from the pair of rolled-up gloves you are carrying at the same time.

"In the dust on that sill—Elliot himself commented on the dust—there were no such smudges. There were no smudges at all except, well to each side of the fingerprints, certain marks where the sill had been touched with gloved hands. Elliot announced this; I confirmed it for myself; the meaning became obvious. When your uncle opened that window, striking the catch with the side of his fist and rolling the sash upwards, he opened it with hands still gloved. That is what it means, and the only thing it means."

"Look, Solon!" Nick almost wailed. "Uncle Pen's prints *were* on the window. You mean they might have been old prints?"

"They might have been," Dr. Fell said sharply, "but they were not."

"Then when did they get there?"

"You will see at any moment."

In that quiet corner of a quiet lounge-bar, where only a few other customers had gathered on Sunday evening, the necessity of keeping lowered voices imposed a strain on this group. It imposed particular strain on Nick and Dr. Fell; it imposed strain even on Fay Wardour.

"Please!" she interposed, moving her glass back and forth on the table. "I wasn't there when you were arguing about fingerprints; I wasn't there when you were arguing about most things. But that doesn't much matter, does it? What matters is the scheme for murder and the one who planned it. Andrew Dawlish—whom Deidre thought infallible! While all this was going on, what must have been in his mind?"

"As, yes." Dr. Fell sat back with a flourish. "The point is well taken. What was *he* thinking? What was *he* doing? How his brain must have churned, his inner eye rolled round, to find some way of plucking back good fortune! Was all his forethought to go for nothing and Pennington Barclay remain obstinately alive?

"No, by thunder! He also thought himself infallible. Nor were his gods slow in granting him opportunity.

"For what came next? Into the library from the cloakroom rushed Estelle Barclay, talking excitedly of a great bundle of papers she had discovered in her father's study and left in the cloakroom when she ran out.

"She really had discovered all but one of those papers in a false compartment of her father's desk. Since the secret is to be kept among ourselves, I may mention the one paper she had not discovered. This was a forged codicil to the old man's will, bequeathing herself ten thousand pounds. She herself had forged it and put it there. I believe her oath, sworn afterwards when she was detected, that she did not do this for the money; she did it to prove dear Father had not forgotten her.

"Having planted the forged codicil among valueless papers, the tactics she employed were her customary ones. She would nag her brother; she would nag the loyal solicitor. Believing in Dawlish's absolute honesty, she would compel him to take away and examine those papers. The codicil would be discovered; it should prove the vindication of Estelle Barclay's devotion; all would be gas and gaiters.

"This, I say, was what *she* planned. Andrew Dawlish had other ideas. He had been seeking a way to accomplish his own design. He would have said fortune favours the bold; let him act with boldness, not to say brazen impudence, and his gods would not have deserted him after all. For here, it might be, lay golden opportunity."

"Half a minute, Aristotle!" said Nick. "They're coming over the plate too fast for me. Here was golden opportunity for what?"

"Don't you see?" inquired Dr. Fell. "He agreed to take the papers out of the cloakroom. But he did not want the papers; he would not have the papers just then. He marched into the cloakroom, shutting the door in Estelle's face when she tried to enter. There was something else he wanted from the cloakroom, something he could carry away in the brief-case, something that *might* open the way to success. Well? What was it?"

"I think *I* see," supplied Garret, groping hard if not quite understanding. "He wanted one of those two smoking-jackets in the locker."

"Bull's-eye!" said Dr. Fell. "Whang in the gold! Since he

was familiar with every detail of his victim's habits, he knew that too. In the locker were hanging up two smoking-jackets very much like the one Barclay now wore. Barclay had attempted suicide with a blank cartridge. One of these jackets must now bear a bad scorch and burn. The other would be untouched. He must walk away with that undamaged jacket.

"Dawlish marched into the cloakroom, I say. The bundle of papers, which for the moment he did not want, he thrust under the couch to get them out of sight. That was why I looked under the couch afterwards, but by midnight they had been removed. No matter; we are following Dawlish before the attempted murder. Having put the papers under the couch, he shoved the undamaged smoking-jacket into the brief-case.

"And so, good friends, under your eyes this master of impudence stalked out again fastening the catch of the brief-case. Did you actually *see* the load of papers he claimed to be carrying? No, you did not. As a decoy, as misdirection to convince you, he took one piece of paper—a receipted bill—and thrust it under the flap of the case so that it obviously protruded. Estelle snatched at this; he made her give it back. You were almost willing to swear you had seen all the papers. And he could walk away with what he really wanted: the undamaged jacket from the locker."

"But how the hell," exploded Nick, "would it help him to steal an *un*damaged jacket?"

"Because it left a damaged one. Suppose the prospective victim could be tricked, trapped, or forced into changing the jacket he then wore? Barclay *believed* there were two coats hanging up in the locker. It was not so now. If by some irresistible move he could be compelled—against his will—into putting on again the powder-burned jacket he had worn before, the way to murder would be easy. On the writing-table lay a loaded revolver; under cover of all the confusion, this daring and swashbuckling lawyer could steal it at any time he chose. A bullet could be fired: from a distance, if need be. Provided Pennington Barclay could be shot through the heart, the powder-burn already on the coat would make this seem to be the near-contact wound of suicide.

"But how, you ask, could Dawlish manoeuvre him into donning the burned jacket? At that moment (here I indulge my fancy) he was not yet sure. He ought to have left the house; Estelle, indeed, tried to drive him away. He would not go just yet. The indomitable brain of Dawlish—the chosen one, the gods' favourite—still sought a means. While he was still seeking, there entered another of the cross-currents which have so confused us. Dr. Edward Fortescue appeared and confirmed Barclay's story of the masked intruder.

" 'Don't stay too long,' Barclay is quoted as saying at another time, 'among the people in this house. They are addicted to lies and folly, most of them.' He spoke truly; each person, innocent or guilty, had some little secret to hide. But each person spoke and behaved exactly according to his or her own character. Bear that in mind, I beg; don't judge Edward Fortescue too harshly."

"Fortescue lied in his story?" asked Nick.

"He lied, of course; and yet remember my warning. Dr. Fortescue is not a bad man; he is not even particularly dishonest. You have seen him and heard him; you can assess his character. Even in our Welfare State, for which I confess small affection, no law compels a doctor into the National Health Service. And Fortescue loves an easy life, as he will tell you. His position here, an unambitious medical man not overburdened with duties, might be described as nice work if you can get it.

"His conscience is forever at him, let's allow. He sees himself as a hanger-on at the table of Maecenas. But this hanger-on's position is still a favoured position. He must do his job, or so he conceived; he must earn his keep. And so, hearing Maecenas tell what he knew or felt to be a thumping series of lies, he backed Maecenas to the hilt. That is all."

"If you'll excuse *my* saying so," protested Fay, "it's not all or even an important part. It's completely aside from the main story, which——"

"Which, as you were about to say," Dr. Fell agreed, "is the story of a brutal, rather brilliant attempt at murder. Good! we return to Andrew Dawlish, sweating with perplexity among his companions in the library.

"How *can* he impel his victim into that burned coat? Already, I believe, he had somewhat unnecessarily drawn your attention to a tube of glue in the writing-table drawer. Was it in his mind—again I indulge my fancy—was it in his mind to spill glue on Barclay so as to necessitate a change of jacket? No, impossible! In addition to the fact that glue smeared on a sleeve does not drive any man into a different coat, Barclay would hardly be driven to the jacket bearing such unmistakable signs of his try at suicide. Every prospect seemed hopeless.

"But it was not hopeless, nor had the gods deserted their favourite! You know what took place. Estelle, involved as usual in a violent row with her brother, waved the jar of honey much too wildly. We must not, I insist, suspect Estelle of any complicity in Dawlish's design. Estelle, considered as a *conspirator*, would be the very worst conspirator who ever lived. She is merely what they nowadays call accident-prone; she walks open-eyed into every accident; it is a part of her character. For some time she had been flourishing that jar. The flourishes became too extravagant; the jar smashed against the mantelpiece; the honey inundated her brother's coat.

"Well, good friends?

"The murderer's design had been completed for him. Assuredly Barclay would change his jacket. This was no mere matter of glue smeared on a sleeve. Even when he found that an undamaged jacket had disappeared and that there remained only the coat with the powder-marks, a fastidious man would prefer even powder-marks to the mess and stickiness of the one he had on. Barclay could not leave the library; he could not attend the birthday-party. But why should he leave the library? Nor could anyone enter to drag him out; he had bolted both doors. Napoleon Dawlish, of course, had a different fate reserved for him; Barclay was going to die.

"As for what Dawlish did when he left Greengrove with the presumed intention of going home——"

"Yes, what did he do?" demanded Fay, opening and shutting her hands. "The room wasn't yet locked up, was it? The left-hand window was still wide open?"

"The left-hand window," agreed Dr. Fell, "was still wide open."

"Then what did he do? Aren't you going to tell us?"

"I am going to tell you, Miss Wardour, after I have mentioned another cross-current of innocence in this affair."

"Cross-current of innocence? Why must you mention that?"

"Because it made me certain Andrew Dawlish must be guilty," replied Dr. Fell, "and also because it concerns you."

"It concerns *me?*"

"Yes, Miss Wardour." Dr. Fell, picking up his pipe, looked blandly at Garret and Nick. "Here is a young lady," he continued, "who just under two years ago became innocently but frighteningly involved with a poisoning case in the West Country. Elliot and I knew this. Elliot recognized her; he also knew her to be guiltless. Late Friday night—or rather early Saturday morning—he taxed her with this innocence. Hitherto the lady had been uncooperative. Now emotion burst its dam; she poured out the whole story.

"Up to this time, in my idle musings, I had believed the dashing Dawlish was probably guilty. But I had only speculation to go on; I might be completely wrong. If he had proceeded as I thought he had, he was trying to turn this shooting into a suicide. But he would have a second line of defence: these knowing ones always have. If all else failed, if the police refused to believe in suicide, what better second victim could there be than a girl who herself had once been suspected of murder: in short, a ready scapegoat?

"And yet how could Dawlish have known anything about her? According to Miss Wardour's own account, only Mrs. Barclay was acquainted with her history. Mrs. Barclay, much concerned, had thought of asking Superintendent Wick whether the police were on her friend's track. Miss Wardour made her promise not to do this; Mrs. Barclay promised, and kept her word. But Mrs. Barclay, a good friend, was still anxious to learn where the other woman might stand in the eyes of the law. What *would* she do? Whom *would* she ask?

"Loudly and clearly the answer came back from my Freudian subconscious. In terms of strictest confidence she would ask Andrew Dawlish: the man of law, the man whose profession it is to keep secrets, the one man on earth she absolutely trusted. Subsequent questioning of Mrs. Barclay proved she had done so; and but for the luck of the game, Miss Wardour too would have been delivered into his hands.

"This still remained speculation, if you like. But I felt it was nailed down; I felt I could sing hosanna and write Q.E.D. My idle maunderings had been correct: Dawlish was guilty. We could now say with some certainty what he must have done.

"Under cover of a confusion on which he himself commented, Dawlish stole the revolver from the writing-table before the guests were turned out at twenty minutes to eleven. The revolver was in his pocket when he talked to me in the drawing-room. He put on the long blue raincoat—prematurely, since the rain did not begin until the not-so-small hours of the morning; but he is a cautious man. He put on his bowler hat. He picked up a brief-case filled only with a stolen smoking-jacket. He went out to his car.

"But he did not drive far. He drove only just outside the grounds, where he left the car and came back. He slipped into the garden by one of its entrances away from the house. He was at the eastern entrance to the garden, facing towards a window still open and brilliantly lighted, when his scheme came to full maturity.

"The time was shortly before eleven. Pennington Barclay, wearing a powder-burned jacket as Dawlish had anticipated, was in the library. Not far away, in the music-room, a Gilbert-and-Sullivan medley soared towards its end to cover noise.

"A triumphant Dawlish was sixty feet from that window, the regulation distance for target-shooting. Any sort of hail or call would have summoned Barclay to the open window. Anyone standing in that window, as you saw for yourselves, is brightly cross-lighted. And Dawlish had a target: the black powder-burn on the left breast of the maroon-coloured jacket.

"Dawlish lifted the revolver and fired.

"But that is not all he did. The weapon must be returned to the library so that nobody shall know it was ever removed; it must be found near the body of a presumed suicide. And so the would-be murderer took one more risk. He ran across the lawn towards the window so as to throw the revolver inside. It was not too great a risk. The moonlight was dim; he ran head down, left arm up to shield his face.

"But Barclay? In that last frightening moment of near-death, when he is saved only by a bullet lodging too low, what does *he* think?

"He is summoned to the window. There is a flash from the dark. Something which is not the wad from a blank cartridge strikes him a blow in the same place. He has been talking much of ghosts, or at least of an intruder in a black robe. Out from the garden towards him runs a figure whose long, dark-blue raincoat may seem a robe or anything else you like. He does not recognize his assailant, so that it took patient questioning on Saturday afternoon to make him sure what he had seen. In that uncertain light even the bowler hat was indistinguishable; he felt only that the hat was wrong or the headgear was different.

"Well, do you begin to see?

"Shock and terror Barclay knew; it was as though his own imagination had recoiled on him. He acted from pure instinct. He must guard himself against that approaching figure; he must put some shield between them; he must close the window. He staggered, but he reached out for the sash.

"Dawlish, of course, had no intention of playing ghost then or any other time; he was a practical man who wanted to kill. And yet, at the supreme moment, his nerve almost cracked. He wanted only to get the weapon away from him and into the library. But his victim was closing the window! Careless of fingerprints, which in any case did not register because he had handled only the grip, Dawlish flung the revolver past his victim into the room, where it skittered across the carpet near the tapestry chair.

"Lawn, figure, moonlight were all reeling before Pennington Barclay's eyes. Something *had* got him; it might well be the end. With his bare hands, leaving the prints we found, he seized the sash and brought the window down. The edge of his hand forced over the catch and locked it. Trying to hold himself upright, he retreated from the window. He turned, took a number of faltering steps back into the room, staggered, and collapsed beside the fallen revolver.

"There!" said Dr. Fell, taking a long draught of ale and setting down the tankard with a thump. "There's your locked room, simple and complete. A locked room, as I suggested to Elliot, because at the beginning we persisted in misreading the evidence. And yet a proper locked room after all, since each person in the drama acted exactly according to his character. It was Pennington Barclay, this time with no intent to hoax, who nearly did hoax us at the end."

"But Dawlish?" demanded Nick. "Of all the treacherous dogs who ever . . ."

"His conduct," Dr. Fell conceded, "was hardly exemplary. Yet the rest of what he did is soon told. He could not yet go home. He *must* retrieve that bundle of papers, which he professed to have taken away but which he had actually pushed out of sight under the couch in the cloakroom.

"And so he waited. At some time between half-past eleven and a quarter to twelve, when the rest of us were otherwise occupied, he slipped into the house by way of the open window at the end of the western passage. At a quarter to twelve, fifteen minutes before Elliot and I first visited the library, he slipped out again with the bundle of papers under one arm and, I suspect, his hat under the other. Phyllis, seeing him at a distance, mistook the mackintosh for a dressing-gown, the bundle of papers for a parcel, and added one more element of fantasy to the total.

"Did he learn then that Barclay was not dead? He may have, but I think not. He did not learn, it seems more probable, until Nick Barclay told him on the telephone next day.

"Meanwhile, having examined the papers at Estelle's insistence, of which he had already voiced suspicions, he found the forged codicil and used that too. In order still further to guard his own position, he would first denounce Estelle and then offer to protect her.

"A fine show, we must all acknowledge, he put on for our benefit in his office! Yet more than mere suspicion whispers that it was not quite good enough. He had told you he could not remember the date on which the 'ghost' first appeared to Clovis Barclay; he said he had only looked up the date that morning. Yet the bookcase-section in which he professed to keep his diaries (you recall?) had a glass door so thick with dust that clearly not even housekeeping had touched it in some time. He remembered the date; he had remembered it all along; but like so many criminals, he was trying to make his story too good.

"Having failed at murder once, would he try again? It seemed more than possible he would—if he thought he could get away with it. Very carefully I told him Elliot was inclined to suspect what happened to Barclay as an attempt at suicide; up to late Friday night, in fact, Elliot did wonder. Yes, most thoroughly I played tempter. Dawlish alone did not know there was a police guard on his near-victim. One more small incident occurred before we left the office. Among so many trophies of the gentleman's sporting prowess I observed a cup which showed him as runner-up in the national revolver-shooting competitions at Bisley. I somewhat incautiously muttered, 'Bisley!' but, since two of you interpreted this as 'grisly,' under the circumstances I forbore to explain.

"Subsequent conversations with Elliot and with Superintendent Wick later that afternoon and in the evening disclosed that both Elliot and Wick had come to the same conclusions as those on which I had been lucky enough to stumble. Superintendent Wick was readily convinced; Dawlish & Dawlish, it seems, have been in a shaky financial position for some time. Pennington Barclay, sunk in an abyss of remorse, completed the picture by giving details of the attempt on his life.

"One more event needs to be clarified. Estelle, leaving the lawyer's office *again* convinced her brother was in some fashion conspiring against her, rushed home to pitch into him. The accident-proneness overtook her. She had started upstairs; she mistook her direction and pitched from the landing in the way we know. No permanent harm has been done; the lady will recover. But June thirteenth, I fear, cannot have been altogether a happy birthday.

"Enfin!

"Dawlish might or might not make one more attempt on his victim's life. Barclay insisted, in a manner with which you are acquainted, on being bait for the trap. A 'phone-call to Dawlish, tactfully and sympathetically made as to an old family friend, enabled me to tell this beauty of Barclay's latest neurosis: to be transferred downstairs near his beloved library.

"If Dawlish did make the attempt, what weapon would he use? Another revolver was possible; but the police had the original one, and this time there must be no doubt about suicide. Barclay shaved with a straight-bladed razor; and though Fortescue had locked up all his razors, a razor is impersonal; it may be owned by anyone.

"A police watch was set on Dawlish. On the other hand, there could be no certainty of an attack merely because this versatile gentleman left home late in his car. He must be followed; he was followed. Not until he was passing through Beaulieu, rather less than fifteen minutes' distance from here, did Elliot receive a 'phone-call saying our man would probably pay a call. The trap was set; a too-confident criminal entered by the front door and walked into it; and apart from any emotional undercurrents which may be left, I really think there is no more to the story."

Dr. Fell drained his tankard and set it down.

"Yes," agreed Fay, "it's an explanation of all the *facts*. But where does it leave us? What do we do now?"

"What we do now," Nick almost bellowed, "is have another drink. The glasses are empty, every one of 'em. What'll it be? Same again?"

"It'll be the same again," said Garret, "but this is my round and my shout. Sit down, can't you? For the last time . . ."

Nick was on his feet, hand in pocket. Before there could be too much argument, Garret gathered up the glasses, put them on the tray by which they had been brought to the table, and carried the tray to the bar-counter across the lounge. Here the barmaid replenished all glasses and faded away. But a kind of suppressed tension had followed Garret. About to pick up the tray again, he glanced round. Nick stood at one side of him, Fay at the other.

"Look, old son!" Nick said in a portentously lowered voice. "About these emotional undercurrents Solon mentioned. . . ."

"Yes?" said Fay.

"Yes?" said Garret.

"Old Solon hasn't spotted *those*. He's seen everything else, but he hasn't spotted those because they've got nothing to do with crime."

"Are you sure he hasn't? Fay and I, for instance . . ."

"If I'm not speaking out of turn, Garret, what about you and Fay?"

"And if *I'm* not speaking out of turn, what about you and Deidre?"

"Look, old son! I don't take back one word of what I think or feel about Deidre. But . . ."

"But what?"

"It's a beautiful dream, my lad. That's all it is or was or ever could be. Unless the cops want me for something immediately, I'm off to New York in a few days. And I'm going alone. If Deidre went with me, her conscience would never let *her* alone. I'm not sure my conscience would be easy either. I kind of think, in her heart, she never really cared a damn for anybody except Uncle Pen. And what did *I* feel, honestly and sincerely? These great romances: hell's bells, they're the world's greatest snare and delusion! That's why I want to ask you something. There's been some talk in the past twenty-four hours about you two getting married."

"Has there?" inquired Garret. "But let's be sure of our facts. I asked her to marry me, and she as good as told me to go to the devil."

"Oh, what on earth are you talking about?" Fay's gesture upset a glass on the counter; it was somebody's empty glass and hardly mattered. "I never said anything of the kind. I said ⁓."

"All right; what did you say? Pub or no pub, will you marry me?"

"Look!" insisted Nick, bending a powerfully gloomy gaze on Fay. "Think well before you answer that one. I like you both; I want to see you happy. Two people like you can get on very pleasantly as long as they don't call it love. Think you're in love, get married, and you're sunk and done for. I ought to know; I've been married. What chance have you got in this day and age? None at all! Listen to your Uncle Nick; listen to the voice of experience. Don't do it; don't be crazy! No matter how hard you try, what hope have you got against the accumulated wisdom that says no?"

Fay's blue eyes lifted towards Garret.

"Well, anyway," she said happily, "we're going to try."